"Who *Are* You?" Paris Croaked.

"Now, darlin', that's not the words a man wants to hear from his wife the morning after their wedding."

"Wedding? What wedding?" Paris screeched. She looked down at the big-ass ring on her finger again and screamed out loud—again.

"Let me order up some breakfast for you, dear. A big ol' pot of coffee will help you remember."

"Don't call me dear! I'll take that coffee, though."

Hunka Love got out of bed and rose to his full six-foot-four-inch naked glory. Paris got hot just staring at him.

"Well at least you remember the package, if not the name. I guess that's a good start. And, oh my, you are a mess, woman. There's an eyelash on your left breast, you know."

By Suzanne Macpherson

SHE WOKE UP MARRIED
IN THE MOOD
TALK OF THE TOWN
RISKY BUSINESS

SUZANNE MACPHERSON

She Woke Up Married

AVON BOOKS
An Imprint of HarperCollins*Publishers*

This is a work of fiction. Names, characters, places, and incidents are products of the author's imagination or are used fictitiously and are not to be construed as real. Any resemblance to actual events, locales, organizations, or persons, living or dead, is entirely coincidental.

AVON BOOKS
An Imprint of HarperCollins*Publishers*
10 East 53rd Street
New York, New York 10022-5299

ISBN: 0-06-051769-7
www.avonromance.com

First Avon Books paperback printing: April 2005

Printed in the U.S.A.

10 9 8 7 6 5 4 3

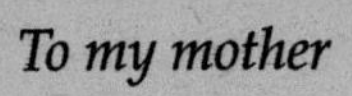

To my mother

Acknowledgments

I'd like to thank the best Elvis impersonator ever, Danny Vernon, for providing inspiration and research data. Thank-yous to Reverend Dee Eisenhauer, for her amazing grace; Susan Sanderford, for her amazing insight; and Dan Brown, for writing *The Da Vinci Code* just when I was ready to read it.

1

Heartbreak Hotel

Paris groaned and forced one eye open by an act of sheer redheaded willpower. Only one eye opened because the other one was stuck shut with a false eyelash. It was hard enough opening the one, because she'd really, really, had too much to drink last night, and it hurt to move her eyelids. She didn't want to try moving the other parts of her body.

What a crappy, stupid way to start the second day of being thirty. Her brain felt like it had cotton balls glue-gunned to the inside of her skull. Come to think of it, the inside of her mouth felt the same way.

A horrid light pierced through a six-inch gap in the hotel curtains. She saw the distorted outline of the Eiffel Tower in the distance. She knew damn well she wasn't in France; she was in Las Vegas. A fuzzy sort of Vegas at the moment. What *had* she done last night?

A deep and extreme need arose in her. She needed coffee. Java. Mud. Hot and thick. Right now. For a minute she wondered if room service might just this once read her mind so she wouldn't have to move any more of her body until a nice big cup of hot coffee was within reach.

The horrid light from the window kept glinting into her open eye. Actually it was glinting off something else in the room, causing a sort of disco-ball effect, which only made things worse. Paris wondered if she'd been so stupid as to wear that red sequined dress last night. Sequins made anyone look fat—and that dress had practically been sprayed on, like Ponytail Barbie's Moonlight Serenade dress. She should throw it out, but sometimes a girl needs to put on red sequins—like maybe on her thirtieth birthday.

She blinked at the glittering disco light, and her sight focused on a white jacket hanging on the hotel desk chair close by. What the hell had she bought now? She raised her head an inch off the pillow and moved her hand up to the stuck-together eye, pulling at the false eyelash. All of that was extremely painful, and her need for coffee increased tenfold. She groaned. She sat up partway and flopped her head forward, a curtain of her own red hair blocking the view. Paris lifted her head slowly and parted the hair curtain, but something got stuck in her long curls. She yanked and freed her hand and looked down to see a very large, square-cut diamond ring on her left hand. When did she buy that?

Her two eyes refocused across the room to that white thing on the chair. It was an Elvis-style jacket with a big-ass collar and broad shoulders, and it was dancing in the sunlight. Her eyes moved to the floor below. There sat one pair of men's white cowboy boots, complete with silver cording and silver studs to match.

What the hell *had* she done this time?

"Good morning, Mrs. Pruitt."

Paris moved her head painfully, quickly, to her right. She sucked in a quick, searing breath and let out an involuntary, long, loud scream, clutching the sheets against her naked breasts and scrabbling herself to the far edge of the bed.

Beside her in the king-size bed was The King himself. Elvis incarnate. His sexy Elvis mouth was smiling at her. He was buck-naked, his head propped on his elbow, a hunk of his wavy black hair curled down on his forehead.

And speaking of hunks, at least he was a hunk a hunka burning love Elvis—the early years, instead of a hunka big ol' later Elvis.

"Who the hell are *you?*" Paris croaked. Her voice was still asleep. She wished she were too.

She knew full well she'd gotten herself into this mess, but she needed some facts, *fast*.

"Now, darlin', that's not the words a man wants to hear from his wife the morning after their wedding."

"Wedding? *What* wedding?" Paris screeched. She looked down at that big-ass ring on her left ring finger again and screamed out loud—again.

"Let me order up some breakfast for you, dear. A big ol' pot of coffee will help you remember."

"Don't call me dear. I'll take that coffee, though."

Hunka Love got out of bed and rose to his full six-foot-four-inch naked glory. Paris actually got hot staring at him. She felt a flush of heat run up her neck and into her face.

"Well, at least you remember the package, if not the name. I guess that's a good start. My, oh, my, you are a mess, woman. There's an eyelash on your right breast, you know."

She looked down at her exposed right breast vaguely, still lost in a lustful thought. He leaned back over the bed and reached for her. She flinched with surprise.

"Hold still now, this won't hurt a bit." His eyes were deep chocolate brown—almost black—and he stared into her eyes as he peeled the offending eyelash off the top of her breast and handed it to her. "There now, you just sit tight. I'll ring up some grub."

Grub? There was no way she'd actually married this cowboy Elvis dude, drunk or not. But she had to admit that she could see clearly why she'd seduced his gorgeous behind into her bed. As he walked away and gave her a terrific view of that behind, she had some scattered memories of unzipping that white Elvis jacket off his incredible body.

It dawned on her that since her birthday had been March 31, this was April Fool's Day. Someone must have put this guy up to this. What a grand joke, really. It sort of reeked of Anton's style.

It was actually a shame she didn't remember more. Maybe she'd just have to ask him to recreate the fictional wedding night for her. Paris giggled to herself and pulled the sheet all the way off the bed, wrapping it around her like a toga. She just had to brush her teeth this instant. But handsome boy went in the bathroom ahead of her, so she'd just have to wait.

It didn't take long, and when he came out of the restroom, he stood naked by the desk, talking on the phone. He seemed so comfortable in his nakedness.

"Yes please, ma'am, that's Mr. and Mrs. Pruitt in the honeymoon suite."

Honeymoon, my ass. She was going to have to

set him straight, right after she had her coffee, and maybe some Elvis aka Mr. Pruitt for dessert. . . . Yum.

She ran her hand down his tan, muscular back as she rustled by him wrapped in her sheet. He twisted round her way to smile at her before he set the phone down. He was obviously happy to see her; a glance downward confirmed that. Oh, yeah, she'd already been a bad girl, so she might as well be bad again. Then she'd explain to Mr. Pruitt that the wedding had surely been a fake and that she had a plane to catch back to New York, and Thank You, Thank You Very Much.

Turner set down the phone and watched his new wife saunter into the bathroom, humming. He had always wanted to see Paris James happy at least once in her life, and he was damn glad it had been him who'd put that smile on her pouty lips, but he felt like he'd been hit by a freight train, waking up next to her this morning. What had happened? He steadied himself on the wall and let the shock wave run through him.

How the heck she'd ended up in his chapel in Las Vegas was something he'd wonder about for the rest of his life. There he'd been, belting out "How Great Thou Art" for the midnight service, when suddenly he'd looked down to see Paris James in a red sequin dress, staring up at him.

She'd been like a vision: same crazy red hair,

same beautiful, flashing green eyes. Granted, she'd had a champagne bottle in one hand and had been swigging straight out of it every few minutes. Also, it had been slightly indelicate of her to catcall at him to "Take it off, preacher boy! Take it all off!" But he'd thrown her his silk scarf just the same.

Turner pulled on his tighty-whities and his white double-knit Elvis pants. He wished he'd had the foresight to stop at his place and grab a change of clothes. His shirt was still in good shape—he'd hung it on the chair under his coat. He slid the shirt on and buttoned it up. He felt for his keys and wallet. Nothing. He'd probably done what he always did. He opened the hotel dresser top drawer and saw his wallet and keys, plus some papers. On closer examination, he realized it was the marriage certificate, a bad photograph, and a coupon for ten bucks' worth of chips at The Dunes.

When Turner had seen Paris last night, he'd known it was fate. But marrying? How had that happened? He must have lost his mind, because what else could explain it? She'd seen him again, remembered him, and convinced him to make her his wife in one night. He turned to the dresser mirror to adjust his collar and saw a shocked, hardly-slept-at-all face looking back at him.

What the hell was he going to do now? He, levelheaded Turner, had done the most impulsive, crazy thing he'd ever done in his life last night. He just wasn't a drinker, and the last time he'd had that much champagne had been . . . never.

What a night. Truly, all his fantasies of her from the past paled in comparison to holding her in his arms and making love to her all night long. She was his completely. They'd taken their vows and consummated their marriage, and well, dang it, he was going to have to deal with it. There were some details to work out for sure. He didn't want to hurt her.

Turner fussed with his collar. He wasn't real clear on everything, except how he'd declared he couldn't just have sex with her unless they were married. Obviously, that problem was solved. It was all pretty fuzzy after a certain point, but he started to remember what Paris had said to convince him to climb into her bed. She'd declared her modeling days were over. That at thirty she'd decided to quit and settle down, get married, and raise a family and that he was the guy for her. He'd been swept away in her birthday bash and had ended up with a wedding night. Kind of a combination special.

Room service knocked at the door and Turner went to answer it. A uniformed man smiled and rolled a cart in the door as Turner held it for him. He proceeded to set up a nice breakfast on the hotel room table, complete with a red rose.

Turner reached in his jacket pocket and paid the man a generous tip.

"Thank you, Reverend." The server gave a nod and rolled his cart back toward the door. But Paris was blocking the way, having just emerged from the bathroom, still wrapped in a sheet. Her eyes were as wide as a green river and she was staring right at him, clutching the doorjamb for support. Very melodramatic of Mrs. Pruitt, Turner thought to himself, although he recalled he had to brace himself on the wall just now, too.

"Reverend? *Reverend?*" Her voice went up a notch.

"S'cuse me, ma'am," the uniformed man said. He looked at her like she was nuts, shook his head, and pushed on out the door.

Turner cocked his head at his wife and smiled. "I see we've both forgotten more than a few details about last night. Come and have some coffee. We'll talk."

"I-I wasn't expecting you to be a reverend. Listen . . . um . . . I have this habit of being a very naughty girl sometimes. I guess I really stretched myself last night, seducing a minister and all. I feel sort of . . . bad." Paris had been inching toward the table, staring at the coffee. At least he'd figured out how to make her slow down. "So you aren't someone's April Fool's joke on me, are you? Did someone put you up to this?"

"No, I'm not an April Fool's joke. I swear. Sit down and join me, won't you?" Turner was polite, but insistent. He could see Paris needed a refresher course straight off the bat. She seemed to have forgotten more than he had.

Paris sat. He reached in the hotel dresser drawer and pulled out the papers. He couldn't believe she didn't remember him from high school. Could he have changed that much?

He recalled that he hadn't actually told her his first name since she'd woken up. He smiled to himself and wondered how long it would take her to remember him. She was still just staring at him and his clergy collar. Perhaps the light was starting to go on. He set the photo down in front of her but kept the certificate in his hand. Then he poured them both a cup of coffee and sat down across from her.

She picked up the coffee with two hands and took a big slurpy sip, her green eyes never leaving his face. Turner felt his mouth turn up into a smile. She was still the girl he'd known thirteen years ago. Still the same Paris.

Paris finally picked up the photograph of the two of them at the altar in front of . . . she guessed it right . . . *another* Elvis—but the heavier, fat, sideburn-years Elvis. They were kissing—she and Reverend Pruitt, that is. She had a fake rose bouquet and, amazingly enough, was wearing a wedding dress. A white satin Marilyn Monroe in *Gentlemen Prefer Blondes* kind of gown, with a little veil perched on her head.

"Now this just proves it's not real, buddy," she said as she pointed at the photograph. "I would never wear white satin to my real wedding. I look like a cow. Look at this picture. Look at my hips, for Christ's sake. I look like two-ton Tessie. Oh, sorry about that Christ's sake thing."

"I forgive you," he said. He smiled at her, stirred some milk into his coffee, then set the spoon down on his saucer.

"Ha-ha."

"You rented the dress. That's my own wedding chapel. It's called the Graceland Chapel. That's a friend of mine doing the ceremony. Let's eat. This breakfast looks great." Turner lifted the silver covers off each of their plates and set them aside.

"I rented a wedding dress and got married by an Elvis? That's just too surreal." Paris felt sick. She was too hungover to eat eggs. Turner, on the other hand, put enough pepper on his eggs to hide their color, added Tabasco sauce, then dove into his breakfast with gusto. Yuk.

She picked up a piece of toast and nibbled. As she nibbled and sipped coffee, dipped toast in her coffee and sipped more, it started to occur to her that preacher man here was less likely than most to lie about the authenticity of their marriage. Paris slowed her nibbling and sipping down to stop-action and stared at the man across the table from her with his clerical collar and Elvis pants. He seemed so familiar.

Oh my God. *Could* she have married him?

"Paris, we've got a great deal to talk about," Turner said. He pointed at her with his fork. "Even though we've known each other a while, we did rush into this marriage, and now we'll have to catch up with ourselves. We need to decide what to do about it. I have to tell you that despite the fact that we acted rashly, I consider marriage a sacred vow. After all, I own a wedding chapel in Vegas. If someone like me doesn't consider it sacred, who will?" Turner laughed. He went back to eating his breakfast.

Paris's stomach screwed up into a square knot. This guy was talking crazy. "Why did you marry me?" she asked.

"Well, now, Mrs. Pruitt, you finally said yes. Besides, I couldn't very well take you to bed without a proper wedding ceremony. I don't believe in premarital sex."

"Oh my God, don't tell me you were a virgin."

"Okay, I won't tell you that."

"No way. I do have *some* memories of last night, vague as they are." She did. They were very vague, but they involved massage oil and something about that large tub in the honeymoon suite bathroom.

"I wasn't always a reverend."

"Well, it shows. Now, look. I'm really sorry about accidentally marrying you. I must have seriously tied one on last night. I swear I'll never touch the stuff again. But we can't be making any plans for a future, for heaven's sake." Paris looked at him hard, then chugged down the rest of her coffee and set the cup down with a clunk on the saucer. "I have a plane to catch back to New York. I have a life. You were undoubtedly a wonderful lover, and I'd even like to have another go at it, but I have a horrible headache, and you'll just have to tear up that fake marriage paper and get on with your life, Mr. Pruitt. In this case, what happened in Vegas is definitely going to stay in Vegas," she snapped.

Turner Pruitt looked at her with his deep brown eyes in a sort of patient, holier-than-thou manner that really irritated the hell out of her. He went back to eating the last bite of his breakfast, which irritated her even more.

"Tearing up the paper doesn't change the fact that we are man and wife, Paris," Turner said between bites.

"Listen up, Elvis, I don't even know you. I don't care what that paper says; I am not your wife. I'm going back to New York, and I suggest you get a grip on that fact. As a matter of fact, I'd like you to put on your blue suede shoes and hit the road, buddy." Paris crossed her arms and let her one nasty eyebrow flare up. Her sheet slipped, so she readjusted the toga fold and re-crossed her arms.

She really didn't remember him, or the wedding. Amazing. Turner sat up and looked at her pretty, pissed-off face across the breakfast table.

"Cowboy boots."

"What*ever!*"

"Paris James, I'm surprised at you. Or should I call you *Patricia Jamison?*" He picked up his bacon and chewed on it, waiting to see how she'd react.

She reacted all right. She went pale, and her hand went up to her mouth in shock. Her green eyes got wider.

"What did you say?"

"You heard me. As a matter of fact, it was me who renamed you Paris. We'll always have *Paris*, remember? My Humphrey Bogart imitation and your Ingrid Bergman farewell? Here, maybe this will help." He handed her the marriage certificate he'd kept on his side of the table.

She looked down at the marriage certificate. Yep, that was her scrawled signature, obviously written under extreme champagne exposure. And his—*Turner Pruitt*—a clear, bold signature. Yep, there were witnesses, too. Turner Pruitt—she used to know a guy named that . . . long ago. But this couldn't be him, could it? She glanced up at him, then back at the paper. She felt herself freaking out.

So what. So what if she'd signed this. This was Las Vegas. They'd been married by another Elvis impersonating preacher. There were probably a dozen of them on this end of town alone. That didn't make it *legal.* Plus it was still April first, after all. This had to be a joke. He couldn't be the same Turner Pruitt. But how would he know her real name?

"Turner?"

"Lightbulb going on? Sister Agnes's poetry class? My senior year at St. Mary's? Paris, how could you forget?" Turner finished his bacon and drank down the last of his coffee. She couldn't believe he could stay so calm. She felt electrified. "Oh my gawd. I can't believe it. *My* Turner Pruitt?"

"In the flesh."

"You look *so* different. It can't be you. I would have known. You . . . you were just a scrawny boy. Now you're a . . ."

"Man?"

"It's really you?"

"It is."

Paris leaned back in her chair and studied Turner. She began to see the essence of the boy in the face of the man.

"Oh God, Turner, it is you. How could I not remember this? You say I did know you last night?"

"You did."

At that moment Paris James decided that she would never take a drink again in her life. She'd obviously been out of control if she couldn't remember anything but the sex.

She paused a long time, reeling back to high school, a place she didn't visit in her mind often. She and Turner Pruitt at seventeen and eighteen years old. It all came back quickly. Turner's parents had put him in the only boarding school in the Nevada area, where his elderly aunt lived. His aunt had passed away right before he'd graduated. How could she dredge up old stuff like that and not remember her own wedding?

"What are you doing in Las Vegas? I thought you were going back to the Cook Islands and rejoin your parents' mission?"

"I did. I went back, remember? Then I decided to go to college. I'd gotten a taste of life on the mainland that year I spent here. Besides, I figured out there are lots more sinners in Las Vegas than on the Cook Islands, by far."

"That's for sure." Paris laughed. "Where did you go to college?"

"Stanford University, then Denver Seminary."

"Woo-hoo, Mr. Intellectual. You always were a brain."

"So were you."

"Get real, I wouldn't have passed that class if you hadn't helped me."

"And you? I've seen your face on a dozen magazines over the years."

"Oh, I traveled all over and just did the modeling thing. It's not as easy as it looks, but the money has been great."

"Last night you said you were going to retire."

"I did? Did I tell you what I would do for a living after that?"

"No, you were too busy kissing me. But you did remember me a little more clearly last night."

"I did?"

"Enough to say I do." Turner pushed the breakfast things aside and reached for her hand. "Paris, I know you. The real you. I was in love with you once. I think our marriage, our coming together after all these years was not an accident. I am willing to make this work. I know you live in New York, but we can live anywhere in the country. I could dust off my credentials and go into private practice. I have a clinical psychology degree."

"What about your ministry?" Paris's hand felt jumpy under his.

"That's my calling, but I can counsel as a minister without being affiliated with a particular church. As I said, I do own a little wedding chapel here in town, but I have options. I can sell it, or just manage it from anywhere. I've always been sort of a roving minister. I can rove wherever I like. Sometimes life changes."

"How did you end up doing this Elvis gig? A nice missionary kid like you?" Paris asked.

"It was a fluke. I did some professional church singing in the area, then a friend of mine had cancer, and I took his place in the Graceland Chapel to help him out. I could see that I was really helping the people that came in to see me. Unfortunately, my friend died. He left the chapel in my hands, and I took over as new owner, but like I said, life changes. I can relocate and rearrange things."

This was just plain insane. At least Paris felt better that she knew Turner. That it was really *her* Turner, from long ago. That relieved her of thinking she'd just up and married some stray Elvis in the middle of the night. They'd been best pals their senior year, both boarding at St. Mary's, each for their own reasons. It seemed like a million years ago. And here Turner's family was still in the Cook Islands. Her family—that wasn't even worth thinking about right now.

"It was swell of your folks to let you come to the States for your senior year. I'm glad I got to provide you with that true teenage experience that you'd missed out on, having that sheltered childhood in paradise, like you did." She smiled, remembering what hell they'd raised. "Like howling at the moon out in the desert, drunk on beer."

"You left Charles Barnes out there broken-hearted. I went back for him later, you know."

"He deserved it! He didn't really love me any-how. He loved Sheila Broach. I can't believe you rescued him. You should have let the coyotes have him."

"A trail of broken hearts, and me picking up the pieces."

"Turner. We have to get this marriage thing annulled. I don't have enough time to take care of that with you. I'm going to trust you to do the right thing." Paris withdrew her hand from Turner's warm touch.

"I know you're going to find this difficult to understand, Paris, but I don't want to annul the marriage. As a matter of fact, I think it's fate we ended up together."

Paris got up from the table. "Fate? That's ridicu-lous. It was a bottle of champagne. What hap-pened to the people I started out the night with?"

"Trail of broken hearts."

"Very funny. Turner, I can't stay here with you. I can't be Mrs. Pruitt. I have to catch my plane back to New York and get back to work. I . . . I don't want to be married." Paris talked as she walked across the room. She looked for her suitcase and seemed very relieved to find it. She threw it on the unmade bed and unzipped it.

Turner turned in the chair to watch her. "Yes, you do. You said you were tired of it all and wanted to settle down like your friend Marla."

"Quite the memory on you."

"Practically photographic."

"I was drunk."

"I think you said what was really in your heart."

Paris looked around for her clothing. She gingerly picked the offending wedding dress off the floor, untangling it from the bedding. Paris carefully hung it on the chair across from Turner. He could return it for her, since she had no idea where she'd rented it.

She grabbed up clothing in her arms. "S'cuse me, I have to do some things in the bathroom," she said. She just needed to be out of this room, more like it.

Turner watched Paris scurry around. She was the original runaway girl. Whenever love would get a little too close, Paris would bolt.

He drank down a full glass of water and refilled it from the metal pitcher the hotel had brought with breakfast. Darn, he was thirsty. He wasn't used to alcohol.

He might as well just sit back and watch the show, because nothing he said right now was going to make Paris stop.

It's not like he could just pick up and leave

anyhow. He'd have to find someone to take his place at the chapel, and Millie would need a new roommate. It looked like he hadn't thought things through too clearly himself last night. That wasn't like him. He wondered how he could have been so impulsive. Look at the mess it had caused.

He heard the shower running. A flash of the evening before tumbled out of his short-term memory. Paris in the bathtub. It was suddenly quite clear to him why he'd jumped at the chance to marry Paris. It was a chance he would quite literally never get again in his lifetime. Something must have snapped in him—and a more primitive instinct had won out.

Her wallet was on the dresser, splayed open. Such a trusting girl. He thought of getting her address so he could keep track of her no matter what happened next, but he just couldn't bring himself to dig through her wallet.

However, her driver's license was in plain view.

Dang, she might be a model, but the DMV can make even a beautiful woman look like a dawg. Turner laughed to himself as he looked at her DMV picture. He copied her address onto a piece of hotel stationery.

As he jotted down the numbers, he saw several pictures slipped in opposite the license. One was of a stunning blonde holding up a frilly baby girl—that must be her friend Marla she'd talked about so much last night. And one more photo. He lifted up the edge of the plastic folder a tiny bit—a very, very old picture of Paris as a child . . . with her mother. It was very seventies and Paris had braids in her hair, all dressed up for Easter Sunday in some kind of a psychedelic hot pink and lime green dress. Her mother had on a matching outfit. She looked so much like Paris did now. Full of life.

He heard the shower stop and stuffed the note he'd scribbled in his coat pocket. He felt suddenly guilty for prying even that much. Paris's life was so private. Even the relentless press hadn't unearthed the truth—which he knew so well.

Paris reappeared with a small suitcase, a fully done-up face, her hair pulled back into a ponytail, and dressed in a white knit sleeveless wrap dress that clung to her every, lovely curve. She looked just like a wife would on a honeymoon. There was no way in hell they were done with all this. He'd married her, and he had to come to some kind of squaring of that fact. Marriage was a sacred thing. He knew that was a very old-fashioned concept in this disposable society, but he was firm in his belief. He'd let her go for now, but she was going to have to deal with this very soon.

He decided to leave her with a good memory for the next few weeks.

"Well, Paris, I see you are ready to go." Turner stepped up close to her and took her in his arms. She seemed a little stunned and dropped her round suitcase with a clunk onto the floor. "I wanted to say a proper good-bye to my one-night wife." He tipped up her chin with his finger and gave her a toe-curling, remember-me-forever kiss. The future hung clouded and uncertain before them, so this kiss was going to have to last until the fog lifted. He made sure it was a good one.

2

All Shook Up

Paris felt her lips still tingling from that amazing kiss Turner had given her. That devil. Marrying her when she'd been in a compromised state. Of all the low tricks.

"Champagne, Miss James?"

"No possible way," Paris snapped. The stewardess looked at her sharply. "It's just that I've sworn off alcohol. Could you pour me a nice ginger ale, please?"

"Certainly. Vegas has that effect on lots of people." The stewardess smiled and poured out a ginger ale, handing Paris the cup and the can.

"Thanks." Paris took a sip. The stewardess pushed the cart onward toward the main cabin, leaving Paris in first class sipping ginger ale and watching the on-flight movie, *Down With Love,* with sound coming through headphones. It was giving her a headache.

The flight was bumpy, and her stomach was still unhappy about her recent . . . bender.

Vegas has that effect. What an understatement. She just hoped that Turner would carry through with the annulment. When she'd given him specific instructions on that, he'd just sort of winked at her and said, "Of course, dear, I'll do the right thing." Which didn't give her the greatest sense of confidence.

Turner Pruitt. What an amazingly small world. He used to write the most wonderful poetry in Sister Agnes's creative writing class and had even put some to music. Paris had always been amazed at his ability to be so open and confident. In some ways he'd given her the courage to run away to New York and start modeling. She even remembered being self-conscious in the early days and telling herself to be like Turner—brave and bold.

No one had known more about her than Turner, Paris remembered. She'd written two sets of poetry for that class. The set she'd turned in to Sister Agnes, and the set she'd let Turner read. Poems about her family and the heartache they'd caused her.

Paris felt the old pain surface, and wished she hadn't sworn off alcohol.

The plane bumped again and she took off her

headphones. She adjusted her pillow and decided to try and get some sleep. Maybe she'd wake up tomorrow and find out this had all been a dream. Not a bad dream really, waking up married to Turner, having spent a wonderful, passionate night together, but a dream anyhow, because she'd just left Turner behind and was going back to her life in New York.

That would work out for the best. This way she wouldn't break his heart, and if she remembered Turner right, he had a very big heart.

Something was itching her. She excused herself and went to the tiny little horrid airplane powder room to take down her spandex panties.

Paris let out a gasp that half of first class must have heard, because what she found rolled up in her waistband was her Nortrel patch. It must have loosened up during their bathtub adventures, or from the massage oil, and been hanging by a thread since last night. She grabbed onto the tiny sink station for support and felt herself swoon with fear. *Oh my God Oh my God.* She'd gone on a honeymoon with Turner Pruitt and had compromised her birth control. He had used a condom, hadn't he? Him and his old-fashioned no premarital sex thing, he could have decided since they were married it was okay to just go *natural.* He was like that.

Paris decided to spend the rest of the trip praying for mercy. Turner had reawakened her spiritual side, all right, Amen and *Please* God; don't punish me for my sins. She decided to try and remember how to say Hail Marys on her long string of pearls.

"Where's the coffee, and why are you sitting in a chair like a lump? You never sit in a chair like a lump. What's up?"

"I got married last night."

"Well I'll be a ring-tailed no-boobed old showgirl. Where the hell is your bride? Did you lose her in a poker game?"

Turner looked up at his roommate, Millie, standing in the doorway. True, she'd seen better days, but she had an irrepressible spirit. She looked just like the greeting card cartoon character Maxine at the moment, with her floral robe gaping over a slinky negligee, her hair in curlers, and a cigarette in her hand. Where do old showgirls go in Las Vegas, anyhow?

Turner looked at her with gratitude. They'd been together quite a few years now. She was a great cook and great support. He felt the arrangement was more in his favor.

It made him feel a little odd that Millie made a living doing phone sex, astrological charts, and telemarketing, but she made fairly decent money, so who was he to say what she could or couldn't do? He sometimes got a good laugh over her "gentleman callers"—if they only knew what the woman on the other end of the phone was really like.

But hey, she still had great legs. She'd survived a bout of breast cancer and was still kicking strong. He just wished he could get her to stop smoking.

Millie sucked on her cigarette and stared at Turner. "Well? Who was she?"

"A woman I went to high school with came into the chapel and we had a great reunion. I took her out dancing, and she told me she was ready to settle down and have a family and that now that she'd found me again, she wanted to get married right away."

"Was she drunk?"

"Yes."

"Were you?"

"Way."

"Oops."

"She's a little confused today. She doesn't quite believe it was legal—or real. She hopped a flight back to New York."

"And you're sitting here? Have you gone soft in the head?"

"We both just need to think things over. I believe she'll get back to the fact that she married me for a reason. I'm just going to give her some space."

"Space is highly overrated." Millie came over to Turner, sat on the arm of the old overstuffed chair, and ruffled his curly black hair with her thin fingers. "Do you love her?"

"I was in love with her in high school. She's very special."

"She'd have to be to get a guy like you to take the plunge just like that. Did you at least have a wedding night?"

"Unbelievable. Wilder than my wildest dreams."

"So what's the deal, are you going to let her forget the whole thing and call it a wash?"

"I would like to talk to her again and find out if there is anything to it. I'm pretty darn conflicted. I took vows, I married someone I know, but it's all under questionable circumstances. At least we should sit down and talk it out. I'm not happy with the outcome."

"Well, what are you waiting for, preacher man? Get on your horse and go get that gal!"

"It's not that easy. I said I loved her in high school. That was then. I need to get to know her again. Besides, I've got responsibilities here. I'd have to get a replacement at the chapel, and I'll need to be sure you're okay, Millie."

"That's you—Mr. Responsible. Well, then, take care of your business, then go on. You don't have to worry about me; I'm tough. Tina Hicks has been looking for a place to stay. She was one of the original Sparkle Plenty girls, remember?"

"I remember." Millie had a scrapbook of Las

Vegas showgirl history that should be in a museum. But he didn't trust Tina to make the rent. She was living off a boyfriend who would probably dump her for a younger version and bail someday. "I can arrange to have the rent on this place taken out of my bank account automatically," Turner mused.

He helped Millie off the edge of the chair and stood up. He needed to pace.

"What that girl needs is another dose of Turner Overdrive love, darlin'. You've left her reeling and she'll start missing that good loving before you know it. She'll miss that burning, huge, throbbing . . ."

"Millie darling, we're not on the phone sex clock, so you can spare me the shop talk."

Millie snorted. "That's why you have to be there—to fill that yearning when it comes, so to speak." She headed toward the kitchenette for her "morning" coffee. It was noon. Millie would never be a morning gal.

Maybe Millie was right—about some of it, anyway. He and Paris had made contact. Fate had crossed their paths, and they had connected so strongly that they'd ended up married. Their brief honeymoon had been like Fourth of July fireworks.

But he couldn't just walk out on his job. The Graceland Chapel needed someone special to minister to his flock. He'd have to find that special person and train him to take his place. And finding a good minister that could belt out an Elvis tune and look good in a gold lamé jacket was no easy task.

Turner took his fourth return lap from the kitchen to the living room. It was a very small apartment, and it was hard to get a good pace going.

He made his decision somewhere around three-and-a-half rounds. He'd take a leap of faith and figure Paris would at least talk it out with him. Something in his heart told him Paris needed him. But he was willing to give her some time. He needed to get things in order. She was not a woman who could deal with uncertainty. He'd been living a very simple, low-key life. Those were not words that applied to Paris. Some major changes were going to have to happen.

Change was good. Who knew what would happen? They'd talk, she'd either convince him they should ignore the whole incident, or that they should give their union a try. So much of this went outside his values and conviction. He could see that this whole event was going to take him on a very new and amazing journey.

3

Reconsider Baby

"Foil me. I've been bad."

"You don't have to tell me, I'm reading it loud and clear." Anton teased Paris's long red locks into strange forms and put plastic clips here and there to emphasize the oddness. "Where the heck have you been? Did you know that Venus went into your seventh house while you were gone—*on your birthday?* I mean, last time it did that you almost married that senator."

"Well this time I married Elvis."

"Get *outta* here." Anton's rattail comb paused in midair.

"Actually, his name is Turner Pruitt." Paris smiled weakly at Anton. He was going to give her *so* much shit. She might as well tell him and get it over with, because he was the only person on the planet who would understand.

She'd hidden out in her apartment with some sort of nasty flu since she'd returned, watching *Days of Our Lives,* eating cheese puffs and drinking Mango Madness Snapple.

She'd only been on one cattle call, for a headache commercial, and that had been some kind of nightmare. Usually she didn't even have to audition, so that had been humiliating enough. She'd had trouble getting something to fit her, no doubt due to her slothful ways and nasty diet of late.

When she'd arrived they'd already cast it to some snot-nosed brat of an eighteen-year-old model from California named Sweet and she just so *wasn't!* She'd looked like Barbie's bad younger cousin, or one of those Bratz dolls, and Paris had known for a fact those boobs hadn't been the genuine articles. She knew silicone when she saw it. No bounce.

When her hair had gone dull, she'd known it was time to spark up and face Anton.

She reached in her leather bag and pulled out the photo of her supposedly legal wedding.

Anton let out a shrill shriek. "*Satin!* Were you drunk?"

"Apparently."

"Oh this is a do-over. You had planets. You

were drunk. Just tell the Pruitt you want a full wedding with a nice Vera Wang and we'll do a tiered dessert thing, a little white chocolate ruffled cake from Sylvia Weinstock, and some Roederer Reserve champagne. I mean, *really*." Anton gestured wildly.

"I left him back in Vegas."

"You know, honey, you really look like hell. And hot pink is not your best postmarital color, sweetie. You look Grace Adler pale today."

"Did you hear what I said?"

"Oh, I heard you. You've misplaced your new husband. Don't worry. He'll turn up. Hmm, something is just not right. We're going for the cap today, honey. You need highlights, not chunks." He took all the plastic clips out and slapped a rubber cap on her head, then started pulling strands through the holes with a crochet hook.

"Ouch. I do know him, you know. We went to high school together at St. Mary's our senior year.

"St. Elvis."

"He's very good looking," Paris said.

"This is true. He looks like a complete stud muffin in that picture. Is his hair that black for real, or is that Elvis hair?"

"It's for real. But when you're up close it's got brown highlights, not blue. He also sings really well."

"Now we're defending the missing bridegroom? And where's the ring?" Anton did a combination Brooklyn/Bronx twang on that one.

"I left it with him in the hotel. Did I mention he's a reverend?"

"Let's see now—a little overview. Paris James went on a bender and married Turner Pruitt the singing preaching Elvis—on accident—as my baby sister used to say."

"So what's your point? I told him to get it annulled. It was just a mistake." She made a face.

Anton studied Paris's twisty features in the mirror for a moment—a long moment—without batting an Anton eyelash. That made her squirm. He then resumed pulling strands of her red hair through the rubber cap. "There was that solar eclipse in Gemini. That might account for it. Something is just way weird, girlfriend, I can't tell you what, but hang on to your garters because all will be revealed as soon as that damn Mercury goes direct again."

"You and your planets. I just made a little itty-bitty mistake, that's all. I'm going back to work, Turner will get this annulled, and that's all there is to it. Now make me pretty and shut up."

Anton raised one eyebrow at her and pulled on her hair again.

"Ouch!"

"Beauty requires sacrifice, you cranky bitch."

"Fine. Sacrifice me."

"Grab that jar on the table and slime some of

that green stuff under your eyes. You look like you didn't unpack the bags."

"I haven't been feeling well. I've got a flu bug that just won't leave me alone."

Paris leaned forward and grabbed the jar, twisted it and inhaled the soothing mint scent. She took a few fingersful and smeared it under her eyes—and on her temples. That damn headache was coming back.

She leaned back and endured Anton and his hook. He was muttering to himself now, his full sleeves billowing over her. She closed her eyes and rested. She was still dog-tired for some reason. You'd think months of rest would have helped. Or maybe it was the fine diet she'd been on, or the late-night documentary shows on UFOs and the true story of Courteney Cox's life. Why did she watch this stuff?

"Excuse the interruption. Is that you under there, Paris?" a deep voice boomed from behind her.

Anton and Paris both jumped like rabbits. Paris stared into the long studio mirror in front of her and could not believe her eyes. Turner Pruitt. In cowboy boots, jeans, a sheepskin-lined suede jacket, and . . . the hat.

He took off the hat.

"Wow. That explains a lot," Anton said. He turned to look directly at Turner. "Forget the planets, you've roped in the real McCoy, Paris!"

"Turner!" Paris shrieked into the mirror. "What the *hell* are you doing in New York?"

Turner tried to keep a straight face as he gazed upon Paris in her rubber cap with strands of hair sticking out like sprouting long grass, along with the blobs of green stuff on her face. He tried. He failed. He started to smile.

"Did you come all this way to have me sign something? Because that's the only reason I can imagine." Paris put her hands on her hips, the silky black salon cape flapping around her elbows like bird wings.

"I figured you might have had enough time to change your mind, darlin'." He couldn't stop smiling, and he knew he was going to laugh out loud soon, so he figured he'd better cover up his mouth—with her lips.

He strode over, grabbed her chair, spun her around to face him, and angled his head so as to miss the green spots and just get those luscious lips. He did good. She melted against him for a moment. Then she shoved him away.

"I didn't change my mind, and no big Nevada kiss is going to change it for me, either," Paris sputtered. She wiped her mouth. She got green goop on her hand and tried to wipe it on her cape. Then she slowly turned the chair back to her reflection in the mirror and screamed again. She ran from the room like an Irish banshee, shrieking little short shrieks all the way out of the room.

"Women," Anton said.

"Yeah. What's that about?" Turner said to Anton.

"I knew it was a bad day to mess with her hair. This just proves it."

"Mercury is retrograde for another two days anyhow. Maybe after that I can talk some sense into that woman," Turner responded.

Anton looked at him like he'd cursed or something.

"What?" Turner scratched his head.

"I'm reeling from your comment about Mercury, my fine cowboy. Can I call you cowboy?" Anton said.

"Turner would be fine. Turner Pruitt." He took a step over to Anton and shook his hand. "Sorry about that, my roommate Millie, back in Vegas, does astrological charts on the side. I guess her planet talk just rubbed off on me."

"Oh, no apologies necessary. Cowboy Turner, I think you could use a little trim. Saddle up the chair there, I seem to have an opening. Is that your natural color?"

Turner thought about it for a minute, and figured he might as well get a haircut. "Yup. I have a touch of Native American in my ancestry somewhere way back there. Just a little off the sides, please."

"That explains it. Are we keeping those sideburns? Because here in New York they're a little passé."

Turner shed his big rancher's coat and sat in the chair. "Sure, take them off. My Elvis days are over for a while anyhow. I think. I'm just not sure which end is up these days. Paris and I need to talk."

Anton whipped a black cape around Turner and snapped it closed. "Paris showed me the wedding picture. Love that sequined white jacket."

"You can get stuff beaded in Vegas for very little money."

"No kidding. I'm Anton, by the way. Confidant of the beautiful girls here at the Rita Ray Agency."

Maybe Anton could give him a hand with a few things. "Pleased to meet you, Anton."

"So tell me everything. How long are you here for, where are you staying, and how do you think you're going to get wildcat Paris to climb back in your wagon?"

Turner laughed. "Slow down there. Let's see. I checked in at the YMCA at West Sixty-third yesterday. It took me a day to find this place."

"The Y." Anton paused. "Primitive, but decent."

"I grew up on the Cook Islands in a native village. *That's* primitive."

"I should say. All*righty* then. How long, and what's the plan?"

"As long as it takes, and I'm hoping a miracle will occur with Paris so we can get this all straightened out. Also I'd like to pick up a little spending money if I can get a quick gig doing Elvis, or singing or something."

"Miracle with Paris, huh? Okay, so you'll be here a few months maybe." Anton ruffled up the dark curls on Turner's head. "You'll need a guide. You could pass for Irish, you know. I'll have to take you around to all the various districts and show you the ropes. We'll have to tour all the Irish pubs, starting with Dolan's. I know Stephen would love to hear you sing. Paris says you've got the voice of an angel."

"She did?" Turner was surprised to hear that Paris had said anything about him. "I'd be extremely appreciative to be given a tour of the city. I don't know why people think New Yorkers are so rude. I've met nothing but friendly people so far."

Anton switched on the clippers. "You've seen Paris in the morning?"

"Yes. Well. There is that."

"Exactly."

"She has her good moments, and I'll have to catch one. I've caught one before. I'm going to stay till the job is accomplished. I married her. I came here to settle things with my wife, so I'll just have to deal with whatever comes up."

Anton stared into the mirrored eyes of Turner Pruitt and saw a brave, brave man staring back at him.

Not only did Turner Pruitt have some nerve but also he was a complete fool to think she'd change her mind about this little marriage thing. However, she did have a very important question about condoms to ask him, so in some ways it was fortuitous that he had arrived in New York. It saved her the trouble of tracking him down in Vegas, which she'd been considering over the last few weeks.

After wiping off the green mint mud, Paris brushed her hair out with gusto, thinking bad thoughts about Turner at every stroke. Didn't he know she'd make a terrible wife? She was a bitch, plain and simple. She had terrible PMS, she didn't sleep well or eat well, she drank too much—before she'd reformed on that habit, and that made her even bitchier, because a nice glass of wine would sure take the edge off for an hour or two. She was also lazy and self-centered.

For heaven's sake, how could he even have considered marrying her?

And worst of all, he knew all this about her from before. He really was a fool, plain and simple. He'd been a romantic-headed songwriting geeky-looking preacher's kid in high school, and now he was a romantic-headed Elvis-impersonating preaching, great-looking *man*. Someone better talk some sense into that man.

Paris's brush stopped in midair. She stared into the mirror at her thirty-year-old face and wailed. It was kind of involuntary. A sobby sound just rose out of her middle and escaped through her mouth. She sat down on the dressing room chair, in front of the mirror, and bawled. Big piles of Kleenex started forming on the counter as she mopped up the waterworks and blew her nose repeatedly.

She'd never planned on getting married ever. Ever, ever, ever. She was not the marrying kind. She could not be any man's wife. Besides that, her PMS was just beyond horrible today. She just had to start her period, right now, today, this minute. She was seriously overdue, and every time she thought about what might be the real reason she felt so rotten lately she just freaked out, so she'd stopped thinking about it.

The door to the dressing room flew open. Through her blurry eyes she saw Turner and Anton staring at her.

"Are you okay?" Anton asked.

"Shut up and shut the door. Leave me alone," Paris sobbed.

"Paris, honey." Turner took two steps in her direction.

"Don't you honey me, Turner Pruitt. Damn you for marrying me! Get *out*."

Turner wisely backed out of the room. Anton was already out. They closed the door quietly behind them.

"I've never seen that girl cry in all the years I've known her. Ever. She usually just yells at people when she's got PMS."

"Wow." Turner scratched his head, puzzled. He'd been doing that a lot lately. 'Course he'd just had his hair cut, and it felt odd. As odd as being married to Paris.

Turner resumed his seat in the salon chair. Anton resumed his position behind him, scissors in hand, and got back to work on Turner's trim. This was some setup—a hair salon right in the modeling agency building. It made sense though, with all those high-maintenance models to deal with. And it was starting to look like Paris James . . . Pruitt . . . was on the top of the high-maintenance gal list. She really was a she-devil, just like in high school. But Turner knew more. He knew Paris's deep secrets. He knew her heart. Underneath that nasty exterior was a real woman. He was going to figure her out and get this mess of a situation sorted out. Talk about a challenge.

Anton finished up his trim, gave Turner's neck a brush with a soft whisk, and whipped the cape off Turner's shoulders.

"There. You look ma-a-a-velous. Well, I don't know about you, but I've got the rest of the afternoon off if Paris doesn't want highlights. Would you like to bunk at my place instead of the Y? I've got a guest room. I don't think Mrs. Pruitt is going to be flinging open the door to connubial bliss this particular evening."

"I'd be honored, Anton. We'll have to get my things out of a locker, there," Turner replied.

"We'll just grab a cab. Can I interest you in a steak?"

"Sure. It's lunchtime in Vegas." Turner put his coat back on.

"Lunchtime in Vegas. Sounds like a musical. *Lunchtime in Vegas . . . ,*" Anton sang in a very Nathan Lane–style voice.

Turner laughed.

"Have you seen *Cats*?" Anton went on.

"Bored the livin' heck outta me. What's up with that? But *The Producers* was fantastic. And *the Fantasticks* was fantastic, too. We get the road version of most shows in Vegas. My current favorite is *Mamma Mia!* It's playing at the Mandalay Bay hotel."

"Get out! A fellow Abba fan!"

Turner walked out of the third-floor salon with Anton, and they headed toward the elevators singing excerpts from *Mamma Mia!*

He was glad he'd made it to New York and found Paris. She'd reacted pretty badly. He'd get himself settled and have a long talk with her. Probably more like five long talks.

Paris finished blowing her nose and hiccupped one more time. She refilled her glass from the watercooler and took a sip. These overhead fixtures were nasty. Rita should put some full-spectrum lights in this room and cheer them all up on these gloomy Manhattan days.

She suddenly thought how ghastly and nauseating the colors were in here. She was going to have to tell Rita to repaint: magenta, teal, gray, bleah. The eighties called, and they wanted their décor back.

But she did love this old place. The Rita Ray Agency had been like home to her for so many years. Modeling had been an adventure. She still loved it. It wasn't being very kind to her right now, but things always picked up in the spring.

She wet a makeup sponge and reapplied some foundation to her weirdly pale face, covering up the red blotches around her eyes. Damn it, no wonder she never cried. It ruined your face. Now what do you suppose had gotten into her to bawl like a kid? She'd probably just been too mad to do anything else.

For some reason it dawned on her that it was way too quiet out there. She jumped up and flung open the door. A few girls were passing through, their heels clicking against the black-and-white tiled floors. Other than that, no Anton, no Turner.

This made her stomach pitch. She really had to talk to Turner. The other thought that made her very queasy was thinking about Turner telling Anton about her childhood. He wouldn't do that, would he? There were parts of her she kept very separated. In a locked box. Hidden in the back of the closet. That's where they belonged. They didn't belong in her New York life.

Turner was so honest that he might not think about keeping her secrets. He might think everyone here knew every detail of her life. That was so far from the truth it was funny. But she wasn't laughing now.

And Anton had a big mouth. Pretty soon the whole town would be talking about her horrible family life. She couldn't bear that.

Knowing Anton, he'd invited Turner to stay with him. Well, she'd just have to change that plan. She started to bite her nail, then stopped herself—that last manicure was really too expensive to bite to pieces. Well, there was no way she could just wait around Anton's hallway till they showed up. She'd have to go on a manhunt. She'd have to check out all of Anton's regular haunts.

Paris went back in the dressing room and grabbed the purple dyed faux fur coat she'd arrived in and its matching hat. The sun had gone down and it had been chilly as hell out there this whole week. She relaced her purple boots and tucked her hot pink leggings back into place, then put on her hot pink leather gloves.

She glanced in the mirror, but the great outfit didn't even cheer her up. Where was her old swagger? Here she was dressed to the teeth, and . . . nothing.

Clothes were her best friends. She could make them draw all the attention in the room by filling them out nicely and walking in a particular way. She loved the colors and fabrics and the way designers played with her body. She'd been the muse for an Italian designer named Vittorio Saladino for a while, back in her younger days. He'd loved her look, and everything he'd made had been perfectly suited to her. In turn, she'd made magic for him on the runway. It had been a perfect marriage of their particular talents. But that was when she was twenty. Now she was thirty.

Paris picked up her Galliano slouch bag, got out of the stuffy dressing room, and attempted a little walking action. After ten steps she gave up. Maybe some lunch would help. She had an intense craving for a cream cheese Danish from Zabar's. Or maybe six.

4

A Little Less Conversation

"I knew you'd adore him," Anton said to Stephen Banyan, proud owner of Dolan's Pub.

"A classic. The body of Adonis, the voice of Pavarotti, and nice—he's *nice,* yet."

"Sorry, he's straight, and taken. He accidentally married Paris James."

"Accidentally is right." Stephen rolled his eyes and kept twisting his dishtowel into a bar glass.

"I gotta tell ya, she's one lucky woman that fate dumped him in her lap."

"And what does that make him? A lion tamer?"

"Saint Turner." Anton and Stephen collapsed in laughter, slapping the counter.

Turner stepped offstage to the sound of applause and shouts for him to do a few encores, then he walked toward the bar. Anton and the bar owner were laughing. He hoped they hadn't found his set too corny. Those old Irish standards were pretty quirky.

"Turner Pruitt, you've got them weeping in their Guinness. You're hired. If I were Irish I'd be cryin' too. 'The Fields of Athenry' is a killer."

"At least they cheered up on 'Whiskey in the Jar.' I noticed your accent—Australia?" Turner asked.

"New Zealand, mate. I never say *mate,* it just makes everyone feel like I'm more authentic."

"I hear that. I've been doing an Elvis gig for the last few years and said, 'Thank you very much' at every wedding I performed. The veil better be pretty thick or the customers might come down to reality, and we wouldn't want that."

"Well, mate, you're a smash on the mike. Would you come in every once in a while during your visit and give us a tune?"

"Sure. I'd love to. I used to tend bar back in college, so I'm comfortable around a good pub. It didn't go down too well with the seminary, but I enjoyed it."

"I'd say being a preacher and being a bartender are fairly similar jobs. Here, I made this for you. Welcome to Manhattan." Stephen passed Turner a very odd looking drink.

"What's this?" Turner asked.

"Red Snapper. Like your wife. Now go sing us a tune. Something about a redhead." Stephen winked at Turner.

"That's my Mrs. all right. Redhead through and through." Turner took a small sip, winked back, and headed for the small stage again. He bent over the piano player and had a brief discussion, borrowed her other songbook, then got himself behind the microphone. He sang his own version of the "Rose of Tralee."

Though lovely and fair as the rose of the summer
It was not her beauty alone that won me
Oh no! 'Twas the truth in her eye ever beaming
That made me love Paris, the Rose of New York.

"My God, that man is a die-hard romantic if I ever saw one." Stephen leaned on his elbows against the bar, listening.

"If Paris can get over herself long enough to see that, she'll be the luckiest woman in Manhattan," Anton said as he sipped his drink.

"Thanks for bringing him to me. You just don't find blokes like that every day."

"Blokes, what is that, the New Zealand Irish barkeep's version?"

"Right-o, mate. Oh my gawd, here comes the redhead herself. Duck."

Paris was standing in the door, framed in

light, listening to the last refrain of Turner's song. She was damn stunning in that purple faux fur, Anton thought to himself. She came over to him, trying to act calm, but in his opinion she still looked a little blotchy around the eyes. "I figured you'd take him to Dolan's."

"You've got cream cheese right here—this corner." Anton pointed to his own mouth.

Paris picked up a bar napkin and dabbed at the corner of her mouth. "Stephen, darling, how are you? How's business?" She feigned pleasantness.

"Lovely, fine, booming. Can I get you a drink?" Stephen gave her a fakey, twangy, nasal comeback. Anton watched them face off and come to a silent agreement that they'd behave. After all, it wasn't Stephen's fault that Anton had dragged Turner there, and Paris was smart enough to figure that out.

"I've sworn off the stuff. Just have Nadine fry me up a single and get me extra vinegar. Oh, and a cup of chowder. No, a *bowl,* and a ginger ale. Did you actually give him a job?"

"He's just going to drop in and sing a number here and there. He's got a hell of a voice. But I'd give him a permanent job if he was staying in town longer," Stephen said. He looked like he regretted saying that as Paris glared him into a charbroiled smoking bit of New Zealand barkeep. "Or not." He turned to stack glasses, out of eye contact.

"I need to have a talk with him. Can you direct him to that dark little table over there when he's done?"

"You bet," Stephen said over his shoulder.

"I'll join you for a bit." Anton followed Her Majesty at a safe distance.

"I'm not speaking to you."

"What is my crime?"

"Fraternizing with the enemy."

"I couldn't help myself. He's so *piacevole*, so nice to be around. So genuine." Anton lapsed into his family's creative Italian and gestured toward Turner, who was now done singing and was headed her way, no prompting necessary from Stephen.

"Yeah, yeah," Paris muttered.

"Give the man a chance, Paris. He came all the way to New York to prove to you he's serious about this marriage thing. I told you, Venus was in your seventh house. It's an excellent aspect."

"This marriage is not legal. It's not real, and he's not real. It will all fade away and we can get back to work."

"This from the woman who has had a serious drop in bookings? Darling, the universe is giving you a big sign. It's ten feet tall and glowing red. Can't you see it?"

"Shut up, you are so . . . so . . ."

"Honest?"

By now Turner was standing in front of her table. "I'm glad you stopped in, Paris. We should talk."

"Anton, get lost."

"Yes, dear. Turner, I"ll have your steak sent over."

"Thanks. Thanks for everything, Anton."

Turner couldn't take his eyes off Paris. She was shielding herself quite nicely with a thick layer of fur. It was darn cold out there tonight. And unfortunately, darn cold in here, as well—when he got near Paris. Turner said a silent prayer for Paris's soul. She needed healing, he could see that much more clearly here than he had in Las Vegas.

"Turner, I'm glad you're here."

"So am I. Your friends are great. Shall we . . . ?"

Paris interrupted him. "See, there is no we. I can take care of myself. I don't need you, I don't need anyone. I can't be anyone's wife, Turner. I just can't." Her voice was matter-of-fact and harsh. Paris peeled off her gloves and shoved them inside her purse.

Turner just sat back in his chair and stared at her. It was very unnerving. She was glad when Nadine the cook showed up at the table with Turner's steak and placed it in front of him. Nadine wiped her hands on her white apron and thrust one of them in Turner's direction. "I just wanted to meet the man with that voice. I'm Nadine, the cook."

"How do you do, Nadine the cook, I'm Turner the part-time musical entertainment." He shook her hand, then nodded toward his steak. "Very nice work, Nadine, it looks delicious."

She blushed and looked embarrassed. "Tanks."

"Single? Chowder? Anything?" Paris glared at Nadine.

"Keep yer pants on. I'll have Mary run them out. I can only carry so much." Nadine glared back, turned tail, and left.

Turner poured ketchup on his steak, baked potato, and carrots.

"Good Lord," Paris said, disgusted.

Mary showed up with Paris's food. She was Nadine's niece, with the same mousey brown hair and buggy eyes. She smacked the plate down so hard that the food jumped and a fry landed on Paris's coat.

"Crap." Paris picked it off her fur quickly and threw it on the table.

"Sorry." Mary threw a napkin down with some silverware and handed an extra one to Paris, then stared at Turner with what looked like unabashed adoration.

"Thanks." Turner smiled at her, then picked up his fork.

"Shall we eat?" Turner paused, waiting for

Paris. So *polite,* Paris thought. Mary curtseyed to him and ran off. *Curtseyed,* yet.

Paris waved. "Go . . . eat. You're starving."

"Long flight. Peanuts." Turner had a mouth full of steak now.

Paris picked at her deep-fried cod and poured vinegar on it. She'd thought she was hungry, but now she felt sort of—not. She took one bite. It was good, but she was feeling nervous about what she wanted to ask Turner.

"Can you answer a few questions while you eat?"

"Sure."

"So, forgive me for being so blunt here, but I have to ask you about our *so-called* wedding night. I remember a few things . . . tubs, bubble bath, lots of fun."

"Thank you. You did seem happy and kept coming back for more."

"Oh, great. So my question is, did we have any kind of intelligent adult discussion about birth control?"

"You showed me your patch and swore you'd had the appropriate tests and were disease free and had been on a long dry spell—at least a year. You made quite a point of it, and I told you I was also disease free."

Paris let the breath she'd been holding out. Her patch had been on in the beginning anyway. Thank God. "Well, at least I was still acting responsibly, despite my irresponsible actions." That didn't make a whole lot of sense, but she ignored it. She picked up a fry, stared at it, put it back down, then decided on the chowder. Pepper, lots of pepper. She was shaking pepper in her chowder when Turner made a comment.

"Of course you were quite adamant about starting a family right away." He didn't stop eating for that, or anything.

"I what?" Paris stopped peppering and set the shaker down hard on the table.

"You said it was a miracle that God had sent you to me after all these years. That you were done working, you wanted to get married and have a family."

"Tell me you didn't listen to any of that."

"I did reserve some sense there. You kept your patch on, and I felt that would give you some time to get settled before we actually started a family."

"Tell me you used a condom."

"I tried. You wouldn't let me. You kept peeling them off. I swear, you were very insistent about that. I finally gave up and figured I'd married you, I was in for better or worse, and I would be honored to have children with you, Paris."

Paris's insides turned into an iced latte. All bitter and too sweet and too cold at the same time. She stood up so fast the chair behind her fell over. She ran for the bathroom.

* * *

Anton came over, picked Paris's chair off the floor, and sat down in it. "My, my. If I ate fried food I'd finish this for her."

"Nadine is a terrific cook. This steak is great."

"What became of our purple princess?"

"I believe she's unraveling in the ladies' room."

"Again? My goodness. So, now, what's the basic plan, Turner?" Anton swirled the swizzle stick in his drink.

"Let's see." Turner put down his fork. "I can bunk with you for a week while I look for a more permanent place to stay. I have to admit it, Anton, I have huge doubts and other night terrors plaguing my mind at the moment. I need to study the situation and find the honorable path. That's all I've got so far."

"No kidding? Wow, are you up for a long-term project?"

"As long as it takes. I've got to make some decisions. I've come to New York to settle things with Paris. Part of that might be sticking around long enough to work things out properly. She's never had anyone do that. She just needs someone extremely patient so she can ride out her feelings and get to the other side. Under that prickly exterior is a very vibrant, loving woman. She just doesn't remember that."

"That's true with her men, without a doubt.

She's never *let* anyone stick around. What was her family like? She never talks about them."

"She's very private that way," Turner said. He changed the subject. "I have a very strong feeling that Paris is going to need some help from a man like me very soon. I feel that this is the right thing to do. When I feel that way, nothing is going to make me give up."

"That's quite odd you should say that, because I actually have the same feeling about her myself. I think Paris's time has come. She's needed to make a shift in her career goals for a while now, but she's refused to face that."

"Perhaps I can help her with some of those things." Turner picked up his fork again and dug into Nadine's great baked potato. "I felt quite clearly when I looked down from my pulpit at the Graceland Chapel in Vegas and saw Paris standing there that she had been sent to me. I wouldn't be much of a spiritual person if I didn't see that project through."

"So basically, like Elwood and Jake, you're on a mission from God to help Paris through this time in her life?"

"Blues Brothers, aye?" Turner chuckled. "That's one way to look at it. We're certainly not being aware if we don't see the people coming and going out of our lives and what they have to offer us as far as learning goes. It's no accident who we meet and who we help. On the other hand, maybe Paris was sent to me to change *my* life."

"You and I are going to get along so well, philosophy boy." Anton reached over and gave Turner's arm a pat. "What is your birthday, by the way?"

"I'm a Christmas Eve baby. December twenty-fourth. I just turned thirty-one last December."

"Capricorn. Paris is an Aries, you know. That's what makes her hair so amazing. Aries people have gorgeous heads of hair."

"She is that, isn't she? But it's not so much her looks for me. *'Twas the truth in her eye ever beaming. That made me love Paris, the Rose of New York.'*" Turner repeated the line from the song he'd sung.

"Oy," said Anton.

It must have been a bad Danish. Or she'd eaten too many of them. That was it. That's why she wasn't hungry, and that's why she yakked. That, and the very upsetting conversation with Turner. There was no other explanation. No explanation she could even entertain right now. Paris held a wet paper towel against her forehead and leaned against the wall.

As soon as Turner had started telling her what she'd said to him back in Vegas, it'd all come back to her in a blinding flash, like sequins glittering in the morning light. *All* of it. Her encounter with

Turner, her convincing him to marry her, the wedding, and the oh-so-hot wedding night.

She remembered she'd sobered up somewhere along the line and had kept up with the wild adventure anyway—particularly the part where she'd gotten Turner into her bed. In her flashback of memory she recalled Turner telling her he couldn't have sex with her unless they were married, so she'd just made that happen. Lust is a many splendored thing.

It wasn't drinking so much champagne that had kept her from remembering; it'd been self-preservation. If she'd recalled what a complete idiot she'd been, how badly she'd behaved, she would have had to face her worst qualities. She was a manipulative, oversexed, over-the-hill woman. Turner just happened to have been the recipient of her horrible display of self-centered, sloppy behavior.

Which in some ways was lucky for her. Turner would listen to reason. He'd understand and forgive her for tricking him and using him for one wild night. He was very forgiving. Anyone else might not be so forgiving, and she'd have them to deal with. That ought to be a lesson to her.

She was going to clean up her life and get her career back in order just as soon as she put Turner back on a plane to Vegas.

Anton was so mean to bring up her bookings,

even if it was true. Damn him. This was just another example of Anton's inability to keep private things private. Obviously he and Rita had discussed it, which was just nasty; he couldn't even keep that to himself, ratting out Rita by telling Paris he knew about her bookings. That meant they were all talking about it. She crossed her arms on the dressing table and smacked her head down hard on them. Her life was shit.

It was all true; she'd just been trying to pretend it wasn't. She had seen a significant decrease over the last year. The designers kept wanting younger and younger girls. What did they see in those anorexic teenage snots? It just made her want to puke. Again.

Thirty in model years was like . . . dog years. Paris could see where the seeds of her Vegas outburst had come from. Reality bites—job woes, age woes, and boyfriend woes. But start a family? No way. She would have never said that, drunk or sober.

Paris realized, with her head on her arms, that she hadn't calculated a period into her miserable life for over two months. That wasn't totally unusual—it had happened before when she'd gotten too thin, but presently she was firmly in the fat jeans phase.

What was she going to do if she was pregnant? She was way too Catholic for some of the options she might have had if she'd come to her senses earlier.

Which left her with giving the child away. No matter what career change she made, there was no room in it for a baby.

Paris was a working girl. Period. End of story. That's all she ever wanted to be. Well, except that time she'd thought she might make a good senator's wife. Backstabbing political arenas were right up her ally.

Turner was just way too nice. She'd break his heart in tiny pieces and leave him a damaged man. She did have some scruples. She was just going to have to ignore him until he got the message. But she wasn't going to let him and Anton have a slumber party and tell all her secrets; that was for sure. She'd take Turner back with her to her place and straighten him out there.

Paris moved to go fill a paper cup with water at the sink and rinse her mouth out for the tenth time.

She looked in the mirror at her pale complexion and automatically reached in her bag for her lipstick. Maybe sparkling hot pink wasn't her best shade today, like Anton had said; she should have put on a soft rose color instead.

She tilted her head and smacked her lips together, finding her best angle. There. She might be thirty, but she was still hot. Plenty of companies wanted a slightly older model anyway. She could find work. Look at Cheryl Tiegs. She'd been a spokesmodel for the last zillion years. Of course her own personality wasn't quite as *perky* as Cheryl's.

If worse came to worst, she'd just get fat for nine months and give the kid to someone who would appreciate it. A nice couple. There were hundreds of them out there waiting to adopt. Then she'd get back to work. She just wasn't mother material. Not with her family background.

She blotted her lips, tossed the paper towel in the trash, and pulled herself together.

She just wanted to go home and curl up with one of Marla's books and a cup of hot chocolate. *Murder so Blue* . . . or *Green with Murder*—one of the new color-titled ones. That would make her feel better. This just wasn't happening. She had no proof anyway, and a bad Danish does pop up once in a while. She'd start her period in a few days and laugh about her horrible paranoid moment. Until then she'd just distract herself—keep her mind off it.

Sure.

Paris picked up her purse, slung it over her shoulder, and pushed through the swinging door of the "Lassies" restroom. She marched straight for Turner and Anton.

Grabbing her coat off the chair, she started bundling her shaky self back up. "You," she pointed at Turner with a wrist snap so quick both Anton and Turner jumped. "You are going home with me, Turner Pruitt. Get your stuff."

"Paris, queen of tact," Anton said to Turner.

"On the other hand, I might get lucky," Turner replied. "All right, I surrender, General Paris. Take me prisoner. Slap me in handcuffs."

"Oooh, can I come too?" Anton squealed.

"I'm afraid not, my friend. I'll report in tomorrow."

"Good luck."

"I'd be glad to *slap* you with something, Anton." Paris made her stone face at him.

"Hurt me. Go ahead."

Paris waved him off, disgusted, but having just a little bit too much fun playing word toss. She had to get Turner out of here and stay on track.

"I'll have a word with Stephen and be right with you," Turner said.

"Hurry it up, will you? I've about had it for today," Paris groused.

"Mrs. Pruitt, we're going to have to work on your social skills." He took a long moment and swigged down the last of his dark ale. With that, Turner headed for the bar, leaving Paris fuming.

5

Teddy Bear

Turner dropped his canvas duffle bag on the floor and gaped. "Wow, who's your decorator, The Dixie Chicks?"

"This from a guy who until recently wore a white rhinestone outfit."

"You can take the girl out of the country, but the country must stick in your craw something fierce. Is that a real chicken?"

"Stuffed. And programmable. It's an alarm clock and it crows. The neighbors hate it." Paris seemed genuinely proud of her odd possession. She flung her handbag on an old beat-up hall tree with peeling white paint. Or maybe that was that distressed country look. The fur coat made it on a hook, her boots went flying on the floor.

Turner took in Paris's place and realized he was seeing a whole new side to Paris. A really messy, tacky, interesting side. The apartment was a large studio with tall ceilings and a great huge window that let the light in—unfortunately. Because what it illuminated in the daytime was really scary.

Her large bed in the far left corner was draped with a lace curtain canopy, piled high with pillows, along with unmatched pale pink and yellow quilts. It was unmade, and on one end was a stack of clothes she must have shed. There was a chair—he couldn't tell what kind because it was covered with Paris's clothes. He could see a few almost empty water glasses on the bedside table, along with piles of books and plates.

There was a kitchen, because he could smell it, dead ahead. Pots and dishes were stacked in the sink and take-out cartons from every cuisine known to man littered the countertops.

She had a collection of small bears that took up most of the cupboard space, as far as he could tell, and apparently the collection had taken over every windowsill and tabletop. Turner pivoted around the place and got the full picture. Tall stacks of magazines had old coffee cups and saucers on top, as if the magazines were end tables.

"Just throw your bag in the living room behind the sofa. That's where you'll be sleeping."

Paris flounced over to her bed and shed a few more layers of clothing, which went on the chair.

She did have a closet, he guessed, because she stepped into an area that was draped with plain canvas panels hung from the ceiling. She vanished like a magician's assistant.

Sofa. Let's see. There was a sort of beige plaid blob of slipcovered fabric to his near left. That must be it. It faced the wall, and two tall, skinny windows poured the night lights and neon colors of Manhattan back down on it. It actually also faced an old cabinet television perched in between those windows. He didn't see it at first, because it was piled with papers.

Turner put his bag behind the blob sofa and walked around his new sleeping spot. He picked three dirty sweat socks off one sofa cushion and put them in a basket overflowing with more magazines. He would have considered sitting and contemplating his fate, but the rest of the sofa was occupied by a gaggle of larger teddy bears—in dresses.

Turner tripped over Paris's tennis shoes. Two pairs of them were just underneath the billowing bottom of the slipcover. He caught himself just before his head hit the bears.

Turner Pruitt had married a kitchy, bitchy slob.

He decided to go to the kitchen and find a glass of wine to dull his senses.

Just about then Paris popped out of the canvas

closet wearing gray leggings, thick socks, and a gray-and-white nightshirt with big pink kittens on it. Her hair was in a messy ponytail held back with a pink scrunchy. Hey, she was color coordinated.

"Help yourself to whatever is in the kitchen. I haven't had a chance to spruce the place up since I got back from our little Vegas adventure."

That was quite a while ago. But it looked to Turner like she hadn't spruced up since Clinton was in office. Or maybe Carter.

"Thanks," he replied.

"The bathroom is over there." She pointed to a door painted barn red off to the right. Actually, it was painted just like a Dutch barn door, open on the top, closed on the bottom, with a black-and-white cow's face smiling at him.

Turner felt genuine fear wash over him. What evil lurked in the heart of Paris's cow bathroom? Maybe he should have stayed put at the YMCA. But then he couldn't spend this quality time with his new wife and get her to come to her senses and talk to him.

For a moment Turner wondered if she had any senses to come to. "Thanks again. I'm going to pour myself a glass of wine."

"None for me, thanks. If you think I'm falling for that one again, you're nuts. I'm not getting drunk and ending up in bed with you. I'm going to brush my teeth, get in my own bed, and curl up with a good book. Do whatever you want. There's sheets and blankets in that closet right there." Paris pointed, then padded toward the barn bathroom door in her socks and slammed the cow in his face.

Turner found the blankets and sheets in a small linen closet that dumped its entire contents on him when he opened the door. He picked out a few things and stuffed the rest back in. He better do battle with the teddy bears or he'd never get to sleep tonight. After some careful rearranging, he managed to make himself a bit of a bed. The teddies glared at him from their new home in the corner on the floor.

The kitchen, the kitchen. Oh, my Lord. He just couldn't help himself. Turner located a trash can under the sink, but it was full to the brim. He shut the lid down as best he could. If it wasn't still so cold in New York, there would be more flies. There. He found a blessing. There would be more flies if it wasn't so darn cold.

A box of large black trash bags under the sink caught his eye. He pulled one out, shook it open, and started tossing half-eaten take-out cartons in. When he'd filled it to where it could stand on its own knee-high, he took a break.

Hey, she had a granite countertop! This place was actually kind of eclectic and interesting under her piles.

Turner looked in the fridge long enough to see a bottle of white wine in the door. He grabbed the bottle and slammed the fridge door quickly before any of the science experiments escaped.

A glass was a little harder. He saw that she had a dishwasher, but it only contained baseball hats. How interesting. The cupboard was bare except for a group of ceramic bears.

Oh, and much to his surprise, one thick white china mug with Garfield on it, declaring "I hate Mondays." That would do. There was just enough space on the top of the dish heap to run the water into the cup and clean it. No dish towels to be seen, and no paper towels. He just shook it dry and unscrewed the wine bottle. A mug of bad wine would have to do.

Paris shoved back the tubes and jars of makeup and face junk so she could sit on the edge of the counter and look at the red bump on her nose close up. It looked like a zit—a zit! All this stress was bad for her skin. She opened the mirrored medicine cabinet and pulled out a bottle of acne cream. She'd zap the little devil back into submission.

She put a blob of the stuff on her nose, then hopped down to brush her teeth with her battery-operated Sylvester the Cat toothbrush. Paris looked in the mirror again and smiled with a foamy toothy smile at her reflection. Turner was going to get the full reality-based Paris here. Let's see how long he lasted with that.

No Chinese herb known to man or woman had been able to tame the raging beast that overtook her during days 25 to 28. She put the Incredible Hulk to shame. Most months she tried hard not to appear in public that week just in case she snapped, lost the last of her wire-thin self-control, and murdered someone in cold blood for cutting in front of her for a cab.

This month her boobs were nasty sore—way worse than usual. She must have been a bad man in her last life and they'd made her a woman to get even for it in this life. Karma. That was it. PMS was just not fun.

She'd see how fast Turner Pruitt turned tail and ran back to Vegas after a few days of the horror of PMS. He really should know what an indecent sort she actually was. No manners, no patience, she was just not cut out to be one of those wives that made dinner and ironed shirts and put out whenever the guy was in the mood. Nope, she was not wife material. And neither was she cut out to be a mother to some snot-nose, whiney child with twenty-four-hour needs. She was too selfish and mean.

Paris looked in the mirror again and saw that she was crying. A few tears had escaped her green eyes and streaked their way down her cheeks. She was completely freaking out.

Damn it! Turner Pruit was not going to stir up the past for her and remind her of the pain she'd so carefully buried. She just didn't care to dig it all up. He'd just get all preachy on her anyhow.

She might have to explain why she'd decided to keep him with her instead of letting him stay at Anton's, and that would mean talking about it all again. Turner could be so pushy about trying to fix things. He couldn't seem to accept that some things just couldn't be fixed.

She shifted her head to the side a bit and looked at her reflection. It had come to her lately that she had begun to resemble her mother quite alarmingly. No doubt she had her mother's dark shadow lurking inside her, and one day the shadow would emerge and take her over completely.

No child should have to live through that. And that is why she would never allow that to happen.

Paris grabbed her ratty pink terry-cloth robe off the hook, tied it on, flung open the bathroom door, and shuffled into the kitchen. Turner was leaning against the counter drinking something out of her Garfield cup.

"That's my favorite cup."

"Many pardons, my queen, I'll rinse it out and fill it with anything you like. Hot Milk? Cocoa? I found a teakettle and two packets of cocoa mix, complete with marshmallows. Are you game?"

"Hmph. Fine." She headed to the third drawer beside the dishwasher and pulled it open to find her Twinkie stash intact. One she peeled right away and stuffed in her mouth, the other two she put in her robe pockets. "I'll be in bed when it's ready," she mumbled through a Twinkie.

"You're welcome, dear."

"And don't call me *dear*."

"Yes, dear." Turner smiled big at her and started filling the teakettle with water.

As she walked toward her bed, she glanced back at him. If she didn't know better, it would look like he'd cleaned up the kitchen counters. She could see the blue granite in spots.

Nah, it must have been that way before.

He was humming.

She unloaded her Twinkies on the bedside table and threw her robe onto the chair. She could hardly believe how good it felt to get in between the smooth blue gingham sheets of her bed and pile the quilts and down comforter on top of herself. She squirmed out of the piles of covers enough to prop herself up on pillows and peel another Twinkie rapper.

He made quite a bit of kitchen noise, then he started singing some Irish sea chanty about leaving sweet Bessie behind or some such nonsense. His voice was really marvelous, but the neighbors were going to be banging on the walls pretty soon.

"Pipe down in there, you'll wake the neighbors." She yelled, but she had a Twinkie in her mouth, so it came out more like, "Phm dwine fer ul make the gnapers."

"Whatever you say, darling." The kettle started whistling loudly and drowned out whatever else she might have to say.

"Augh!" she said.

Turner came over to her bed bearing a steaming cup of hot chocolate in her favorite cup, perched on a pretty plate she didn't know she owned. He balanced this for a moment and picked up three wine glasses with his other hand, finger balancing them, so there would be room on the bedside table for the plate. He set the glasses on the floor, arranged the plate, and placed her remaining Twinkie beside the hot chocolate.

Then he picked up the wine glasses and walked away humming again. What an annoying, beastly man he was.

She sipped the hot chocolate and finished up her second Twinkie. It was heaven, really.

A minute later she saw him cross the room with a wine glass of something for himself and head toward the sofa.

After he set his glass on the coffee table, he did the most amazing thing. He took off all his clothes. He did this very slowly, very deliberately, and without any self-consciousness at all.

He had turned down the apartment lights, and the city lights were the only thing illuminating him except her bedside lamp.

She watched him unbutton his faded blue denim shirt, fold it neatly, and set it on the table beside him, atop her stack of *Harper's Bazaar* magazines. Next he peeled off a white T-shirt he'd worn under the shirt. His naked chest was broad and gloriously muscled from biceps to abs. She licked her lips and got hot chocolate foam in return.

He folded that shirt as well, and added it to the pile. She sat up a little taller to watch him remove his boots, set them to the side, then take off his jeans. Slow and easy they slid down his magnificent legs. He folded the jeans neatly and piled them with the rest.

He turned his back to her, and she had to really sit up against her hands to see the final piece of clothing come off Turner's amazing body. His rear was truly a thing of beauty. She gasped, then heard herself gasp, and scrunched back down against the pillows in case he noticed. She quickly grabbed a paperback book off the table and pretended to read it.

Turner stretched out on her sofa totally nude, picked up his glass, and took a long drink. He stared out the windows. He didn't pick up a magazine, turn on the tube, or read the newspaper. He just stared out the window.

After a while he set down the glass and rose from his reclining position. He walked straight across the apartment, still naked, and into her bathroom. She heard water running. She giggled to herself and ate her last Twinkie, washing it down with the last of the hot chocolate. She'd have to go brush her teeth again somehow, but she'd be damned if she'd let him know she'd been watching his gorgeous self get naked.

Turner came out of the bathroom, passed by her, smiled, then lay back down on the sofa, pulling a sheet and blanket over himself. She watched as he again just gazed out the window.

"Paris?" he asked.

"What?" she replied as flatly as possible.

"Your book is upside down."

She glanced at it, then snapped the damn book shut and threw it across the room toward him. It hit the back of the sofa. She heard his deep, steady laugh echo around the apartment.

Paris threw off the covers, marched to the bathroom, brushed her teeth vigorously, marched back to her bed, turned off her light and pulled the cover over her head. Damn him! Damn Turner Pruitt.

Paris woke up with fear pressing in on her like a pitch-black cloud. It was an old fear—an old dream. She struggled to reach out of it.

"Paris." Turner's voice came out of the darkness. His hand smoothed her hair away from her temple and brushed her hot tears away. She reached out, caught his hand, and held it close to her heart.

He slid between the covers and held her with her back to him. She caught her ragged breath as she felt his warmth surround her. He was still naked, and his body responded to her nearness, but he kept holding her quietly until she felt the darkness fold into a softer feeling.

She turned her body to him and let herself have the pleasure of touching his hot, smooth skin. Her fingertips ran from his shoulder, down the small of his back, across his bare hips, and behind him. She heard him groan as she skimmed over to his front and traced lines up and down his thigh, and around his now completely full-blown erection. She smiled to herself as she heard his breath go ragged, and she traced closer and closer with her fingertips, then up and around him, ever so lightly.

She felt a strong wave of desire hit her body. She wanted to be held, and touched, and she wanted him to soothe the fire that was now burning her up. She squirmed out of her leggings and tossed off her nightshirt, then pressed her naked body against his. She took his hand and made sure he felt her patch in place. She was suddenly glad she'd reapplied it, even though she'd had no reason to even think this might occur.

He responded strongly—he must have understood, and that was the end of any control she'd had over him. His lips brushed her neck and he found his way to her mouth, slowly tantalizing her with his tongue on the way.

His arms encircled her, and his kiss was consuming. Paris kept trying to keep her head together, but she slipped deeply into the spell of his lovemaking as he completely took her over. She soaked up every inch of his heat and lust her body could get. It made her forget everything. It made her feel alive. She arched herself into him as he moved her breast into his mouth and flicked at the tip of her nipple with his tongue. This was what she wanted. She wanted him to devour her. He was darkness and pleasure, and his body demanded her. She held his shoulders as he drove her to the edge of unbelievable pleasure, touching her and moving his mouth over her. She wanted to hurry him and slow him down all at once. His body—his amazing body—was all she could feel anymore, besides the burning heat inside her.

Even when she moved herself on top of him, he took control of her and slowly teased her with his fingertips and his throbbing, hot erection. She cried out and begged him. He reached up with his mouth and drew her breast into the heat of his mouth again. As she screamed with pleasure, he moved her gently into place and finally slid himself into her. She stroked her hands across his powerful chest, and he pulled her down into a kiss that made her shiver as he again consumed her with his desire.

Paris thought she would faint. She had never, ever felt anything like Turner. The care and emotion behind his touches, his movements—the slow, pressing, burning movements that brought her to the edge again, so easily, so lovingly. This must be what being made love to was really like. She lost her senses and slipped into the throbbing motion of her own body, screaming in pleasure.

Turner moved Paris under him with one quick motion and let her wrap herself around him. He moved her up against the headboard of her bed so he could touch her better and put his mouth on hers and feel her wanting him. She had reached out to him—not so much for lust but for comforting. He felt that from her with all his senses. It gave him a rare and precious door into her deeper side.

Turner knew she was a sensual, sexual woman, because every part of her showed that right out loud. The way she dressed, her wild red hair, her beautiful lips, her flashing green eyes. But the touches she craved right now were more than that. He could tell by the way she responded to being held and stroked. She was an amazing lover, but Paris ate up love with huge bites—like a starving wild animal.

She also gave back. She was so tender inside her passion that his heart ached as he made love to her. Here was a woman, complex and difficult, but hidden deep inside her was another side—a woman with a huge capacity for love. She'd probably been storing that up her whole life, with no one to give it to, no one to take it.

Turner was so moved that he made love to her with the utmost tenderness and caring possible. Each time he touched her he wanted her to feel what he felt—that he knew her secret. Her eyes told her secret, and he let his body respond to her with his heart and soul.

The heat inside her gathered and exploded around him like a thousand-degree tornado. It made him lose his mind completely. He held her so close that he could feel her heart beating as his own orgasm tore him apart with pleasure. Her fingers dug into his shoulders, and she cried out his name . . . his name—he heard it like a sob. She didn't claw him but held so tight they were one moment as one, not two.

When the time drifted down quietly to where he felt the room around him again, felt the soft light, and the sheets, and her head resting on his shoulder, he pulled her into a soft embrace. He kissed her forehead and across her temple, holding her until finally she drifted back into a gentler sleep.

What dreams were those that had made Paris

cry out so badly earlier? Dreams so bad that she would surrender enough to let him make love to her like this? Turner felt her rapid heartbeat subside to a calmer level under his hand, which she now held clutched to her chest. He rested his cheek against her hair. Her scent was a tangle of her special Paris perfume, her shampoo, their lovemaking, and . . . Twinkies.

She was such a vibrant, sensual woman. He wanted to make love to her all over again. Having her tonight had left him hungry for more. But not just hungry for more lovemaking. He'd touched a side of her he'd suspected was there, buried under the pain of her early memories.

Would she ever come to him again? Or would she lock the door behind her after this time?

He listened to the night sounds of the city around them as he lay beside her. Through the large window the light was beginning to change from ink blue to yellow streaks.

He missed the beauty of the islands of his childhood at times like this. Many mornings he'd wake so early that he'd race the dawn across the beaches, running on the wet sand until the sun pulled full out above the horizon.

Then his mother would call to him. She was the other early riser. They'd sit on the steps and share the fruit, bread, and tea she always brought. She'd put honey in his tea, and milk, and put it in a fat blue willow mug she'd gotten at the local market. After a while his father would appear at his desk just inside, say good morning, and smile at them both. They had no windows, just board flaps for when the rains came, so it was like his father was sitting with them on the porch.

There was something so comforting about that memory. Father writing his thoughts in his old green journal, which might work into a sermon for the following Sunday. Mom with her morning picnic on the steps. The smell of the ocean, the ripe mangos they were sharing, the scent of Father's coffee.

Sometimes his father would discuss ideas with his mother as they sat there, the windowless space between them. Turner had loved listening to them talk.

Turner wondered whether Paris had any comforting memories at all. He wanted to make some for her. He wanted her to know this feeling—to have a backlog of happiness to draw on.

When the light flowed in the window enough to see around the apartment, Turner slipped quietly out of Paris's bed and into the cold morning air. He tucked the quilts around her, then crossed over to the sofa and found his duffle bag. He quickly dressed in some sweats and running shoes and his warm coat. He'd better run out for some breakfast items, because from what he'd seen in Paris's fridge, he'd either shop or starve.

Turner slipped out the door as noiselessly as possible, with Paris's key from the hall tree in his pocket.

Paris rolled over and thought about getting up, but it was so chilly. She pulled the covers higher over her naked shoulders and snuggled back in. But her mind had already started up, and she couldn't slip back into sleep.

She lay in bed and remembered her bad dream. Then she remembered Turner's warm body next to her in bed, and how comforting that had been. Hmm, and then how completely stunningly yummy everything had become as he'd gone quite crazy and made love to her. She let a smile cross her lips and felt his kisses still tingling there. My God, that man could kiss.

Why wasn't he still there? She pouted about that for a minute. If he was still in her bed she might let him have his way with her yet again. He was so terribly good at having his way.

But now what was she going to do with him? He probably thought that all meant something. He probably thought she was going to decide to let him stay and be married to her and all that insanity. The rest of her problems started to pile up on her mind, and she reached over to the bedside table to fumble for the clock.

She found the clock easily, which was very odd. It made her sit up a tiny bit and look at the table. Instead of stacks of plates, her cup from last night, books and Twinkie wrappers, there was a bare surface. You could actually see the painted wood under the glass top. There was her lamp, and the reproduction Big Ben clock, and nothing else. Was she in the wrong apartment?

A sound from the kitchen made her sit straight up and stare. It was the clink of pots and pans. Paris noticed that the kitchen looked strikingly cleaner than it had when she'd gone to sleep. And something smelled good, too.

"Good morning," Turner smiled at her from the kitchen.

She remembered his warm, naked body and him moving into her again in a little rush of a moment that made her head spin. A smile played across her lips, but she suppressed it. She didn't reply.

Sitting up hadn't gone well with her. She felt crappy. It was too early or something. Bleackk. Paris slumped back against the pillows and pulled the covers up and around her bare chest.

"I've made breakfast. Shall I deliver it to you?"

"I don't do breakfast," she croaked.

"Miracles happen," Turner replied. In a few minutes he was walking toward her with a round tray. He set it on her bedside table. Paris took a peek and saw a cup of tea, which smelled divine—peppermint maybe—a bran muffin, split, with butter melting on it, and a bowl of oatmeal. The old-fashioned kind of oatmeal, with brown sugar and a little ring of cream on it.

"I remembered what you liked from school." Turner stood beside the bed. He handed her a cloth napkin. She didn't know she owned a cloth napkin.

"What, Sister Julia Child's lumpy oatmeal?" Paris said from her pillows.

Turner laughed. "I can't believe the names we made up for those poor nuns."

"Remember Sister RuPaul? We swore she was a guy under that habit," Paris said.

"Ah yes, Sister RuPaul. Man, we were mean little brats."

"And Sister Timothy Leary." Paris laughed. "She was a total space case teaching us art. I swear she was on acid."

"And poor Sister Don't Do That. Nuns should never do sex ed." Turner wiped his eyes from laughing and leaned on her bedside table.

"It's a mortal sin for sure." Paris laughed till she choked. She reached for the tea and took a sip. It was very fine. "Why the heck did your non-Catholic parents send you to St. Mary's?"

"They had friends that recommended it, and it was close to my great-aunt. Luck of the draw."

Paris suddenly remembered what she needed to say to Turner. "Listen Turner, pull up a chair. There's something we have to talk about."

Turner stared at her for a moment, then pulled

her newly unearthed bedroom chair into position beside the bed.

"Before you run off with Anton again I . . . well. People here don't know about my early days. About my mother or father or any of that. I've put that part of my life behind me. Do you understand?"

"You don't want me to say anything to your friends about your family. I haven't done that, Paris, I know you are a very private person. I'm not one to talk about anyone's business."

Paris heaved an audible sigh. She fluffed back against her mound of pillows. "Thanks. I guess I just figured you for a little too honest for my own good."

"Have some faith, Paris, I'm on your side." Turner got up and went back into Paris's kitchen.

He was on her side? Paris picked up her plate and silver fork, took a nibble of her bran muffin, and washed it down with tea.

She had yet to go into the part of the story where she explained her bad behavior that night, how she'd tricked him and that she was a terrible woman for getting him to marry her just so she could seduce him. He might not be on her side after that.

She thought about seducing him again before she explained that. He looked so seduceable. Parts of her ached with flashbacks of his considerable skills in the lovemaking department.

She'd have to clean herself up to pull that off, though. A quick shower, a slinky outfit.

She set down her plate and slid out of bed, feet hitting the cold wood floorboards. Her head spun. You'd think she'd been on another champagne weekend by the way she felt.

Then she stood up. Then she wondered if she'd make it to the bathroom without passing out.

She did make it. Barely. She yakked her guts out till there was nothing left to yak.

Paris splashed cold water on her face till the color revived in her cheeks. Then she brushed her teeth vigorously and tried to keep the room from spinning. She turned on the wall heater, pulled on a robe, and tried to warm her icy body.

She must have some serious illness. That was it. She'd been coming down with something for months, and it had finally arrived. That *must* be it. It had to be.

Well, she was going straight back to bed until it went away. God Almighty, she felt terrible. And she felt even sicker knowing she was lying to herself like a bold-faced, corrupt politician. Who was she kidding? Herself? Hardly.

After a while she quietly opened the bathroom door. Maybe Turner had left—if she was lucky. Which she wasn't.

Or maybe Turner was sitting in a tall kitchen chair, leaning on the high counter with his arms crossed across his chest, staring at her with his big, serious brown eyes, looking concerned. Him and his look of concern. She broke his gaze and trudged toward her bed. *Bed . . . give me bed,* she thought to herself.

But he was hot on her trail. He pulled the covers open for her and let her fall into the bliss of her bed without any dignity left. He rolled them back over her curled-up body that would not face him if it had to. She made herself into a ball in the darkness of the down comforter and its many quilt companions. "Uuhhhhh," was all she said.

"Paris, I'm going to the drugstore now and get a pregnancy test. Let's just face the facts and see what we are dealing with."

"Flu. Plague," she muttered.

"How long?" he asked.

"Long."

"We'll see. Drink some water because I'm going to need a few drops of pee."

"Charming," she muttered again.

Turner put his coat on and strode out the door.

Outside in the hallway Turner locked the dead bolt with her keys. He walked toward the elevator and looked at the indicator above the doors. She was on six, and the elevator was hovering on twenty-six. Turner decided to take the stairs. A particular urgency overtook him. What was six flights of stairs compared to obtaining certain knowledge that he was going to be a father?

He wondered how Paris could have gotten pregnant wearing her birth control patch, but it sure wouldn't have been the first time a determined soul had made it through to stir up some couple's life. He smiled thinking of that determined soul meeting up with Paris.

But Paris—she'd be devastated. Fear washed through him as his boots hit one stair after another. What would her reaction be?

As he rounded the landing on the third floor he felt his wave of panic subside. It was replaced by an odd calm. Whatever came up, he was going to be there for her.

In the drugstore he found a friendly guy to grill for information on the entire shelf of tests before him. "Which of these is the most accurate?"

"Well, these are mid-stream tests, and these are strip tests. The strip is faster, but this one detects minute amounts of pregnancy hormone. It's pretty darn sensitive. That's about eight or ten days after conception," the pharmacist rattled on.

"I'll take two of each kind, thanks." Turner went for his wallet and started pulling out twenties. "What do I owe you?"

"Fifty three dollars and twelve cents."

Turner handed him fifty-five dollars.

"Here you go, that makes fifty-four and one more is fifty-five. Good luck, sir," the pharmacist added.

"Thanks, I'm going to need it." Turner took the bagged-up tests and steadied himself against the counter before shoving off.

Outside the drugstore, a kind-looking old man was handing out religious pamphlets. "Bless you, my child." He smiled and nodded at Turner as if he knew something.

"Thank you." Turner took the flyer and smiled back at him. He kept moving down the sidewalk, thinking of the odd string of coincidences that had led him to this moment in time. How strange it was that he and Paris should cross paths after all these years. Or maybe collide was the proper term. He and Paris had collided into each other, each for their own reasons, and now life would never be the same for either of them. He saw his path very clearly, all of a sudden. Like fog lifting off the city streets and leaving a ribbon of road clearly visible. He knew the way.

Paris rocked herself back and forth in her overstuffed rocking chair, her knees drawn up, her retrieved nightshirt stretched over her gray leggings, her arms wrapped around her captive legs. She put her head forward and let her curtain of hair fall around her, blocking out the light. She didn't have much experience with this stuff, but she was pretty sure from the talks she'd had with her friend Marla that she was indeed pregnant with Turner Pruitt's child.

She had about fifteen minutes to prepare herself and be ready for whatever Turner's reaction was. She'd probably have a hard time convincing him to put the baby up for adoption, but if he had a brain in his head he'd see her point. She was going to have to be very, very strong with him. She took a few deep breaths. If she was going to be strong, she better pull her fear back into herself and use it to focus. No one, not Turner, not any man she'd ever known, or woman for that matter, could make her do anything she didn't choose to do. When she made up her mind about a matter, it was written in stone, just like her heart. Her stone-cold heart.

She'd be ready.

6

Catchin' On Fast

The little blue line didn't just faintly hint: it glowed like a strip of neon as Turner stared. Paris glanced, then crossed her arms and braced her back against the white wooden chair.

"So that's it then?" she said.

"That would be the fourth one, so I'd say that's it." Turner placed the test alongside the other three tests of various types they had lined up down the center of the dining room table across the Sunday funny paper section. Turner found that somewhat amusing at the moment, with each test taking up another square of the Garfield comic.

"You're smiling?"

"I was reading the comics."

Paris sat forward in her chair. "Before you start with the bighearted speech I'm sure you have planned, I have something to say to you."

"Actually I don't have a speech planned, Paris, I'm just going to take things as they come." Turner reached for her hand, but she tucked it under her other arm, as if to keep herself from accepting comfort from him even if she weakened and reached out. He left his hands on the table. "I'm listening."

"You are the only person in this city that knows about this. You're also the only person here that knows what happened with my mother and father. I know because of that you'll understand that I can't be a mother to this child.

"I intend on going away somewhere until the baby is born, then finding a suitable family to adopt it. When it's over, I'll return to New York, pick up the pieces of my career, and get back to work. You and I are going to get a divorce, and I expect you'll go back to where you came from. In nine months I'd like to be able to put this unfortunate mistake behind me and that includes you. Do you understand?" Paris let out a breath, as if she'd been holding it, and sat herself back against the chair again.

"Yes, I understand. I understand that you've thought this through for the last hour since I left the apartment, and this is what you've come up with as a solution."

The look on Paris's face told him she was going over what he said carefully. Good, she was paying attention, anyway.

"So we're clear on this? I can't tell from what you just said."

"I have a few questions." Turner laced his fingers together and looked at her with all the love he felt for her. "Do you understand that just because your mother had postpartum psychosis doesn't mean that you will repeat that?"

"I see that she and I have extremely similar temperaments. I'm not even willing to take a chance of that happening. The child needs to be placed away from me immediately. I'd like to arrange to have the adoptive parents at the birth and take the child home from the hospital. I don't want to see it, bond with it, or anything. Don't even think I'm going to change my mind about that, Turner. I've already given it up in my mind. I've suspected for a week at least that I might be pregnant. I'll just be the carrier."

Turner had to keep himself from getting angry with her. It was his only chance to keep communication open between them. He bowed his head silently for a moment to regain his composure.

"I'm only a little ways along anyway, I might have a miscarriage. It's very common, actually."

"I sincerely hope not."

Paris glared at him, but at least she had the wisdom not to pursue the subject.

"I figure I've got a few months before I start to show, but I might as well leave now before I start to puff up and people start talking about how much weight I've gained. This place is worse than high school the way gossip flies around."

"You know the idea of leaving town and hiding out while you're pregnant is pretty old-fashioned. This is the new millennium. You're a married woman."

"And then have everyone ask where the baby went? I don't think so. I'm going to take a leave of absence. Rita will figure I'm having a nervous breakdown or something." Paris smiled a wry smile. "Who knows, I might be."

"They have treatment now, Paris."

"They had treatment then, too. It didn't work. Somewhere out there I have a sister that was taken away from my mother because they couldn't help her."

"Paris, they didn't know what was wrong with your mother back then."

"They were smart to give my sister up for adoption. She was neglected and sick. I didn't realize my mother wasn't taking care of the baby right. Dad was so messed up himself, he didn't see it either. If I'd realized it, I'd have done something." Paris's voice broke for a moment.

Turner watched as she pulled her emotions back up like a drawbridge and shut the door. He got up from the table and went to get Paris a glass of water. "Paris, you were only a child. Your father didn't realize what was happening. Those were different times."

"He should have given me up too. But no, he keeps me, gives my sister away, and two years later I end up in a convent. He killed himself over my mother's illness, Turner. Is that the kind of tragedy you want?"

"Your father died of a heart attack, Paris."

"I watched him do it, Turner. He would never rest. He worked three jobs. He drove himself to that heart attack. At night he'd never sleep or eat right. He did it on purpose. He killed himself all right, just slowly."

"Paris, it wasn't your fault."

"I've got their genes, Turner. I'm not going to let that happen to a child of mine. That baby will be safe with other people."

Turner set the glass of water in front of Paris and put his hand on her shoulder. It was hard as a rock—tensed up to the point of pain, he was sure. He gently rubbed the tight muscle.

Paris let out a cry and jerked her hand across the table. The water glass flew as she struck it. It hit the kitchen counter behind them, shattering. Turner moved as she shoved her chair back and ran from him.

There was nowhere to run in this apartment to get away from Turner, so she headed for her bed.

Paris couldn't take another minute of Turner's kind heart or kind gestures—water, peppermint tea, all his good deeds. His touch was full of sympathy for the pain she'd suffered as a child. She hated that sympathy.

She wanted with all her heart to never have her child know that kind of sympathy. She wanted people to say *Oh, that child was so lucky to be adopted by Mr. and Mrs. Jones. They wanted a baby so much.*

Paris kicked off her slippers and clawed her way back into her bed covers. She wrapped them around herself and made a cocoon. And then she cried until she thought she'd never be able to stop. She cried for her father, for her mother, and for her sister, whom she'd only known for two months. Her tiny, helpless sister, who, she hoped, was in a place where no one had to pity her, ever. Then she cried for herself and for the baby she was going to give away.

Turner pulled the upholstered bedside chair up close to Paris's bed after he let her alone for about an hour to cry. Crying was sometimes the only thing to do to get your soul rinsed out from all the pain. He cried for her as he sat there and wiped away the tears with his shirt sleeve. Then he sat quietly beside her until her cry subsided, her breathing changed, and he knew she was sleeping.

He had a lot of thinking to do. Funny thing was, most of it had come to him as she'd described her plan to him. Now he just had to figure out how he was going to carry through with his part. Paris was a force to be reckoned with. Her strength was amazing. But her strong walls were built on sand, because she didn't have the foundation that loving parents can give. He needed to be the foundation she never had. For her . . . and for their baby.

He looked around her apartment at the odd assortment of childlike things: her bear collection, her dolls, even her piles of pillows and quilts. Paris had never gotten to be a child. She'd taken care of her mother as she'd fallen to pieces after the birth of Paris's sister, and after that she'd taken care of her father. Under such unfortunate circumstances, her childhood had been taken so early from her. She was right about one thing—they should have adopted her out with her sister. He supposed the father couldn't bear parting with Paris too, after having lost everything.

And after all that caretaking she'd done, all those people had died or been lost to her anyway. No wonder Paris felt the way she did.

Turner knew it was his job to get Paris through this. Her pain and her past were a storm that they'd have to pass through to get to the other side. And he would have to be a firmly rooted tree that bowed in that storm but always stood steady. He just hoped he could stand the hundred-and-twenty-mile-an-hour winds that were about to hit.

As the afternoon sun shifted downward from the peak of the tall windows, Paris stirred under her bundle of covers. She was too hot, and she pushed them aside with her feet.

"Good morning again," Turner said.

Paris rolled herself toward the sound of his voice, pulling the sheets with her. He stood next to her bed. He was shaved, dressed in jeans and a clean white shirt. She could smell his clean scent. She breathed him in and felt a smile cross her face. He was the only thing that didn't make her feel nauseous right now. She adjusted her bleary eyes to the clock beside her bed. It was one o'clock in the afternoon.

"I left you some lunch in the kitchen—a pot of soup and a sandwich. Just warm the soup back up. Paris, take a nice shower and put on some clean clothes. You'll feel better. I'm going to the bar and I'll be back late. We'll talk more tomorrow."

"Thank you, *Dr. Phil,* I'll be sure and spruce myself up. I'm sure a shower and some lipstick will fix everything."

Turner sighed, then bent over and kissed her

on the forehead. "It won't fix everything, but it will make you smell better." He smiled big at her, shrugged on the big Nevada shearling coat he was holding, and headed toward the door.

"Go ahead. Leave me," she hollered, sitting up in the bed.

"Good-bye, Paris, I'll be back about eleven tonight. I've got your spare key from the rack here." He held it up in the air, then stepped through the open door and closed it behind him.

She was alone. Alone with her miserable self. She usually liked her own company. No one to tell her what to do. But today she was too horrid to be around. Turner might be right. A nice shower and maybe a little lunch might perk her up.

She showered.

She shaved her legs.

She washed her big red piles of hair and conditioned them. The smell of the apricot conditioner almost made her yak again.

She got out and toweled herself off and wrapped a smaller yellow towel around her hair. Then she stared at her naked body in the mirror. She knew she was barely two months along, but she could swear her belly was puffed. Her breasts were definitely puffed. They hurt like hell. This was going to be like never-ending PMS.

She bolted out of the steamy bathroom and walked naked across the apartment to the wardrobe closet she'd had built on one end of the room to house her big clothing collection.

First she went for the favorite jeans. They wouldn't button. She found her black velvet pull-on leggings and squiggled into them. Then she located the Fat Bra. The one she used when she was retaining water and didn't want to be underwired to death. It was black satin with scalloped edges. Very 1940s.

Last came the black velvet pullover with a cowl neck. She might as well be a lounge lizard today and just pull-on-pant matching-top herself right up.

There was no way she was going to keep herself from thinking about all this. She might as well call Marla in Indiana and spill her guts. Marla might be willing to put her up till the baby was born, and Marla could keep her mouth shut better than any girl on earth. Marla kept her own career as a mystery writer a secret from the entire world for years! Surely she could keep one pregnant coworker-almost-best-friend in her guest house for seven months.

Paris went in the kitchen with her hair still rolled in a towel. It was starting to give her a chill. She nosed around at what Turner had left her; chicken soup, the old-fashioned kind—Campbell's—out of a can, a cheese sandwich on sourdough all wrapped in wax paper, which was probably the only kind of wrap left in the house, and soda crackers. She ripped open the soda crackers and nibbled on a few. That was the only thing she remembered from her talks with Marla during her pregnancy—soda crackers cut the nausea.

Just the thought of eating anything else made that wave of horrible feeling rise up in her again. Surely this must be the worst case of nausea on record. This couldn't be normal. Maybe something was wrong with her. She must have super-nausea. Women couldn't have it this bad and still work and carry on with their lives. Hers must be worse. She leaned against the counter and steadied herself while it passed, nibbling on the soda cracker as best she could. Maybe she should go to the doctor before she left town. Dr. Yee had been watching over her female health for the last ten years.

Then again, maybe his receptionist would talk to her pal at the coffee shop and the pal would tell her hairdresser and it would be all over town in about an hour.

Kakkkk. The crackers were stuck in her throat. Paris went to the fridge and grabbed a bottled water. She glugged it down and got rid of all the cracker bits. Now she had soda cracker crumbs all over her black velvet cowl-neck.

She better just plant herself on a chair and call Marla right now. Surely Marla would take her in. What would she do with her apartment? What about all her stuff? A year in storage? And then the apartment would be gone, and no way was she losing her Manhatten apartment. It would take her another two years to find a big open loft like this!

She'd sublet to someone. Paris walked barefoot across the large open room. Her feet got cold. She slipped back into her bed and warmed her feet under the covers. She found the remote on her recently cleaned bedside table and turned on the Collector Channel. Maybe a nice bear would come up today. She muted out the sound and watched the sales pitch with closed captions.

Her portable phone was on the table beside her, waiting. Waiting till she got the nerve to dial. Finally she grabbed it up, propped pillows around her, and speed-dialed Marla Meyers Riley in Indiana. It had been several years since she'd flown down to Richmond to attend Marla's wedding, but they'd kept in touch. Marla e-mailed her, and Paris called her on the phone because she wasn't that great on computers. Except for eBay. She could now say she'd mastered eBay.

She heard Marla's mellow voice on the phone.

"Marla, it's Paris."

"Paris! I've been thinking about you all week. We haven't talked for months. Did you go to the April showing of Helmut Lang's fall line? I'm dying a slow calico housedress death down here. I need you to send me some goodies. Maybe a nice fringed boot or a new handbag?" Marla jumped right in with their usual girl talk.

In the background Paris could hear Marla's toddler making noise.

"Hush yourself, child! She wants raisins. She'll do anything for raisins. Guess what? I'm pregnant again," Marla announced.

Paris was truly stunned. She'd called Marla to whine about her situation and have a little pity party. Instead her friend had really thrown her for a loop.

"Paris? Is everything okay?" Marla's voice suddenly sounded a million miles away on the phone receiver.

"Yes, yes, everything is fine. I'm just shocked with your news! That's wonderful. When is the baby due?"

"October. We didn't want to announce it too soon, just in case anything happened. But I'm firmly pregnant now, and guess what? It's a boy!"

"Oh, a boy. Wow. Are you morning sick?" Paris asked.

"Not too bad this time. After the first two months passed I really felt better. Remember how miserable I was the first time? I could only eat dry toast and ginger ale for three months, I swear."

Paris wasn't sure whether to take hope in the

fact that her nausea might lift in a few months or to feel ratty because this was the first time for her and it was miserable for sure. She felt a wave of emotion come up. Damn hormones. Her first time. Her last time. She just wished it hadn't happened at all.

"You sound weird," Marla said.

"I'm . . . I got married," Paris blurted out.

"What?"

Paris could hear Marla's shock through thousands of miles of fiber-optic wires. "I got married in Vegas to an old high school friend." There, that sounded better.

"Why didn't you call me? I would have thrown you a wedding!"

"It was sort of spur of the moment. On my birthday."

"Ah, yes, well happy thirty, you crazy redhead! You sure did it up royal. What's his name? Did you get my birthday present? I'm so mad at you for not calling me sooner." As usual, Marla was jumping all over the place.

"I did get your present. She's a peach. I love that hat." Paris looked toward the sofa at her bear collection, which had been restacked by Turner. The biggest, most beautiful bear had come from Marla, and it had cheered Paris up quite a bit on her return from Vegas.

"It reminded me of you in that Southern belle

shoot we did in Savannah. Remember? Our dumb hoop skirts kept flying up in the wind."

"You're right, she does look like us."

"His name?"

"Oh. Turner Pruitt."

Marla laughed. "Mrs. Turner Pruitt. Is he gorgeous?"

"Totally."

"Well, you and Turner just get your booties on a plane and come down here. I have to check him out. Where are you going to live, anyway?"

Paris just couldn't tell Marla the whole story. Marla was her best friend, but Marla's life was so right—so in order. Her own life was like a car wreck, and she just couldn't bear to hear the disapproval that Marla couldn't help but express if Paris told her the truth. Most of all the truth about giving the baby away.

"That's sort of up in the air at the moment. We're in New York right now."

"Honeymoon in Vegas?" Marla giggled. "Did you get married by Elvis?"

"Worse than that, he *is* Elvis."

"Wow. This I have to see."

Paris was thinking of ways to get off the phone. She just had to sort a few things out, and her discomfort was growing with each question.

"Listen, I'm off to work. Congratulations on the new bun in the oven, and I'll call you really soon and let you know where we decide to live,"

Paris said. She could hear the pause from Marla's end.

"Well, okay, but call me really soon. I want to hear all the details next time."

"I will. I promise. Kiss everyone for me." Paris rushed, then she hung up the phone before Marla could add anything else.

Well *that* had been a disaster. Now Marla was going to wonder about her and try and reach her. Marla loved a good mystery.

Paris slumped down against her pillows. She'd just have to go hole up on her own somewhere. She put a pillow across her face and blocked out all the light and sound. She didn't want to hear anyone tell her what she should or shouldn't do. Not Marla, not Anton, not Rita even. That left basically no one for her to talk things over with. Except Turner.

7
Hard-Headed Woman

Turner rolled a large keg of beer from the back cooler and slid it into place. Stephen was having him do much more than sing. The minute Turner had set foot in the bar, Stephen had begged him to help so he could get to his paperwork. Turner was glad for it. Stephen had given him a detailed list of tasks.

The more mindless the task, the better, at the moment. He was having a difficult time concentrating. He felt so off-balance after learning Paris was pregnant. So much to sort out in his head. He pulled up newly washed glasses and began to set them in their slots.

Dolan's Pub was busy with a group of kids from the art college down the street. Turner had examined a few IDs of the younger-looking ones, but they had all been legit, or else *very* good fakes. Their drink of the hour seemed to be light beer anyway, and they all lived a few blocks away in dorms.

They made him think back to his high school days—his and Paris's.

He and Paris had always been on the fringes of acceptability. He, for his unusual upbringing, Paris because of her tragic family background. It seemed to him that she'd felt like an outcast most of the time. Yet at seventeen she had reached out to him in the middle of her pain. They had been best friends. Of course he had been deeply in love with her back then, as only an adolescent boy can be, but she'd never known it.

Her humiliation over her family was something they had talked about on dark, starlit desert nights, laying on the roof of the school in their secret hiding place.

He remembered longing for her then but never breaking the bond of their friendship to reach out and touch her—except to hold her when she cried, or tickle her chin till she stopped crying.

Turner remembered going to visit Paris's mother with her because Paris had been afraid to go alone. Father Gibbs had found a heart that day and granted permission for Turner to go along when he'd seen how nervous Paris had been. Turner remembered that Sister Claudia had also been chosen to accompany them.

It had been one of the hardest things Turner had ever done. The hospital had been frightening. There'd been screams in the distance, even though they'd been ushered into a small parlor, away from the other patients. Paris had held his hand so tightly.

Her mother had been brought in, but she'd been severely drugged up, and could hardly talk. Paris had let go of Turner's hand, walked over, said hello, and kissed her mother on the cheek. Her mother had not recognized Paris, and she'd slapped her in the face.

Sister Claudia had come to the rescue, stepping between Paris and her mother. She had said a prayer over the woman and crossed herself. Lucy Jamison had started crying hysterically. Paris had buried her face in Turner's shoulder. The nurse had then stepped in and escorted Mrs. Jamison out of the room.

That was the last time Paris ever saw her mother. When high school ended, Paris had run to New York without looking back. Turner had returned to the Cook Islands before going to college, and they'd never crossed paths, or letters, or phone calls again until she'd shown up in Las Vegas on her thirtieth birthday.

Turner understood that Paris had had to leave that part of her life completely in order to forget. He'd known that if she'd kept in touch with him, she'd be keeping in touch with that painful time.

He had missed her so much in those first months.

Over the years he'd seen her on the cover of every fashion magazine on the newsstands. He'd told his friends that he knew her, but he'd never told them anything else about her.

Turner was aware that he'd always been known as a guy who could be counted on to comfort someone in a bad situation. He guessed that was still his role in life, and that must be why he had been reunited with Paris. His job with her wasn't done yet.

And his own life was obviously about to take a drastic turn of direction.

Mary Finelli brought him a drink order and smiled a sympathetic smile.

"I know a man with woman trouble when I see one," Mary said.

"You're a wise woman, Mary Finelli."

"Never you mind, Turner Pruitt, there are plenty of ladies in the sea," she replied.

"I think I'm lost at sea today, Mary. I better have a nice cup of your coffee and stay on shore."

Mary winked at him. "That'll do it."

He filled the order quietly and smiled back. He was lost in his thoughts. He better focus on present time.

But then present time held its own complications. He was just going to take one day at a time. Maybe he'd even have to do moment by moment with Paris.

* * *

Turner knocked on the door and said, "Paris, it's me, Turner," before he set the key in the lock and turned it. It was quite late, and he didn't want to frighten her.

Paris was not asleep. It looked like she'd been very busy since he'd left.

Whatever order he had created previously was now chaos. Her dishes and food littered the kitchen, her clothes were strewn over the bedside chair again; it almost looked like she'd been gutting her closet, because the piles had multiplied into mountains.

Well, the woman had a great deal on her mind. He wasn't going to bother about domestic details at a time like this.

"I'm packing."

He shut the door and spun the dead bolt.

"I take it you've come up with a plan?" he asked.

"I'm going to Switzerland. It's a neutral country." Paris flung another sequined something on one of the piles while she spoke.

Turner took off his jacket and hung it on Paris's empty coatrack. "What's the rush?"

"The sooner I get out of here the better. People won't be counting months if I leave while I'm not obviously pregnant."

"Have you spoken to your agency yet?"

"I called Rita today."

"You told her you were going to Switzerland?"

"I told her I was taking a year off. Our marriage has really come in handy, Turner, I have to say that."

"Can I fix you anything? I'm going to have a cup of tea."

"People who try and make me hot tea always have something bad to say." Paris stopped sorting clothes and stared at him. "You aren't actually going to try and talk me out of leaving, are you?"

He went to the kitchen and set down the small bag of tea and fresh fruit he'd bought at the market down the block.

"No," Turner replied, picking up leftovers and dishes as he walked through the kitchen. He disposed of the trash and stacked the dishes in the sink. The kettle on the stove was bone dry, so he filled it with cold water. Tea always tasted better when he started with cold water, then got a good boil going.

"Come over here and join me, Paris. I'd like to talk about a few ideas."

"I don't want to talk."

"I don't think you have a choice." Turner kept his voice calm, but this time, he was determined to have his say.

"I can take care of my own problems." Paris's voice was getting very edgy and loud.

"Paris, your problems are my problems. You are my wife, and that is my child you are carrying," Turner said firmly.

She took one step in his direction. "Our marriage was an accident, and I don't even think it's legal. I know it's not legally binding when you are too drunk to know what you are doing."

"Been consulting attorneys?" Turner got out two cups. The Garfield cup for her. He took Bugs Bunny. He'd never seen Bugs Bunny lose an argument.

"I saw it on *Oprah.*"

"Ah. Come and sit down, please."

Paris crossed her arms over her chest, but she came over to the table and sat herself down. She looked very beautiful in her black velvet, with her red hair flaming, and her angry green eyes drilling holes in him. For a minute Turner wanted to take her in his arms and make the world go away just for her. Okay, for him too.

The kettle started to scream. Turner set tea bags in the cups and poured boiling water over them.

"I bought you green tea with ginger today. It tastes best if you let it steep for three minutes. It might help your nausea."

"Just spit it out, Turner. Cut the tea talk, and spit it out."

These bags were't going to get their three minutes. He took them out, set them on the plate he'd layed out, and looked straight at Paris. Eye contact.

"I want to see you through this all the way, Paris. I don't want you to fly to Switzerland. I want to experience this time. That is my child you are carrying, too. I respect your feelings, but I have different feelings." He leaned forward.

"I am willing to keep the child, with or without you. If you truly feel you can't be a mother to this baby, that is what you feel. I, however, am completely willing to be a father. I embrace being a father. I am excited about being a father! I was just as excited about being a husband to you, Paris. And whether you believe it or not, I am legally . . . and spiritually . . . your husband." His voice was strong with his conviction.

Paris looked stunned. She didn't have a snappy comeback. She stood perfectly still, as if she'd been hit with an unexpected spotlight on an unexpected stage.

Then Turner did what he'd wanted to do for days. He strode over to Paris and broke down the barriers she'd put up. He took her in his arms.

She didn't melt, but she didn't push him away. He tipped up her chin with his hand and kissed her pretty, stunned lips. It was a good kiss. The kind of kiss you get before anyone starts thinking about it. He kissed her deeper and ran his hand into her beautiful red hair. She let out a minute sound of pleasure.

Then she must have started thinking. Then she pushed him away.

"I don't care if some paper says you are my husband. I'm not your wife."

He stood in front of her. She wasn't going to run away this time. "*Yes*, you are. And you aren't going to Switzerland. You're going to come with me to Las Vegas, and I'm going to see you through this pregnancy, and then I'm going to welcome my child into my life. You are free to leave or stay at that point. If at any point you actually decide to *be* my wife, let me know, won't you?"

"Oh the great, patient Turner finally cracks." She put her hands on her hips.

"I don't care if I have to handcuff us together to get you on a plane. You are coming back with me."

Paris looked amused. He was slightly amused himself. As if he'd ever actually do that. Although he might.

"I don't think that will be necessary." Paris gave him an odd smile. "To tell you the truth, it's not a bad idea. I will come back to Las Vegas with you. After all, I'm using this marriage as an excuse, why not take it all the way? And you are right. Why should I go through all this alone? You got me pregnant, and if you want this baby, who am I to say you can't have it? Maybe we can talk more about that, because it would be better from my viewpoint if a settled couple adopted it, but I'm willing to hear you out."

Turner was completely shocked at her reaction, but he sure wasn't going to question it. "Now you're making some sense," Turner said. He turned back into the kitchen, picked up the cups, and brought them to the table. "Come and drink this tea. We'll plan this out and get your place packed up and settled."

Paris, much to Turner's surprise, had turned the tables on him. She came and sat next to him pretty as you please. He wasn't fooled a bit, though; she had ulterior motives. He could see her brain working on twists and turns and devious Paris pathways.

When would she ever just surrender to some kind of peace? He thought perhaps this wasn't the time to go into that. He had months ahead to work with her. To soften that hard heart of hers. To charm her out of her coiled-up, ready-to-strike mind-set.

Turner really did feel like a snake charmer. He was never sure when Paris might strike hard and send venom right into his bones and do him in forever. Charming Paris was not a job for the weak-minded. Turner took a deep breath, brought his spirit some much-needed clarity, and sat at the table. He took a long sip of green tea with ginger. It had a bite to it. Just like his Paris.

8

Devil In Disguise

Paris was on a flight to Las Vegas with her new husband, Turner Pruitt, the Elvis-impersonating minister. Anton had said the words to Marla on the phone, but he still couldn't believe it. Something was afoot in Parisville. Anton's mind spun through their last weeks together like a search engine, looking for links and clues. He was Googling through Paris's words and actions, looking for *something.*

"I can hardly believe our Paris letting some guy be nice to her on a long-term basis." Marla finally filled up the gap in the conversation.

"I don't know what it is yet, but there is definitely something not right here." Anton flopped on his down comforter and let it poof around him. He was still in his pajamas, and it felt great. Besides, he needed to get grounded.

"You don't think the guy is a phony, do you? You don't think she's in trouble?" Marla asked.

"No, I met him. He's like . . . Mr. Wonderful. He's patient, he actually loves her, you can see it on his totally gorgeous face. And you should hear the guy sing. And responsible? Oy. He did fill-in for Stephen at Dolan's Pub like you wouldn't believe. He sang Irish and poured beer like a champ, and the regulars loved him. His bar was a regular confessional. He even got Moss McGuity to stop drinking and go back to his wife in a mere four weeks. And his aura was bright as a saint, I *swear*." Anton fluffed up his pillows and got comfortable for a big, fat gab with his Marla pal. Damn the long-distance bills, full speed ahead.

"Did you ask Rita about Paris?"

"All she had was the same story. Paris is going to take a year off and be with her new hubby. But let me just say there was not a shred of kissy-kissy going on there between Mr. and Mrs. Pruitt. Gawd, can you even believe that name? Paris Pruitt. Talk about your karma. She sublet her place and put most of her stuff in storage, I hear."

"She was very strange on the phone a while back. I thought maybe it upset her that Tom and

I are expecting again. Like maybe she turned thirty and she was feeling, you know . . . her time was passing her by."

"I really don't think Paris has stopped to listen to her biological clock. It could have a nine bell alarm go off and she'd just throw it across the room," Anton said.

"Well, whatever it was, she sounded strange. Maybe you and I should take a little jaunt to Las Vegas. Just a surprise visit from the folks, you know."

"Marla, I never thought of you as that sneaky."

"I write mysteries."

"That's clever, not sneaky. I like sneaky on you."

"We better go soon before I get as big as a house. They don't like you to fly in the last trimester."

"I've got a big show coming up at the end of this month." Anton reached for a celery stick and crunched into the phone. He'd been trying to slim down from all the pasta fungili and pub food he'd been consuming lately.

"I've got a book due at the end of the month, too. Can we wait that long?"

"We just need a quick weekend. I'll check with Rita and see what's coming up."

"I'll check with Tom and see if he minds me taking off for a few days. He's awfully overprotective when I'm pregnant."

"Oh, bring the big lug. He's fun." Anton

crunched. He hated celery. Maybe some prosciutto and Gorgonzola would improve it.

"Tom will be so thrilled to hear that." Marla laughed. "I'll e-mail you. Watch your inbox."

"Yes, ma'am. I'll watch. And congrats on the new bambino. Love ya, hon. Kiss, kiss and kiss to Tom and Lizzy and Max." Anton made kissy noises into the phone, then hung it back on the station.

He lay in his pillow world for a while, thinking. This was the first time he couldn't just nail whatever it was that was making him nuts in the head. He was going to have to get out his tarot cards and his I Ching and whatever the heck else was in the house until he figured it out. Maybe he'd call his favorite psychic, Susan Sanderford, and have a phone reading.

If he was going to do a phone reading, the card, the coins, and whatever else, he better get something on this celery and a fresh vodka tonic, because this was going to take all his concentration.

Turner would have carried her over the threshold under normal circumstances. Instead he managed to twist the doorknob and push the door open with his foot. His hands were full of Paris's suitcases. She sauntered in front of him carrying a round hatbox with one finger and her handbag, which looked like a miniature version of most handbags he knew. The rest of her purse stuff must be in the hatbox. She did make a pretty picture, with her tight black skirt slit up the back, her tight crisscross knit top, her sort of forties high-heeled shoes, her huge picture hat, and her big sunglasses. Very Rita Hayworth, Turner thought.

"Akk, this place is a nightmare. Who's *your* decorator, Mary Kate and Ashley? What's up with the cats?" Paris dropped her hatbox on the floor and took off her sunglasses.

This from the woman with the bears. And Turner figured at least one of these suitcases was full of them—and their brick bear house, by the feel of it.

Millie stepped out of the kitchen into the light of day. She had a cup of coffee in one hand and a spoon in the other. Her hair was in rollers, and she had her famous housedress/peignoir combination on. She waved the spoon at Paris.

"Is this your new wife? Go help your husband with your ten tons of luggage, honey. Unless your arm is broke, he ain't your packhorse."

God, have mercy, Turner prayed. He piled the trunks and suitecases just inside the door and shut it behind him so the neighbors wouldn't hear the potential screeching of two pigheaded women all the way down the hall.

"Who are you, his mother?"

"I'm his first wife. This is what happens after

you've been rode hard for ten years. He done wore me out, and I'm too old to take it anymore. I just sent him out in the world to bring a fresh wife home. I'm so glad he found a sturdy, capable gal like you to take up the washin' and ironin'. I hope you don't mind cookin' neither, because I'm real tired of that. We can share the sex, though. I'll take even days, you take odd. Tonight's your night, honey. Lucky you," Millie said. She stopped and took a long, calm slurp of her coffee.

A long, horrid silence hung all around them like wallpaper about to peel itself right off the walls. Then Paris shrieked with laughter. She laughed so hard that she had to sit down in one of Millie's old kitchen chairs and hold her sides.

When she caught her breath, she looked at Millie. "Go get me a glass of water, old woman, you and I are going to get along just fine."

"Say please or you can go to hell."

"With ice. It's absolutely stifling in here. Can we crank up the a.c.?"

"Fine." Millie went in the kitchen and rattled around.

Turner decided to vanish into his bedroom and try and figure out who was going to sleep where.

Once inside his room, he looked around at his serene, simple sanctuary and knew it was never going to be the same again.

* * *

"So, you're going to hide out here and have the baby, give it to Turner, then hightail it back to New York."

It wasn't a question.

"Yes, Millie, that about covers it," Paris said.

"Well, aren't you just a piece of work. I guess I better stop smoking. We wouldn't want Turner's baby to get exposed to that. It's bad enough it's exposed to you."

"Which is my point exactly." Paris got up and kicked her shoes off on the floor. She stretched like a cat. That flight had been murder. The turbulence had been horrid, the food had been worse, and she hadn't gotten a bit of sleep. She took her hat off and flung it toward the sofa. "I'm beat. I'm going to take a nap."

"You do that, Princess. I'll put a pig on the spit, and we'll have a feast later in your honor." Millie got up slowly from the table.

Paris was pretty sure that pig-on-the-spit thing was bull. She'd have Turner order out. As if you could get decent take-out anything in Las Vegas.

There was a small knock at the door. Paris jumped at the sound. Her nerves were shot from flying. She watched Millie move slowly to the door. Maybe it was the rest of her luggage from the airport.

Paris looked over Millie's shoulder, her curiosity getting the best of her. There stood a pale young girl dressed in a gray suit. She must be a Watchtower church witness or something. She had pretty blonde hair.

"Turner, there's someone here for you," Millie hollered. "Step inside, I'll fetch him," she directed the girl. "Set yourself down on that couch. Be sure and sit right on that fancy hat."

Very funny. Paris went over and picked her hat off the sofa. The room was so small that it was about four big steps across and about eight to the dinette set by the window. The smell of stale cigarette smoke caught in her nose, and she felt a little ill. Not that there was anything in her stomach to yak up after that twelve-hour flight from hell. She really wanted a nap.

Turner came out of his bedroom and looked quite shocked, in Paris's opinion, when he saw the woman on the sofa. His face went from surprise to a broad smile. She decided to watch.

"Sarah!" Turner went straight for the girl, took her hand, made her stand up, and hugged her. She stood with her hand in his and blushed. "What on earth are you doing here? How did you find me?" Turner asked her.

"Your parents."

"You look so grown up. I can't believe it's you."

Paris watched the tender scene with interest that lasted about three minutes, then she yawned and headed in to what must be Turner's room. The simple craftsman-style furniture and earthy colors were so Turner. So . . . earthy.

She hardly paused to look at anything—not that there was much to look at. Beige everything. Paris stripped off her clothes and jumped naked into Turner's bed. The sheets felt cool. The apartment was stuffy and hot. But she was used to New York, and a cold one this year at that. Her thoughts were going fuzzy on her. She pulled up the covers from their neatly tucked in state and gathered them around her.

For just a moment she felt sexy. She thought about Turner's body next to hers. His hard, excellent body. She was so tired. He had such strong arms. After all, it wasn't as if she could get pregnant. She yawned again. Then she fell asleep.

Turner took Sarah's hands up in his again. They sat at the dinette table talking low. Millie had made them some iced tea and gone to do some "phone time" in her bedroom. He hoped they were quiet calls that didn't involve any sexual sound effects. Millie was great at sexual sound effects.

His whole life was just a long, drawn-out hands-across-the-table-cup-of-tea drama these days. After this all faded down, he was going to go play racquetball with his builder buddy Greg Stauffer and get some exercise. He wanted to move his body until he felt that great exhaustion you get from running hard or playing hard. The kind of exhaustion that's followed by a great night's sleep. In the meantime, now there was Sarah.

"Of course you can stay. Millie has an extra bed."

Now he had three women on three different time zones, in a ten-by-twelve kitchen, a fourteen-by-twelve living space, including the dinette table at one end, two bedrooms, and three beds. Worse than that, one—count 'em, one—bathroom. Turner shuddered. Maybe he should consider a larger apartment. Or a house.

Obviously, he was going to be on the sofa tonight. He just couldn't picture Paris letting him cozy up. Maybe they could do that thing where they hung a blanket across the middle of the bed.

She'd made it perfectly clear on their twelve-hour flight that their marriage was in his imagination only from now on and there would be no more sex. He'd believe that when he saw it. She had . . . an appetite. He'd been more than happy to feed that appetite. It was his husbandly duty after all. He smiled to himself.

Sarah asked so many questions that he ended up explaining more than he wanted to. About the marriage, the pregnancy, and why Paris was here.

"It's hard to explain exactly, but Paris is Paris. I intend to keep the child myself," Turner said.

"Oh Turner, how horrible for you."

"It's not horrible. I'm very excited to become a father."

Sarah patted his hand. "Maybe it's not an accident I decided to come and find you. Maybe I can help. I've decided to stay here in Las Vegas and go to nursing school."

"I wish you'd written me, I could have found you a place to rent, helped with registration and all that."

"It was a sudden decision on my part. I turned twenty-one and decided I needed to get away from my parents, your parents, and the mission. I didn't have anything more to offer them until I went out into the world. I did two years of college by correspondence, and I was just aching to learn more than I could get from the mailbox and my computerized classroom. I wanted to know what real college is like."

"I do understand that. I know my mother and father would have loved for me to carry on with them, but it wasn't my path to stay there. Even they knew that. They sent me here for my last year of high school so I could be a broader person.

"Who knows about the future. Maybe after the baby is born I'll go back. I know my parents would be thrilled." Turner patted her hand and let go gently.

"I know they would be, too," Sarah replied. She gracefully picked up her iced tea. "And maybe I can help you when the time comes."

"In the meantime we need to get you settled."

"I'm afraid I'm being a terrible burden under the circumstances. I was rather foolish just to show up at your door. I don't have much money. I'd thought to get a job first, then enroll in school for fall quarter. I can send for some money from my parents."

"If they're anything like mine, they don't have much. I've been working and saving and investing for quite a few years now, Sarah. I can certainly help you out with a place to stay. You are my oldest friend. You're like a sister to me," Turner said. He saw an odd look in Sarah's eyes, but he was too tired to try and figure it out. Maybe there had been some trouble she didn't want to tell him about back on the islands. Maybe a boy.

Millie came out of her room with no curlers, a fresh orange housedress, and lipstick. Wow.

"Lunch break. I sold fifteen magazine subscriptions in four hours. That's some kind of record for me." Millie smiled.

"Hey Turner, I decided to quit smoking for the baby's sake."

"Thank you so much, Millie, I know how hard that is for you."

"I'm tough. I can do it. But I'm going to need some patch or something. I figure a nicotine patch here, a Manhattan there, I'll get through it. What's this gal's story?"

"Millie, this is Sarah Eastman. We grew up together on the Island. Her parents were missionaries with my parents. She's decided to go to nursing school here in Las Vegas, and we're going to put her up until she gets on her feet. Sarah, this is my roomate Millie."

Millie eyed Sarah carefully. "And Las Vegas just popped out of a hat?"

"I wanted to see Turner again." Sarah laced her hands in front of her demurely, nervously placing them under her chin.

"Well you picked a hell of a time, sweetcakes, but pile in. You can bunk with me. I've got twin beds. Can you cook? 'Cause I'm sick of cooking, and from what I gather, Princess Paris ain't going to be much help around here."

"I can cook a little. I can learn."

"Oh, brother. Don't they teach you girls anything these days?" Millie went off into the kitchen.

Sarah looked exhausted to Turner, but he'd have to have had a chart to figure out the whole time zone craziness of these women. Except Millie—she always kept crazy hours. Pretty soon they'd all get on track anyway. Hopefully.

Turner felt the extreme need to go to Graceland Chapel, chat with Reverend Danny Vernon, and have an hour or two of prayer. Patience. He'd pray for patience.

9

Return to Sender

Paris stretched and yawned. She had no idea what time it was except for the fact that it was dark in the room. She hated total darkness. She'd have to put a nightlight in here.

She reached next to the bed, felt for a lamp she vaguely remembered, and pushed the switch over. A blinding light pierced her eyes, and she covered them with her hands. Ouch. Did Turner not know that bulbs came in twenty-five watts?

She thumped herself back against the hard pillows. My God, where was she, anyway, Howard Johnson's? The sheets were scratchy, the mattress was hard as a rock. Paris threw back the covers and stomped out of bed.

This was a calculated error on her part. She

felt the nausea rise like a tidal wave. There better be a bathroom in this place very near, and very empty.

Paris ran out the door of Turner's bedroom, naked. She had no time to think about these kinds of details. That door—the one that Sarah person was just coming out of—that was her goal. Paris sped up and knocked Sarah out of the way. She slammed the door behind her, fast.

"Wow. She's got it bad," Millie called to Sarah from her bedroom. "Why are you up so early, girl? Come in here and chat at me."

Turner groaned. He was used to Millie, who needed hardly any sleep, clanging pots at the crack of dawn, but he was not used to seeing a naked woman streak through his apartment at 5 A.M. That's what his Indiglo Timex watch glared back at him. 5 A.M. Poor Paris.

He tried to stretch out his legs, but they hit the end of the sofa. He'd better try and get back into those pajama bottoms he'd kicked off. Sarah probably wouldn't appreciate seeing him in the buff. But it had gotten so damn hot last night in the sleeping bag that he'd pretty much tossed everything aside.

He felt with his foot at the bottom of the bag and pulled them up with his toes till he could reach them. Hopefully he could just slide into them before any of the ladies hit the room.

* * *

Paris splashed water over her face. She didn't have a toothbrush in here yet, and she didn't feel like using Turner's. She didn't want any more of his contributions to her body—no germs, no sperms. That's what had gotten her into this mess in the first place. Why the hell would a woman voluntarily subject herself to this horrible condition? Why would you willingly say *Oh, let me have your love child, it will be so wonderful. Never mind while I yak my guts up for nine months and get fat and ruin my figure and be ripped open by a ten-pound screaming. . . .* She couldn't even go on. They must be insane. There must be some mind control men do that make women go willingly into this state—pregnancy.

She didn't want to think about insanity right now.

She heard a huge thump, which got her mind back to more immediate matters.

She was naked and needed to get back to the room from whence she'd fled. She was pretty sure she'd seen knucklehead Turner on the sofa, and she knew Sarah had already gotten a full Monty of her, but hey, she'd been naked around women her whole life. Modeling was anything but a career for the modest.

So to hell with it. She flung open the door and marched herself naked right down the narrow hall, with Sarah and Millie gabbing behind her in the end bedroom. She walked across the living room, where Turner was on the floor, wrestling with a pair of pajama pants. He must have fallen off the sofa.

"Give it up, Turner, I've seen the package." Paris flung her comment at him as she passed. She hid the huge smile that hit her mouth by turning into his bedroom door and vanishing. What a clown that boy was. Some things never changed.

Oh, brother. Turner bounced to his feet and finished pulling his pajama bottom on and fastening the button just in time to see Sarah standing at the other end of the room, staring. *Oh, brother, again.*

"I'm so sorry, it got pretty hot last night and I had to shed some layers." Turner apologized.

Sarah smiled an odd smile. "Millie is going to teach me how to make breakfast." Then she scooted back down the hall like a high-strung dog. He better not even think those words or he'd end up with one of those, too. Now, how was he going to get some fresh clothes and a shower around here?

First, he was going to barge in on naked Paris. He'd only gotten a short look at her as she'd passed for the second time, but it was enough to make him wish his wife would reconsider sharing his bed. Her bed. Whatever. She was so round and delicious, and her breasts were so . . . well-proportioned. He remembered her in the tub on their wedding night, all slippery and wet.

That got him all hot. He got a semi-erection thinking about her that way. Enough to make his pajama bottoms bulge. But hey, this was his wife he was thinking about.

Sarah came back in the room. Her eyes just grazed over him as she headed for the kitchen. He saw her cheeks go scarlet. He was just not even going to think about that. Turner headed for his old bedroom with speed and determination. He knocked on the door, then turned the knob and went in. By now, the offending erection had wilted into submission.

"Hey!" Paris groused.

Although why, he didn't know. She was back under his covers. In his nice, firm bed.

"I've seen the package, Mrs. Pruitt."

"Humph. This mattress is hard as a rock. What is this, a reverend thing? Denying the earthly pleasures?"

"If I was into denying myself earthly pleasures, I wouldn't have married you, my dear." Turner danced around Paris's trunks and suitcases so he could get to the large antique armoire at the foot of the bed. There was just enough room for him to manuever the drawers open.

"Sweet-talkin' Turner. I'm going shopping. What the hell time is it anyway?"

"About five-fifteen in the morning. Sarah's learning to make breakfast, Millie is going to consume a pot of coffee, and I'm going to eat and run. I've got business back at the chapel." Turner pulled the clothing he needed out of their neatly folded piles.

"Figures."

"What does that mean?" Turner turned to look at her.

"Nothing."

"I'm here for you, Paris. You can call me any time. I'm leaving you the chapel phone number, and anyone there can tell you where I went if I step out. I'm helping Reverend Vernon go over some music. I'm also going to get the names of a few doctors. We'll need a good OB." Turner turned back to the armoire. "Maybe Sarah would like to go shopping with you later. We'll also need some groceries for this crowd. I'll leave you some money."

"Oh, that kind of shopping. I don't do that kind. Don't you just call the grocer and have it sent up?"

"No, we don't have it sent up. We get up off our fannies and buy milk and bread."

"How very primitive of you." Paris sounded cranky. Then again, she'd sounded cranky since they'd gotten on the plane in New York.

"Why don't you just rest today. Have a good meal, get your bearings. Millie can take Sarah shopping," Turner suggested. "I'm going to take a quick shower and get going." He finished selecting clothes, then shut the armoire doors and all the drawers. He was going to nab that bathroom for a shower before it was gone forever.

"Have a nice day, *honey.*"

"You too, *darling.*" Turner marched out of the room with his clothes and made it to the open bathroom. A shower. A cold shower.

Paris couldn't believe she was wide awake at five-fifteen in the morning. She picked out one of her suitcases and opened it on the floor. Bears. Bears! Well, they couldn't just stay in there forever, they'd get musty and unhappy. She grabbed an armful and placed them on the bed. She'd just unpack everything and make this room more bearable . . . *bear*-able. She giggled at her own joke.

She was getting on the phone to the nearest department store as soon as they opened. This mattress had to go. Maybe even the bed. Plus she'd need her own linens. They should be in one of these trunks. Unless it was a trunk the airline was bringing over later. She'd just buy some new linens anyway, just in case. And since she could not fit into a single pair of pants she owned, she'd have to go maternity shopping. Donna Karan had maternity clothes, didn't she?

Paris busied herself unloading the contents of

her suitcases and trunks onto Turner's bed. She found paper in his bedside table and started making a shopping list. *Her* kind of shopping. Three-hundred-thread-count shopping.

Turner took a two-minute shower to conserve the hot water. Only time for one verse of "You Left Me Cryin' in the Chapel." Plus he had things on his mind, and he'd think much more clearly in his own office—away from here. He had questions to sort out. Like how he was going to support three women, and how he was going to get Paris to stop thinking she'd be the worst mother on earth, and how he was going to keep his hands off her.

Maybe working two jobs would help. Besides his job at Graceland Chapel, there was always work for a good Elvis in Vegas. There were lots of private parties and conventions. Also, summer in Vegas through September was the peak wedding season, then things quieted down until December and New Year's.

It was a good thing that he'd found the interim reverend. Danny could stay on as Turner's assistant. That would be a first, having an assistant. Turner would have some free time.

Turner knew Graceland Chapel could easily support a part-time assistant. He'd gone over the books carefully when he'd bought the chapel a few years ago, and it'd barely been breaking even at that point, but he'd done a few do-it-yourself renovations to class the place up, and business had picked up nicely. Enough to pay the overhead and a little on the side.

But he'd need more than a little on the side if he was going to keep up with Paris, Sarah, Millie, and baby makes four. He'd have to save up for a larger apartment—or a house. First and last months' rent could really add up on a decent place.

He'd just have to put his name in to the Elvi booking agency and get some action going. He wiped the fog off the bathroom mirror and peered at his reflection. He'd have to let the sideburns grow out again.

When he left the bathroom, fully dressed, Turner heard all sorts of banging and thumping coming from his bedroom, so he decided to join Millie for a cup of coffee and a muffin instead of attempting another round with Paris.

"You've got yourself a wildcat there, Reverend," Millie said. She had to remove the Tootsie Pop from her mouth first. Turner figured that was her replacement for the usual morning cigarette.

"Looks like it." He poured himself a cup of coffee in a non-cartoon mug and sat down heavily on a kitchen chair. "Any suggestions?"

"Just let nature take its course." Millie smiled. "Everything will work out." She took a gulp of coffee and stuck the sucker back in her mouth.

"You should be preaching this Sunday, Millie. These are great muffins. Thanks for baking so early in the morning."

"Sarah made them. She's not too stupid in the kitchen."

Millie hadn't bothered to take out the lollypop that time, so it had come out a little garbled, but Turner got it. Just then Sarah emerged from the hallway, looking very conservative in a white high-necked, long-sleeved blouse and a dark floral skirt. Turner hoped she hadn't heard Millie.

Then he remembered she'd seen him . . . inflated. He just hoped Sarah wasn't very observant. Fat chance, but Turner hoped anyway.

"Sarah, good morning."

"Good morning, Turner." She gave a wan smile.

"Millie tells me you made these muffins. They're very nice. Apple spice?" Turner went for the distraction.

"Yes, thank you. Millie is a good teacher." Sarah got a cup down from the cupboard, went to the stove, and poured herself hot water. She squeezed a wedge of lemon into the cup and added a little honey. All this had been carefully laid out next to the stove, Turner noticed.

"I thought I'd go to the chapel for a while, then run over to the college and see about enrollment forms for you."

"Oh," Sarah said. "I thought we'd do that together. Or I'm happy to do it myself." She carefully sat down across from him with her hot lemon water and sipped it slowly.

"I can't let you just wander around Vegas alone. I'll pick you up and we'll go together."

"I'd love to come and see the chapel, Turner. Can I just go along?"

"Of course."

Millie had a smirk on her lollypopped lips. She removed the sucker and spoke up. "I thought I'd hit the Piggly Wiggly early before my calling hours. Can we do that first, come back here, then you and Sarah can go to the chapel?" Plop. Back in it went.

"Sure. I guess we're a one-car family at present, so we better make do," Turner replied. He took a deep draw off his coffee. If this day was any indication of the complications that awaited him, he was going to need more than patience to get through it.

Paris stalked through the bedroom door, sniffing the air. Turner twisted in the chair to see her approaching in some kind of flannel gown. Her hair was all crazy. She looked like Raggedy Ann, but meaner. She also looked more like six months' pregnant. Turner thought this was odd. He guessed he hadn't noticed when he'd glimpsed her glorious body earlier.

"What's that I smell?" She got closer. She spotted muffins. She dove in and practically stuffed one in her mouth whole. "Hmmmm. Good."

Sarah was staring at her.

"Paris, I'm going to take Millie and Sarah food shopping, then drop Millie back here. Then Sarah and I are going to the chapel and later over to Nevada State College to get some enrollment information. Would you like to come along?" Turner asked.

Paris got a strange look on her face. Her left eyebrow twitched up high on her face. She looked at him for at least thirty seconds. Thirty seconds of some women's deadpan stare is very unnerving. Then she peeled another muffin out of its paper wrapper, took a big bite, and chewed. That took some time as well. Finally, she answered him.

"I don't care what you do. I've got some shopping to do too, so when you and *Dara* are all done, you'll need to drive me to the nearest mall. Hopefully there's a decent department store nearby. There wasn't any when I left here years ago."

"Sarah," Sarah said.

"Oh, right." Paris flounced to the cupboard, picked out one of Millie's Siamese cat cups, poured coffee out of the Mr. Coffee, and plopped dramatically in the other kitchen chair, leaving Millie standing.

"Neiman Marcus, Macy's, that's about it.

There's a Saks on Las Vegas Boulevard, and a few other high-end stores out on West Sunset," Millie rambled. "Darn good coffee, Sarah. Paris, you shouldn't be drinking this crap."

"Okay, ladies, we'll get this all worked out. Sarah, Millie, let's roll. I'll bring the car to the front of the building." Turner slugged down the rest of his coffee, got up, backed out of the kitchen, and made a break for it. He heard the sound of female arguing in the distance as he grabbed his jacket and keys and ran out the door.

Turner finally snagged a Load and Unload Only spot in front of the building. He eased the station wagon into the parallel spot and turned off the key. He was thinking very unpreacherlike thoughts by now about how to unload all these women out of his life. But apparently this was his journey to take, and he better make the best of it.

Besides, he was married to Paris now, and he'd have to make the best of it. She just needed some understanding. And a reality check. And maybe a spanking. He smiled at that thought. He better watch himself, he'd get all hot for her again. He thought about bills and baseball for a while.

He waited. And waited. He turned on the radio to the oldies-but-fifties station. He sang along to "Crazy Little Thing Called Love" at the top of his lungs. A few people opened their windows and started to yell, but didn't. He hoped that was because a little music in the morning wasn't a bad thing.

Where were those women? He would go up and get them, but that would be like walking into the jungle . . . at night . . . with a T-bone steak in his pocket. They'd eat him in three bites. So he sang three more songs, this time a little softer.

A glint of color caught his eye, and he turned to take in the amazing trio of women headed his way. Paris was dressed in a black dress and big hat, her standard fare. Sarah didn't have the conservative skirt and blouse on anymore; instead she wore what looked like one of Paris's wrap dresses, even though she'd buttoned a sweater over the top to cover up any cleavage visual.

Millie looked very nice and even had a hat on. Kind of a Mamie-Eisenhower-goes-bad thing.

Millie swung open the front passenger door, but Paris flew past her like a true New Yorker. Millie shrugged and climbed in back with Sarah.

"Where did you get this monstrosity?" Paris said as she slid into the seat next to him.

"This isn't a monstrosity, it's a 1969 Vista Cruiser Wagon," Turner replied.

"It's my car," Millie said. "It's my showgirl car-pool wagon. We'd load up a pile of us long-legged ladies and get to work. It saved us all money, and we had a great time. We all chipped in on the car. Then we all retired one by one and I ended up with it. It's a beaut, isn't it?" Millie settled back into her seat. "I only let Turner drive it," she added. "Turner, you should take the back way. The morning traffic is starting up."

"Don't drive all jerky. I'll get sick," Paris added.

"Can you go through downtown? I'd love to see a few sights on the way," Sarah asked.

Turner sucked his breath in slowly and put the car in drive. God help him, because nobody else would.

10

Double Trouble

Dr. Shapiro ran the ultrasound bar over Paris's gooped-up stomach three more times and stared at the monitor intently. He pointed at the monitor and made humming noises. Turner stood behind him, nodding. This was pretty much pissing Paris off.

"What is it, an alien?"

"It's twins." Dr. Shapiro shifted the monitor so Paris could see. She propped herself up and stared at the wavy gray lines, trying to see what they were seeing.

"See here?" Turner stepped over and pointed. "Two heads."

"I have a two-headed baby." Paris fell back against the hard hospital couch with a thud.

"No, you have two one-headed babies." Dr. Shapiro laughed.

"How the hell will I get them out of me?"

"It's been done before," the doctor replied. He put down the ultrasound bar and wiped some of the gel off her with a soft cloth.

"You did this. You put two in there." Paris felt like crying. She bit her tongue to try and keep the tears in.

"My apologies," Turner said. He went around beside her and took her hand in his. She pulled it away.

"How can you tell so early?"

"The size of her uterus, for one, and the ultrasound quite clearly shows two separate sacs. Why don't you get dressed and we'll have a chat about it in my office. I'll answer any questions you might have."

Swell. A chat. Paris grimaced at the doctor. Trust Turner to come up with some happy jolly sort of obstetrician. The two of them were just beaming. Turner shook the doctor's hand.

Paris sat up by herself. "I'm so glad you two are so happy. It's peachy, isn't it? Now I have two huge kids in me and I'll be stretched till I pop." She swung her feet over the side of the bed and slid down. She got dizzy. Turner steadied her.

"You can get dressed, and I'll be with you in a few minutes, Mrs. Pruitt." Dr. Shapiro did his vanishing act.

"And now you'll have two babies to take care of, Turner. Have you taken that in?" Paris tore off the flimsy paper gown they'd given her.

"Look at you! I should have known. I thought you were a bit bigger than average." Turner patted her belly.

"Cut that out." She pushed his hand away. "This is horrible. It was bad enough before."

"You're going to be fine, Paris. But we need to take even better care of you now," Turner said.

She wrestled away from him. "Get out. I want to be alone."

"I'm not going to leave you, Paris. I'll be here for you, no matter what." Turner put his arms around her.

She felt herself be unresponsive. She wanted to lean on him and cry and be comforted, but she just couldn't bring herself to break down and let him in. He let her go, but he kissed her gently on the cheek, then walked out the door and shut it quietly behind him.

Paris sat down in the green leather chair next to the ultrasound bed. She felt the tears roll down her cheek. She wiped them away. What was she going to do? It was bad enough, the whole idea of her handing one baby over to Turner and getting on with her life, but two? Everyone would think she was a monster.

But deep in her there was a monster. It was just like her mother's monster. And two babies would make it twice as bad. She'd never be able to make it. She'd crack up, and it would be just like her mother with her little sister. She remembered how her mother would cry for days at a time, not change the baby, and even gave up nursing her. Paris had started feeding it and changing it and trying to cover up for her mother. She'd cut school until they'd come to get her.

Then they'd started with the doctors, and her father just hadn't been able to deal with it, and everything had gone so, so wrong. Paris remembered the day when they'd taken her mother away in a car. A nurse had stayed with her and the baby. Her father had just put his head in his hands and cried. If she'd just been older than eight, she could have taken care of her broken-up family. If they'd just left her alone and let her stay home with them.

After that she'd ditched from public school so many times they'd finally put her in St. Mary's Boarding School. She'd suddenly felt bad for the trouble she'd added to her father's life. She'd wondered if it had contributed to his death. She'd wondered if he'd somehow killed himself. No one had really told her that, and they'd all talked about his heart problem. She'd known it was his *broken* heart that had killed him.

She grabbed five Kleenexes out of the box on

the table next to her and bawled into them until she hiccupped. She wished she knew more about everything that had happened. But one thing was for sure. She wasn't going to let her history hurt these babies. Turner would take good care of them. He'd see to it they were happy. He'd probably marry some nice girl, and the babies wouldn't have a mom who thought that passing car lights were spaceships and hid her children under a bed.

Paris sobbed again and blew her nose. She grabbed another bunch of tissues. These memories were killing her. She'd just have to shove them away like she always did and get on with life.

She'd just have these babies and give them to Turner and return to New York. She could lose herself in New York. She'd go back to work for Rita and make a comeback. Or maybe Rita would even let her help out with the agency.

They always needed models to mentor and teach the new ones. And she'd be a ruler-rapping, tough teacher at that. She stuffed all the used tissues in the trash can and took out another pile to wipe all the leftover ultrasound goo off her stomach. Yuk, she was a mess. She cleaned herself up and finished dressing. She could do this. She could. She sucked in a big breath, grabbed her canvas-and-leather handbag, and braced herself to walk out the door.

* * *

Turner had listened to Paris crying in the exam room. He'd been guarding the door for the last twenty minutes, redirecting staff and letting Paris have a few moments alone. He was hoping she'd think over her decision now that they'd confirmed it was twins. But he was prepared either way. These were his children. It was actually a blessing having two. They'd have a brother or a sister, and even if Paris left, they'd be a little family.

He'd asked himself almost every night how Paris could leave her baby and walk away. How could her heart not ache for her child? He knew she truly thought that it would be better for the child if she was out of the picture. How she'd become so completely convinced that she would follow in her mother's footsteps was not so clear to him.

He was going to bring this up in the doctor's office. He himself had some questions that needed answers. Maybe if Paris heard the answers from a medical professional, it would help.

It made him ache to hear her sobbing in that room and not be able to go to her. But she was still not ready to let him in. Somewhere, long ago, Paris James had had her heart broken so badly that it might never be fixed.

But he had to try. He loved her. He loved those two babies she was carrying.

Turner decided at that moment that he would find out everything there was to find out about postpartum depression and psychosis, and about Paris's family. When she talked about that time, about her father and mother, rare as that was, it was always from the perspective of a young child. He was pretty sure she had never looked into the actual facts. Maybe, just maybe there might be something there that would help her.

Paris came out of the room at that moment. Her eyes were red from crying.

"I'll tell them you're ready," Turner said.

A few minutes later they were both seated in front of Dr. Shapiro's desk. Paris was nervously twisting a strand of hair. Turner was staring at the plastic model of a womb with a plastic baby in it. It was all such a miracle. Dr. Shapiro had his hands laced in front of him and was smiling at Paris.

"Well now, we'll just get right to it, shall we? From the ultrasound we can see you've got fraternal, or dizygotic, twins in there. That means they are in separate amniotic sacs and are not identical. Identicals most often share one amniotic sac. Identical twins are one egg that split into two babies at some point. Fraternal twins came from two different eggs. Are there twins in your family, Patricia?" Dr. Shapiro paused his hand gestures depicting dividing eggs and looked at her.

"Not that I know of," Paris answered.

Turner looked at her to see if she'd correct the name thing. He guessed she wanted to stay as anonymous as possible wherever she went, so they were using her real name on the chart—Patricia. She didn't say a word, but her face was pale and her hands fidgeted with the strap of her handbag. He put his hand over hers gently. She didn't push him away this time, probably for the doctor's sake. But he could hope.

"Well, many factors can up the percentage of twins, including maternal age."

Paris tossed her red hair back with the hand Turner had captured, escaping his grasp. She harrumphed.

"Don't sweat it, Mrs. Pruitt, you are still a young woman. These days I see many patients in their forties having babies. The most important thing I need to tell you is to take extremely good care of yourself. I'd like you both to go to a prenatal class we have here that talks about maternal care during your pregnancy.

"I would've liked to have had you in here a bit earlier, but I'm glad you are here now. We like to monitor twin pregnancies a bit more closely." The doctor handed them a pile of pamphlets with pregnant women on them and kept talking.

"You are in good health generally, and things looked fine on the ultrasound. Because it's twins we'll want to see you every two weeks from now on. Twins deliver anywhere from thirty-five to thirty-eight weeks rather than the full forty. If we get to thirty-eight, we're really doing well."

"Oh, are *we?*" Paris snarled.

Dr. Shapiro seemed unfazed. "Yes, we are. We are a team. Me, you, and your husband. Our goal is to get those two babies delivered healthy and happy. Right?"

"Right," Turner answered. He felt bad that it had taken him so long to get Paris on track with an OB. But what Dr. Shapiro didn't know was that they'd gone through three other potential doctors before this, and Paris had dismissed each one for whatever whim she'd come up with.

This time Turner had put his foot down and insisted Dr. Shapiro was the one. Turner liked him. He was easy to talk to. Which reminded him; the moment had come to bring up the subject he was determined to know something about.

Turner spoke up. "I have some questions, Doctor. I'd like to know everything there is about postpartum depression. My wife's mother had a severe case, and Patricia is convinced she will have the same problem."

Paris looked at Turner as if she might slap him. Her face went red as flame and her green eyes snapped with anger. He didn't want to bring up old pain, but this was his chance to get her to listen to reason. It looked to him as if Dr. Shapiro was on his wavelength. The doctor paused to look at Paris, sat back down, and appeared as if he was choosing his words carefully.

"We've made some real advancements in this area. I had a patient that helped educate me on this matter more than anything I learned in med school." He looked up at his bookshelf and pulled down several books. He handed them to Turner and indicated one particular thin blue paperback book. "My patient participated in a study with this woman, Dr. Katharina Dalton, in London. We did a natural progesterone treatment following the birth of her second child, and it was extremely successful in her case. I myself was very impressed with the overall theories presented in this book. It changed the way I treat my patients who have difficulties with postpartum," Shapiro said. "There are many new approaches."

Turner thanked God for sending them to this particular doctor. Someone who didn't autopilot through the issue—someone who had taken the time to listen to a patient and read new research. It truly seemed like a miracle at the moment. Perhaps Paris would see that as well.

"Is it hereditary?" Paris asked coldly.

"There are hereditary factors, yes. A predisposition to depression and severe premenstrual syndrome as a reaction to the hormonal drop in progesterone present in both the natural cycle and more severely after delivery of a child. But again, we've been having some success with natural progesterone treatments for all of those conditions in combination with other things."

Turner knew that all Paris had heard was *yes, it's hereditary,* and he already knew that her PMS was the stuff of legend. He sensed that she had not even heard the part about treatments.

"But even severe cases can be treated and recover to normal levels, yes?" Turner tried hard to get that fact back into the conversation.

"With the kind of support Patricia has, I know we could diagnose early and make sure she gets the help she needs."

That's what Turner wanted Paris to hear. But when he looked over at her, she was up and out of the office door. It slammed behind her.

"Problems?" The doctor pressed his fingertips together.

"Big ones. I'll read up and we'll try this conversation again. I can't go into too much detail, but this is something we will have to deal with as we go."

"Let's just take things a step at a time. Just because her mother had it doesn't mean she is made of the same genetic material. It could bypass her completely. But a family history is something to pay attention to. We'll talk more after you've read that book. I think it might help."

Turner looked at the book in his hand. *Depression after Childbirth* by Katharina Dalton. "I hope so, Doctor."

"The class is Friday. Please get Patricia there. I think it might help her to be around other pregnant women."

Turner didn't think so. But who knew? He only knew he had to find the key to unlock Paris's fears. And he *was* going to find it. He wouldn't stop until he found it.

Turner thanked the doctor and went to find Paris. He wondered, for a moment, what was driving him. He came through to the waiting room and saw Paris standing by a large fishtank, her back to him. Her red hair spilled down her back in soft waves of curls. She had on simple clothes today—a pale green shift dress. She looked like any other woman in the waiting room, not a formerly famous model.

He came up behind her and put his arm around her shoulders. She looked up at him with all her jumbled-up emotions showing on her face—anger, fear, hurt. He felt his heart ache for her. This is what drove him. He loved her. He'd probably always loved her, since high school. He leaned toward her beautiful hair and breathed in the scent of her. She was an odd mixture of expensive perfume, shampoo, and ultrasound gel. His insides flip-flopped with feeling for her.

"Come on, I'll take you home," he said softly.

Paris went directly into his formerly sane, simple room and shut the door behind her. Turner followed her.

"Thank you for doing the exam. It's quite a surprise, twins."

Turner looked around. The whole room had been amazingly transformed into a Paris moment if he ever saw one, which he rarely did, because she shut herself up in there most days. The simple bed had become an ornate four-poster with lace curtains. His simple wooden dresser had taken up a spot in the living room so he could get to his clothing without disturbing her.

Of course there were bears everywhere in there, and flowery artwork, if you could call it that, on the newly painted walls. Ornate whitewashed reproduction antique furniture had replaced his own simpler items and was now holding Paris's clothing. There was room to walk around the bed and that was about it. His small former closet was stuffed to the gills with more of Paris's clothing. Clothing she actually couldn't fit into at the moment.

Paris wasn't talking. He knew by now when to leave it be.

"I'll just be out here if you need me." He backed out of the room.

Sarah and Millie were putting together a jigsaw puzzle of a very hunky movie star with his shirt off—Russell Crowe, it looked like. Turner had to laugh about that. Millie was certainly influencing Sarah.

He hung his jeans jacket up in the hall closet, which also held all his hanging clothes, which fortunately were modest. His Elvis costumes he kept at the chapel.

"Well, guess what, ladies, it's twins!" Turner announced.

"I just knew it. She was just too big. I figured either twins or one big huge Turner hunk of baby." Millie clapped. She jumped up and hugged Turner. "You sure are one stud-muffin there, daddio."

Turner hugged her back. "Thanks, Millie, but it's all about the eggs in this case."

"Did she change her mind about going back to New York after the birth?" Sarah asked. She'd turned herself toward Turner.

Turner had noticed that Sarah had been extremely direct lately, even a little cruel. He was sorry in a way that Millie had shared as much information as she had with Sarah. At least neither of them really knew Paris's motives, which was, he was sure, the way Paris would have wanted it.

But that left them both thinking she was truly a heartless woman.

Turner suspected that Millie had a broader view of it and knew Paris must have deeper reasons. That left Sarah thinking badly of Paris—a sad state of affairs Turner was not able to correct without betraying his wife's confidences.

"That remains to be seen, I guess. She has some deeply personal reasons, Sarah."

"What possible justification could there be for leaving two newborn babies without a mother?" Sarah straightened herself back around and carefully placed a puzzle piece in Russell Crowe's navel.

"I'm praying she finds peace enough to change her mind. I suggest you might do the same, Sarah."

Millie smacked Turner on the butt. "Don't you worry, Rev, we'll do just fine with those babies. We'll teach them to deal blackjack before they're five. And if they're as cute as their ma, we'll just make them baby models and rake in a mint of money."

"Thanks, Millie, I appreciate the enthusiasm," Turner said.

Sarah turned his way again. He noticed she had makeup on. That was so unusual for her. Maybe she'd met someone in school and was trying to improve her usual bland looks. Most likely it was Millie's work.

"I'm sorry, Turner. I shouldn't have said that. And I will pray for her."

"Apology accepted." Turner went over to the table and put his hand on her shoulder. She looked up at him with soft brown eyes, and he saw that tears had welled up in them.

Just then Paris opened the door to the bedroom. She stopped in the doorway and stared at Turner and Sarah.

Millie broke the awkward moment. "My goodness, girl, two in the tank! We'll have to get busy and paint your toenails fire-engine red before you can't see them anymore. Just let me know when you want to do a pedicure. I've got all the stuff. We showgirls were very good to our feet."

Paris finally moved her eyes from Turner to Millie. Her voice sounded strained. Her reply seemed forced. "I hear you on that one, Millie, modeling is all about your feet, too. I'd love one. I'll go soak them in the tub after dinner."

Paris stood very still, with a look on her face Turner thought might be anger.

"I'm starved, people, and I'm eating for three now, so what do you say we order in an entire Chinese feast?" Paris continued.

"I'm meeting with a bride and groom at seven, so I'll have to miss the feast and grab a sandwich before I leave." Turner had removed his hand from Sarah's shoulder and felt somehow awkward standing there.

"You mean, couples don't just walk in and get married?" Sarah asked.

"Most of the time, but we are a full-service chapel, and we do plenty of prenuptial planning with anyone that is willing. I love to get them early. Even two weeks gives me a chance to counsel them. Can I get you a glass of water, Paris?"

"No, thanks," Paris snapped.

Turner turned into the kitchen to get one, whether she wanted it or not. He needed something to do. He stuck his head in the fridge and grabbed sandwich stuff, pitching it on the counter beside him.

The doorbell rang. Now, who the heck was this? He hoped it wasn't his couple, mistakenly meeting him at home instead. He'd given them his home information in case they needed him. It'd be a little hard to explain his current situation to anyone, and it had an endless array of possible twists anyone could jump to just by standing in this room for ten minutes.

All three women seemed startled and did not move.

"I'll get it," Turner said, grateful for any interruption. He flung open the door and stared into the piercing blue eyes of a very tall, very beautiful, very pregnant blonde woman. Not another one! She had on a brilliant blue coat that looked like it was from the fifties—very wide and circular. Mighty warm for Vegas.

A shriek came from behind him and Paris streaked by, into the arms of the blonde woman.

"Oh for pity's sake, Turner Pruitt, move these broads and help me with these bags. You'd think we were on a European cruise instead of a weekend jaunt." Turner recognized the voice of Anton behind the blonde. Thank God, another guy. Gay or not, he wasn't pregnant, he wasn't going to hang panty hose in the bathroom . . . well. . . . Turner stopped because you just never know, really. The lines between everyone had grown very fuzzy. Well, for sure he damn well wasn't a woman, no matter what.

"Anton, buddy ol' pal!" Turner looked over the blonde's shoulder.

"This is Marla Meyers Riley, also known as M. B. Kerlin, author of the Mike Mason Mystery series. Just thought I'd bring you up to speed." Turner watched Anton hop up and down from behind Marla, trying to see, trying to talk to Turner over the tall ones.

"It's an honor to meet you, Marla. Paris has told me so much about you."

"Nice to meet you at last, Turner Pruitt." Marla smiled for a moment at Turner, then directed her gaze back at Paris. She held Paris out from her by her shoulders as if to examine her carefully. She made a scrunched-up face like she was trying to figure something out, eyebrows knotted together, then she looked like she'd discovered America. Her eyebrows shot back into place, and her eyes got very large and blue. Spooky blue.

"Oh my God, you're *pregnant!* You *bitch!* How could you not tell me! I'm going to kill you," Marla Meyers shrieked, then she started to cry. Not just a little weepy, whispy cry, no-o-o. A big fat bawling, sobby cry.

From behind her Anton handed her a white linen hanky and sighed. "It just figures. I should have known the day I couldn't get anything on her hair. Ladies, ladies, can we move it aside? We'll yell at her when we're inside the door." Anton gave Marla a gentle nudge and moved her enough so Turner could help him with the three suitcases in the hallway. There was no room in this inn, that was for sure, but they could figure that out later. Not in the hallway, with the weepy sisters.

"Cut it out, Meyers, just stop it." Paris stood with her hands on her hips.

"How could you not tell me?" Marla hiccupped.

Turner stacked the suitcases against the end of the sofa. "Anton, this is my roommate, Millie, and my friend Sarah." Turner gestured.

"Hello, ladies. Oooh, Russell Crowe." Anton picked up a puzzle piece and added a chunk to Russell's right bicep. "*Hellooo* Russell."

Paris could not believe Marla and Anton had flown to Vegas. What had they been thinking? She was already upset and humiliated, and now everything was going to get *so* complicated.

"Give me some Kleenex," Marla sniffled.

Paris grabbed a nearby box and pulled a bunch free. "What the hell made you get on a plane and show up on my doorstep? You could have called." Paris shoved Kleenex at Marla.

"I e-mailed you fifteen times."

"I don't have a computer here."

"Don't you turn this around on me. I am so hurt, I can hardly even speak."

"Then don't. Come in my room and we'll talk."

"Just let me say hello." Marla went over to Turner and Sarah and Millie and graciously introduced herself.

Paris could not believe this endless craziness. If one more person, or one more suitcase, or one more piece of furniture came into this apartment, the floor would give way and they'd all be on the fifth floor instead of the sixth. She folded her arms and tapped her foot until Marla came back to her. She led her into Turner's old room.

"My goodness, you had this room decorated, didn't you? It's just so . . . *you*. What does Turner think? It's a little over the top for a man, isn't it? Land of precious and all that?" Marla asked.

"Now that you've pushed your little perfect blonde nose into everything, you might as well hear the whole story. Turner doesn't sleep with me."

Marla put her hand over her mouth in shock. Then she removed it, gave Paris a look, and took off her voluminous blue coat, handing it to Paris. "It's too damn hot to comment on that," Marla said.

"Nice coat. Nice dress too. And *whoo-hoo* on the shoes. Are those Manolos?"

"Whew, Vegas is an oven. Yes, they are, and swollen permanently on my feet right now. I figure I have two more months before my feet can't fit into *any* of my shoes, so I'm treating myself for now. Besides, I don't get to wear them on the farm too much. I'm usually in Wellies—those fancy English mucking boots." Marla flopped down on Paris's pink floral down comforter cover and propped herself up on a pile of Paris pillows.

"What are you now, fifth month?" Paris hung Marla's coat in her French country armoire.

"Going on seven. I'm due in late October. And you look about the same. Oh . . . damn it." Marla started to cry again.

Paris handed her the whole box of tissues.

"I'm due in December. It's twins."

"Oh my gosh." Marla reached over to grab Paris's hand. "That is wonderful."

Paris flopped down on the bed beside Marla. They lay side by side, Marla holding Paris's hand. Paris started to cry a little herself. They shared the tissue box. *Damn it,* Paris said to herself as she sucked her breath in and tried to calm down.

"I have to tell you some things, and you're going to have to be a good friend and not get crazy. Do you promise?"

"No."

"Well, great. You are really insufferable, you know?" Paris sniffled. "First off, do all women just cry for nine months?"

"Pretty much," Marla answered. She rubbed Paris's hand. "What happened with you and Turner? He seems like the nicest guy ever."

"He is. That's part of the problem. He just doesn't deserve someone like me messing up his life." Paris wiped a few stray tears from her left eye and let tears from the right side fall onto the pillow.

"Just tell me the whole story. I came here because I knew something wasn't right. So now I'm here, and now I want to help. So tell it, Paris. Tell the whole truth, and don't leave out your usual gigantic details."

Paris took a breath and started in. Marla was going to be a total pain in the ass about this whole thing, so she might as well get it out in the open and deal with whatever came up—for once. She was feeling quite determined about her own particular part in this drama, and what was going to happen, so she might as well test-drive it on Marla.

Suddenly she wished Turner was here to help her explain things. He was so good at it.

11

Don't Be Cruel

"You know her better than I do." Turner kept his voice low so Paris wouldn't wake up. She'd fallen asleep after her big talk with Marla and was probably exhausted from the whole day's ordeal.

Marla sat across from him at the table and shook her head. She leaned her head into her hands in a gesture of sadness—and what Turner interpreted as complete disbelief.

"I never knew *this* about her," Marla said. Turner slid a few more tissues under her bent head. He watched Anton clear off the sandwich plates from the snack they'd had and step over into the kitchen. A few minutes later Anton poured himself a beer and came to sit with Turner and Marla.

"I knew," Anton said. "She's scared out of her wits. Paris has always had terrible fears. It's what's kept her from having a committed relationship for all her adult life. I don't know where they came from, but we all have skeletons in the closet, don't we?"

"Look. I know you came with good intentions, but I don't know if there's anything you can do. I have my own theories, and I hope to dislodge the pain enough to get some healing going on in her. I feel that our paths have crossed in this way for that very purpose. And apparently I'm about to have *children* in my life as well. I have to confess, I'm completely thrilled about that.

"My greatest wish is for Paris to have a complete change of heart—where *everything* is concerned. I can't imagine the course of action she's chosen bringing her anything but pain. I seem to have fallen in love with her, and I don't want to see that happen," Turner said.

Marla looked up at him and took his hand in hers. "We'll do whatever we can to make that happen, Turner. Right now I'm going to get her dolled up and take her with us to our hotel, if that's okay with you. Why don't you come as well?"

"Yes, come along with us, Turner, there is no way I can schlep all that luggage again. Never travel with pregnant females who overpack. I said we should just check in first, but no, Miss

Determined here wanted to come straight to your place. Come, it'll be fun. We'll have dinner and stick some nickels in the slots."

"I hate to abandon you, but I have a meeting at the chapel at seven. But Anton, if you take half, I'll bring the other half with me in a few hours. Where are you staying?" Turner asked.

"The Four Seasons. No casino, fabulous food, and the best views in town," Marla answered.

"I wanted Treasure Island. All those dashing pirates running around." Anton stuck out his lip in a pout, then finished his beer.

"I think it would be good for Paris to get out. She's pretty depressed. She did one big shopping spree right after we arrived, then I'd say she's been curled up sleeping most of the time."

"Well, the first trimester of pregnancy you are really tired, but by now she should have perked up. We'll get her cheered up. Maybe it will help." Marla patted Turner's hand again. "So you go do your meeting, then join us at the Four Seasons when you can. I'll give you my cell phone number so we can keep track of each other. We've got adjoining rooms—I'm keeping Anton out of trouble."

"No, I'm keeping *her* out of trouble. Her husband, Tom Riley, will kill me if she so much as breaks a nail." Anton got up. "I'll leave you the heavy stuff, big boy. I've pretzeled myself into a knot and will surely need at least three massages to recover."

Turner rose as Marla got to her feet. "I'll leave her in your hands. I'm going to be late if I don't leave now." He headed for the door. "Millie, I'm taking the car."

"Go for it," Millie answered from her room.

Turner was grateful that Millie and Sarah had hightailed it back there to give the visitors some room—after a proper amount of grilling Anton for details of life in New York while Paris and Marla had been locked in . . . *her* room.

Turner felt his dispossessed feeling again. Oh, hell, he had the chapel office, and maybe the grand plan was to get him used to having lots of people around. After all, he was going to be the father of twins. He smiled to himself as he left the apartment at the wave of fear that went along with that thought.

Money, space, his ability to balance his life between two babies and work. *Lord, give me strength,* he thought. But really, none of that mattered. He was going to have a family. He could hardly wait to tell his parents, and to hold those babies in his arms. What a wonderful gift. A complicated package, but still wonderful.

"That's enough rest, sleeping beauty, haul that fat ass of yours out of bed and throw on something that glitters."

Paris groaned. "That's what got me into this mess in the first place. And my ass is not fat . . . yet."

"It will be if you don't stop laying around like an orca whale. But for now, think food."

She rolled onto her back. "Hmmm, now you have my interest. Steak and lobster?"

"Every woman's friend."

"Go through my closet while I pee for the ninetieth time today. What's up with that?" She slid slowly off the bed and got her bearings.

"Body adjustments. Haven't you read anything yet? For pity's sake. We'll stop at a bookstore and load you up with books. My favorite is *The Girlfriend's Guide to Pregnancy*. Very irreverent."

"Up to this point I was sort of hoping it was a bad dream. But today it became much more real. I know I owe these babies a healthy ride, so I guess I'll read up. But let's have them delivered. Books are heavy."

Marla had flung open the armoire doors and was riffling through Paris's new "fat" wardrobe. "What the hell were you thinking with all this black knit? It gets hotter than hell in Las Vegas. Plus it's good to throw in a little color now and then, ya know? It brightens the spirit."

"Everywhere I go is air conditioned. And I thought it might slim me down—visually anyhow." Paris straightened out her current black dress and took a quick but fatal look in the dressing table mirror. "Whoa. Can we get a makeup crew in here?"

Paris saw Marla glance back at her over her shoulder, then do a double take and stare head-on. "Wow, you are a train wreck. We'll have Anton pretty up your hair. What the hell have you been doing to yourself, Paris? Just because you are pregnant is no excuse for all this letting yourself go. I've never seen you like this. You are one of the most vibrant women I know. It was hard to get you to hold still back in New York. Lazy, yes, but full of life."

"I've been tired."

"This is *not* tired, this is depressed." Marla's voice got serious, and Paris could see the strain in her friend's face. She wondered for a minute if she really wanted to go out with Marla. Maybe she'd just crawl back in bed and watch Ellen DeGeneres.

"I know what you're thinking, Paris. Now look. You've told me your story, and I know I'm not going to get anywhere by being a big, bitchy nag. I told you how I feel, but I am your friend. Right now I just want to help you feel better. We'll save the lectures for another time.

"You need to get out of this apartment and get some perspective. Fresh air. Lobster. Maybe I'll buy you some new jewelry to pretty up for the coming months. By the way, why *are* you holed up in this apartment? Why not just get your own place?" Marla took her hands off her hips and kept digging in the closet. She threw a black slinky sequined dress on the bed.

"I can't fit into that." Paris avoided the rest of the conversation, but one comment stuck in her head. Why was she in this apartment? Oh, yeah, she was hiding out from the world.

"It's actually really sexy when you put on a slinky knit with your new belly. Look, it's stretchy. You'll look great. Like Barbie in the Spotlight with a bun in the oven."

"Two buns. And why would I even want to look sexy? I seem to be temporarily married."

"My, my, how conventional of you." Marla threw a fake mink stole at her.

"Don't even try that reverse psychology stuff on me. No man would look at me like this, anyway."

"Your *husband* would. Why don't you let him show you?"

"I'm going to pee now."

"Just let these questions roll around in your mind. I'll be here when you get back," Marla said.

Paris stalked out the door of the bedroom and headed for the bathroom. It sort of felt good to be mad for a change instead of just upset. Or just dull. It made her smile. It didn't make her smile when she saw the hotel door hanger they'd rigged up as a marker on the bathroom door. Do

Not Disturb. She knocked on the door. "Hurry up in there."

"Please. It's hurry up in there *please,*" Millie's voice came from the other side. "Do I have to make a damn chart for you and give you gold stars when you get some manners?"

"What*ever.*" Paris tapped her foot and leaned against the hall wall.

"I'm waiting." Millie's voice again.

"You mean you actually want me to say it or you won't come out?"

"I'm teaching you manners, remember?"

"Why bother?"

"It's really fun. Kind of like Mission Impossible."

"Fine. PLEASE. Please, *please*. There."

The door flung open and grinning Millie stepped out.

"There you be. You catch more flies with honey, honey."

"Why in God's name would I want flies?"

"When you get as old as me it would be nice if you had some friends left to take care of you. Remember that."

"I'll try." Paris pushed past her and shut the door.

This place was a nuthouse. She peeled off her spandex panties and plopped on the john.

No toilet paper. Damn it!

She grabbed Kleenex instead. And then, of

course, the toilet, the stupid, low-flush, stupid toilet, clogged up. She just wanted to scream.

Why was she staying here again? Sure, she used to be on every magazine cover, and her wild life used to be tabloid fodder, but that was ten years ago. She'd bet no one would even notice her around here. This was Las Vegas, a fairly small town in reality.

She could get her own place. She certainly had the money for it. She'd taken to dumping all her money into an investment account and having her financial planner pay whatever bills came around since she was so bad at keeping track of stuff like that. Last time she looked there was over thirteen million in there, with interest.

But what if people did point her out? It was nobody's business whether she left a set of twins with their father for their own good. Maybe hiding out here wasn't such a bad idea.

Paris washed her face and hands and straightened up to brush her teeth. As she stared at herself in the mirror, she saw how washed out her face was. Even her teeth looked dull. Everything about her seemed run-down and pale.

Maybe she'd check into the Four Seasons and play with Anton and Marla for a few days and treat herself to that wonderful luxury hotel feeling where they pamper you like crazy and the spa is right down the hall, and room service is a phone call away. Oh man, that would feel so, so good.

Whoa, she'd really fallen asleep in cat's pajamas here. Marla was right. She needed to escape. Paris finished brushing her teeth.

She opened the bathroom door to the hall only to bump into Sarah. For some reason she didn't feel like explaining the plugged-up toilet or lack of toilet paper to her. Maybe Sarah would flush it and the entire thing would gush over into the bathroom and cause a flood and Sarah would be swept away right out of the building. Yeah. Maybe.

"Be my guest." Paris held the door open for Sarah and smiled at her. Sarah looked at her wierdly.

Paris stomped across the living room and noticed that Anton and Millie were back at the Russell Crowe puzzle, and that Turner must have left.

She threw open the bedroom door. "Pack me a bag, I'm checking into the Four Seasons with you for a spa week."

"We're only staying three days. And pack your own damn bag." Marla gave her the fakey smile.

"I don't care. I'm tired of laying around this place. I'll need a week to get myself back in shape. I need a full body treatment, nails, hair, the whole bit. That will take a week right there. Most of all I want my own bathroom." Paris went to her armoire and grabbed a few more black dresses, then opened drawers for a pile of lingerie. She threw it all in a pile on the bed. She pulled one of her suitcases out from under the bed and dumped the contents—bears and assorted clothes—on the floor, then kicked it all under the bed.

"Careful there, you're in a delicate condition."

"Excuse me, aren't you the one that just gave me the *get up and go* lecture?" Paris kept packing.

"I guess I overdid it. Here, let me help you."

"Let's go dancing like we used to."

"Sounds great. Did I mention that your husband would be joining us later?"

"No, you didn't mention that."

"Think steak and lobster. Shimmy into this dress. We'll check into our rooms and get you one, and Anton can spruce up your hair. We'll get some red lipstick on you and you'll be good as new."

Good as new. Paris had the feeling she'd never be good as new again. "Whatever. I'm going to indulge myself. Turner can have his bedroom back tonight." Five pairs of shoes and six bikini panties later, Paris zipped the bag shut. "Anton will have to take this one. We don't want Turner to get all worried and ruin my escape."

"You break it to Anton. I'll run to the ladies' room."

"Um. You might want to wait on that one. It's currently occupied."

Paris heard a muffled scream through the thin walls and grinned. That gave her a small twinge of guilt. Then she remembered the scene she'd walked in on earlier with Turner's hand on Sarah's shoulder, and Sarah gazing at him in a way that Paris knew full well was . . . love.

Why should she even care? Maybe it was because she was stuck here being pregnant with Turner's babies and the idea of Sarah moving in on Turner and making him feel warm and loved was just really shitty. Right in front of her nose. Hey, why should Turner get to feel warm and loved when she didn't?

But of course she could feel loved if she let him in. She just couldn't do that. He'd get all involved with her, and she'd leave, and he'd be even worse off. The truth was, she was doing him a favor keeping him at a distance. Yes. A favor.

12

Are You Lonesome Tonight?

"Last time we were here in Las Vegas together you had Tom Riley in tow and we were dripping in fake jewelry and not much else." Paris held her menu down and looked Marla in the eye.

"Ah yes, I remember it well," Marla replied.

"Remember how you lied to me about Tom?"

"I remember that, too."

"Well, now we're even."

"We will never be even, I told you that a zillion times."

"Shut up, girls, and decide what you want. I'm starving. It is a sign to the waiter when you put your menu down. And he's cute, so hurry up!" Anton slapped his menu on the table.

"Okay. Okay! I can't believe I haven't had a

night out in forever. My temporary husband spends all his time singing 'Love Me Tender' to these crazy people who get married down here, and most of them are in the evenings. He's a real late-night soul saver and marrying man."

"Have you gone and watched him?" Marla asked, setting her menu down on top of Anton's.

"Hell no. He's got Sarah helping him down there when she's not in school. I think they make a lovely couple, don't you?" Paris gave her menu a particulary hard slap down—enough to get the cute waiter in their corner right away.

"Hello, I'm François, I'll be your waiter tonight."

"You aren't really French, are you?" Paris asked.

"I am *really* French, madame, I assure you. I'm here studying hotel and restaurant management, and enjoying myself working at Charlie Palmer's. I am actually the wine steward, but we are a bit shorthanded tonight."

"Well, François, I am Anton, but not French, just very pleased to meet you. We'd like to start with the oysters on the half with apple cider mignonette, and the ahi tuna tartar sushi roll."

"Eeeeuuuhhh," Paris shuddered. "I'll have the surf and turf just past rare with lobster instead of prawns. And can you bring me a chocolate milk shake?"

"She's expecting twins." Anton rolled his eyes.

"Certainly, madame. I'm sure the bartender can create you a superb chocolate milkshake. We have a nice Caesar salad to go with that steak and lobster if you like."

"Swell."

"Anyway, François, what's good tonight?" Anton continued.

"Our beef is really exceptional."

"Then I'll have the filet, medium rare, and the duck salad. That looked divine. Pick me out a nice wine for that. I'll be drinking alone tonight, I fear."

"I have a very oaky Shiraz I'll open just for you."

Paris sensed some flirting going on and caught Marla's eye. They both gave each other the "look."

"And the lady in blue?" François indicated Marla.

"The roast beef salad, and as long as you're making her a shake, I'll take one too."

"Moo," Paris added.

"Merci, and I'll return shortly with your appetizers." François vanished with the menus under his arm.

"Look, you made him go away now," Anton pouted.

"That's his job. Besides, he'll be back. Anton, shut up about the twins and the whole being pregnant thing, will you?" Paris glared at him.

"I hate to tell you this, but your shape is a big giveaway." Anton glared back.

"I'd rather not announce it. I came here to hide out. At a dinner table I can pass for retaining water," Paris said.

Anton and Marla both laughed.

"Okay, a whole lot of water." Paris put her napkin in her lap and covered up the bump, which didn't cover too well.

"Hiding out. Why is that?" Anton asked.

"I want to be able to go back to work without everyone knowing my business. I'm just a very private person anyhow."

"This all sounds very lame to me. Why don't you just get some maternity modeling gigs?" Anton pressed her.

"I don't want clients knowing I'm pregnant and fat, and most importantly no one needs to know I'm giving up a set of twins to their biological father and getting on with my life. I don't want to talk about this anymore. I just want to enjoy my escape from crazy Millie and sulky Sarah and the smallest apartment in the universe."

There was a very prickly silence at that point. Paris just wanted to scream at them all to leave her alone.

"Yes. Well, we'll have a two-day spa blitz. Did you see they have a maternity massage package?" Marla changed the subject, thank goodness.

"And a four-layer seaweed and mineral mud

facial, plus hair, nails, feet, all that." Paris could almost feel the relief she'd get from all that pampering. Relief from all the tension and all the body changes and a million other things. How do you spell relief? M-a-s-s-a-g-e!

"You'd let someone else touch your hair?" Anton put a hand to his heart and feigned a swoon.

"Well, duh, you can't be everywhere," Paris replied.

"I'll go along with you and give him your formula."

"Fine."

"And by the way," Marla interjected, "no, I don't think they make a lovely couple. I think Turner is madly in love with *you*, Paris."

"Thank you for that keen observation, Mrs. *Rittley*." Paris crossed her arms and sat back in her comfortable chair, which wasn't feeling very comfortable at the moment. "I thought we agreed to drop the lectures for now."

"I'll try harder. Steak, lobster, facials. How's that?" Marla said.

She looked upset. Paris didn't care. She was going to take care of her own self for the next two or three or four days. And she was going to have a selfish, self-indulgent, jolly old time of it.

Turner watched the couple sitting across the desk from him. They were young. Maybe twenty-two for her, and maybe twenty-five for him. The potential groom held the girl's hand the entire time. She leaned close to him while he talked about what they wanted to read to each other during the service.

They wanted something fun and campy for their wedding—a fifties theme. Turner smiled to think how the whole getting-married-by-Elvis-in-Las-Vegas thing had reached across the generations.

He made a few notes in his leather-bound notebook under Watkins-O'Conner Wedding. How he envied them being so in love. They'd chosen the "Blue Hawaii"–themed Elvis wedding.

"That's pretty much all we need for now. Let's have one more meeting before the wedding, say, next week at this same time? We can set up the limo pickup time. And let's plan on a short rehearsal with the whole wedding party so they all know their cues." Turner rose from behind his dark antique wood desk and came around to shake their hands. "I'd wish you luck, but as we talked about, it takes more than that to make a marriage work, and you both seem to have a good grasp of what you're doing."

"Thanks, Reverend Pruitt. You've been awesome."

Turner escorted the happy couple out through the chapel and to the street door. "Let me know what day would be good for a rehearsal and we'll get our calendars matched up."

They agreed and waved good-bye. Turner closed the door, locked it, and walked down the aisle of his chapel. Since he'd removed the orange carpet and repainted the ghastly yellow walls a soft beige, the place looked great. The pews had been reupholstered with red velvet, the lighting made more dramatic and updated, and the altar refinished. It looked pretty darned elegant now.

He'd had a local artist renovate the stained glass windows on either side of the altar. Right now they were sparkling in the sunlight, dancing colors all over the room. Over the last few years Turner had put a great deal of effort and work into his chapel. His bookings had doubled, and he was glad that Danny Vernon was on board to assist him. Danny's Elvis was really a knockout, and he seemed to get better every time Turner saw him.

This would really help when the twins came along. He'd have to take a leave of absence for the first few months, and he knew he'd better think about getting a second minister in here to fill in during that time. The doctor had told him that twins deliver around the thirty-fifth week of pregnancy instead of the usual forty. That only left him till the beginning of December.

Man, he had a great deal to put into motion, get into order, and make happen. Turner walked up behind the pulpit and looked across at the empty chapel. What was he going to do with Paris? He had a vision of her standing in the doorway in her red sequined dress, yelling out to him. She'd looked gorgeous with her flaming red hair.

When he'd seen her there he had to admit it was like she'd been sent to him. He'd been buried in his work, enjoyable as it was. He'd been so busy marrying people, preaching on Sunday, and doing late-night services that he'd let his personal life slide into a corner. He'd dated, but no one special had caught his heart. When he'd seen Paris, it was like the years had fallen away. Only this time he was a man, not a boy, and she was a handful of woman.

Well, she'd always been a handful.

He tried to muster up some regret for marrying her on the spot, and getting her pregnant, but somehow he was actually glad. He was glad his life had been shaken to the core, and that Paris was the one doing the shaking. It was truly a miracle they had been brought together. If only she'd reach out to him.

Turner stood poised at his pulpit with the light streaming in the windows behind him. As the sun went down, the brilliance of the reflection through the stained glass seemed to flare into a kaleidoscope of color that filled the chapel with bursts of light.

Suddenly he felt a strength and direction that had eluded him over the last few months. It filled him with determination and spirit. His path wasn't easy, but he knew he'd find the way to make order. He knew in his heart that Paris was going to have a complete change of heart. It might be painful, but he was going to be the one to unlock the doors that kept Paris from letting love in.

Turner left the chapel ready to take on whatever was necessary to tame the tiger that was Paris. He'd have her sitting in his lap purring like a kitten before this was all over.

The next thing Turner's eyes beheld was his wife's fanny doing the boogaloo to an updated version of an old Rolling Stones tune, "She's So Cold." Now, of course, she wasn't on a dance floor—that would be too conventional. She was just grooving down the halls of the Four Seasons hotel. *I'm so hot for her* is right, Turner thought as he heard the lyrics to the song. And how did she manage to squeeze into that black sequined number? It was pretty shocking seeing her out of her flannels and back in her strutting clothes. She had on strappy black high heels to top it all off . . . well, to tip it all off if you think shoes.

"Hey, Paris," Turner called.

"Look, it's the old ball and chain!" Paris turned and boogied backwards.

Both Marla and Anton stopped. Turner took three big strides and grabbed Paris before she fell on her cute fanny.

"Oops. I guess I'm a little off-balance."

"It's probably the extra boobs. You're moving on to prereduction Dolly Parton there, Paris!" Anton smiled.

Being pregnant had certainly increased her cleavage, that was for sure. And her thin-strapped, low-cut dress was showing that off well.

Paris looked down at her chest. "Oh my gawd, where did those come from?"

Marla put her arm around Anton. "I swear she hasn't had anything to drink, Turner, she's just naturally unbalanced."

"Now that I'm here I'll provide the balance. You can keep on dancing."

"Anton wants to go next door to the Mandalay and get tickets for *Mamma Mia*. He really wants to get out of this dignified, elegant joint and party," Paris said. She swiped a spray of red hair out of her eye.

"Sounds great to me. I haven't had a night out in . . . well, since April Fool's Day."

"Oh yes, our wedding anniversary. Has a great ring to it, doesn't it?"

"Unforgettable," Turner replied.

"Move it along, you fools. I'm having an Abba attack right here." Anton fanned himself.

Turner fell in beside Paris and took her arm.

"What's this? Trying to get on my good side?" Paris asked.

"Stability, Paris, I'm just here to provide stability."

When they stepped through the lobby doors, the Nevada heat hit like a tidal wave. It felt good to Turner, being out of the air-conditioning. It was going to be a hot night, no doubt about it.

The Mandalay Bay Casino gaming floor was resplendent with red patterned carpets and dazzling lights. It always amazed Turner to watch people gamble their money away like water. He knew the gambler's anonymous group was overflowing with reformed addicts, and his own church's late-night Sunday service attracted quite a few reformers looking for a little spiritual strength. He always kept that in mind when he gave his sermons.

He was glad to see the tables didn't hold a big attraction for Paris. She always seemed to be heading toward the music and dancing.

"C'mon, Marla, let Anton go get his tickets and we'll make Turner dance with both of us."

"I'll come with you, but my feet are pretty swollen. I think the change of climate has thrown me out of whack. I can't wait for that massage tomorrow," Marla said.

"Me neither. Which reminds me, Turner, I have a few things to tell you."

"That makes two of us." Turner kept Paris pointed toward the Coral Reef bar dance floor. "We'll talk while we dance."

"To this? They're on the slow end of the set. I want to groove."

"Well, groove to the slow." They'd reached the edge of the wooden floor, and Turner took Paris in his arms. He saw Marla park herself at a side table and smile at him.

The music was being provided by your basic top forties oldies-but-goodies band, and he knew the guy well. Tony had played at quite a few wedding receptions Turner had ended up attending. He did a great Huey Lewis dance set, but he was a blues ballad guy deep at heart. He was just finishing up the Shirelles' hit "Will You Still Love Me Tomorrow?," which was just about perfect. Turner knew the universe had a way of providing just the right moments to bring your life to another level of understanding if you listened well enough and paid attention.

Turner pulled Paris closer to him, and she didn't resist. She was letting the music take her away. Not taken away by him, exactly, but that was good enough for Turner. Her voluptuous body was enough to drive him nuts. She was a good dancer. So was he. He made sure she remembered it.

"Great song, Paris, it's so us. That night you were mine, completely, you gave your love so sweetly. That night, the light of love was in your eyes, but did you love me . . . tomorrow?" Turner paraphrased the lyrics of the song into his own version.

"Shut up and dance, Reverend." Paris pressed herself closer to him.

He felt his body respond to her. Lust shot through him like a hot Vegas night. His mind flipped back to their wedding night, when he'd made love to Paris for the first time. She had been his, completely.

He would never forget unzipping the red sequined dress to reveal her naked back. He'd slid his hands across her smooth skin and slowly moved the straps off her shoulders until the dress had fallen to the floor. Then he'd spent quite a while learning her body from the back. He'd glided over every valley and curve with his fingertips until she'd leaned back on him, overcome. Then he'd turned her body toward him and learned the front of her just as slowly. Every time she'd moved to hurry things along, he had moved them toward a slow, smoldering, aching heat instead.

That night it had seemed that every touch had made their desire stronger. He'd taken his time with her that night. She'd reached an orgasm at least three times before he'd even entered her, and he'd known the deepest pleasure imaginable as she'd finally begged him to slide himself into her. Even then he had done one teasing, smooth, motion at a time so she'd climax as he moved into her.

Now he was so glad he had taken so long that night. That night, and their time in New York, might be the only memories he'd ever have of making love to Paris.

Tony caught Turner's eye when he moved by the bandstand with Paris, and he gave him a thumbs-up. Turner hoped that meant he'd keep up the slow set for a while.

As they danced he ran his hand from her neck down her bare back. The dress was similar. Low in back, low in front, and clinging to her every curve in between. He felt the desire for her rise in him so deeply that it shocked him.

She felt it too.

Whatever was going through Turner Pruitt's head right now, she could feel the results pressed up against her. Paris had her eyes closed, and her body felt delicious in Turner's arms. Something about this hormonal roller coaster called pregnancy must have hit the hot-to-trot track tonight. A wave of pure lust hit her hard—mostly in every spot where his body was touching hers. He had one amazing, throbbing, hard-on there. She just hoped they moved into another slow song so she could enjoy it longer.

As if in answer, the singer started a slow grinder with a deep base beat. "Unchained Melody"—the old Righteous Brothers' song. A very sexy song. And she felt every word of that line about *I hunger for your touch.* Because Turner Pruitt was nothing if not a man with a slow hand.

He could make love to her for hours and keep himself under control until she thought she'd either scream or just pass out with pleasure. She remembered finally begging him to let her have him inside her. Even then it had been the most intense *entering* she'd ever experienced.

She'd had many lovers over the years, but nothing, *nothing* compared to the talent of the ever-so-talented Mr. Pruitt. She was glad she'd finally gotten her memory of their wedding night back, because no girl should forget a night like that.

Her breasts ached against him as she remembered his mouth on her—his sweet mouth.

Mmmm. She felt herself seriously considering taking Turner back into her bed. And what better place than the Four Seasons hotel. No roommates to walk in or hear her scream with the pleasure he would undoubtedly give her.

"Turner," she said. She noticed that her voice gave away her desire right off. He noticed too.

She put her lips next to his ear and brushed against his earlobe when she whispered.

"I have a hotel room next door in the Four Seasons."

Turner pulled back a little, and she saw that his eyes were full of a faraway kind of dream. She hoped it was of her.

"I was going to tell you that I'd decided to hang out with Marla and Anton for a few days . . ." She got that much out and had to take a breath in as he moved her into the dance.

". . . and have a little spa break." She let him lean her into a not-too-far-down dip. He was so strong, the way he led her, and his body moved with hers in perfect rhythm.

He wound his arm around her waist and put his lips against her temple, then slid down to her mouth, where he just gently played at a kiss. It made her crazy.

"So I was wondering if maybe we could have a little alone time. I mean, no Millie, no Sarah, just . . ." She lost her ability to speak when his mouth slid down her neck and across her shoulder. She was only aware he had danced them into a dark corner. She felt for the key card to her room in her tiny evening bag.

"Let's go." She showed him the key.

"Wait," Turner whispered in a husky, dark voice next to her ear. He kept her there, moving his body against her like he was stroking her.

The heat from his body matched the heat from her own, and she shuddered against him. She put her arms around his neck, and he ground into her even deeper with a sensuous movement that echoed the music.

"I need your love, Paris," he echoed the lyric.

She was beyond speach and felt like she was going to have an orgasm on the dance floor. If he even so much as brushed her breast with his fingertips . . . she would.

The song ended, and he held her close. Then he walked her off the dance floor and past Marla. Marla just waved her acceptance of their departure, and Turner saw Anton coming toward her, so Turner knew Marla was in good hands.

Good hands. He kept Paris close to him as they walked out of the Mandalay Bay and crossed over to the Four Seasons. She'd already handed him the key to her room and whispered the number to him. Thirty-ninth floor. Three-nine oh-one. The very top.

In the elevator he kissed her hard. He took her mouth like a delicious, forbidden fruit and showed her what he was going to do to the rest of her body with his kiss. He wanted to run his mouth all over her again. His hunger for her was so evident that he wondered if he could keep the control he'd had their first night. She moaned and pulled him against her harder, her hips pushing against him, her mouth responding to his.

He found the room and inserted the key. God, give me a green light, he prayed. It blinked green and he pushed open the door. They got far enough in for it to close behind them and he threw the dead bolt. Sealed in.

Paris, Paris. He was in Paris heaven again. He murmured her name against her mouth. He let go of her long enough to strip off his jacket and shirt and pants and anything else that stood in his way.

She started to peel her dress off, but he stopped her. He just stood in front of her, looking at the lust and desire he had created in her. Her lips were swollen with his kisses. Her face was flushed pink. Her breasts . . . he stepped closer and ran his mouth across the soft skin that showed above the neckline of her dress. He put his hand behind her head as she leaned back to let him kiss her neck. Her flaming red hair curled and draped across his hand.

He moved his hand to her shoulder and slid one thin strap off. He ran his tongue down to the rosy tip of her left nipple. He noticed how much larger the dark bloom of her breast was—this must be what he'd read about. He ran his tongue around the circle and held her beautiful, full breast in his hand. She made a lusty, low sound and slid her own hand down to press between her legs. That was just so sexy. He slipped the other strap off while he held her nipple in his mouth, heating it and teasing it with the tip of his tongue.

He wanted to devour her, but he wanted to savor every moment of that devouring. He helped her dress fall below her legs and helped her peel off the silky panties that she had on.

This was the first time he'd gotten to touch her belly. He stopped what he was doing and ran his hand across the small bulge that contained his babies. It was amazingly hard. He felt reverent and grateful that she'd opened herself to him tonight.

If only she knew how beautiful she was, carrying his children this way. Even more beautiful than before, because the spirit of their hearts was contained within her.

He let his fingertips smooth down into her heat. She was dripping wet, and when he pressed inside her he started a fire that made her shudder and grab his shoulders. He knelt down and put the heat of his mouth against her until she screamed and dug her nails into his skin. He stopped and lowered her backward onto the bed. The room was warm, and the darkness outside was punctuated by the sparkle of Las Vegas. In that light he could see her magnificent body, beckoning to him.

* * *

Paris couldn't let this man do to her what he'd done before. She would never be able to stand the slow, wild pleasure this time. She had to have him now. She was going to make him want that so bad he'd have to break down and move into her. She ached to have him throbbing inside her.

If he wanted foreplay, she'd take him to the edge of insanity. His amazing body was too much to wait for. His broad shoulders, his tumble of brown hair, his handsome face that had grown so serious and manly since she'd known him so many years ago.

She pulled him down beside her and pushed him on his back so she could straddle him. Not to set him inside her, yet, but to tease him with her body. She slowly brushed each tender, burning part of herself against him. She brushed her nipples against his own. She trailed her breasts across his strong, muscled chest. She brushed her on-fire, wet darkness against him until his erection got even harder. Still she teased him . . . with her fingertips, with her mouth, until she could feel his resolve dissolving. She pushed against him and arched herself up. He touched her breasts and leaned up to put them in his mouth. She moved downward to let him.

But she was going to be the one this time. She was in control. She was . . .

His mouth gave a gentle suck to each of her nipples. Now those were her weakness. He knew that, she was figuring out. He played that hand to the hilt. Each touch of his tongue drove her deeper into madness. He reached her and pressed his thumb into the heat, gently, over and over. Damn him. She spun out of her mind and felt her body climax hard against him.

But this time he had mercy on her. He lifted her slightly and slid his glorious, full, burning hot, hard and throbbing erection into her at the same time she reached the peak of shuddering waves of pleasure. It made her roll back into her own pleasure once again, and he moved her gently on him until he knew she was done. She rested against him for a moment.

Then he began to move. He was so gentle, but his gentleness was driven by his desire. The feel of him inside her made her head spin and her body ache for more. She moved with him, and lifted herself up slightly, only to slide the entire shaft of him back inside her again. He moaned and she felt him begin to lose control. She loved that. She reached her fingertips behind them and brushed the edges of his thighs and upward . . . so gently, but so effectively, that he yelled out her name again. She quickened her movement and he grabbed on to her thighs, pulling her harder against him. She watched his face this time, with her eyes on his eyes. She watched him lose himself, and still he didn't climax.

"Let go." She heard her mouth move, and the

words came from her. "Just let go," she whispered, bending close to his ear, then moving back up to watch him.

Watching him let go was the sexiest thing she had ever seen. He was destroyed with pleasure. She had destroyed him. And she let go again, herself, tingling from the tips of her nipples to the tips of her toes and every other place she had. It was so strong she was shocked. A black sky engulfed her and filled with spinning stars. He kept moving ever so gently until the stars became the lights from the night sky again, and she collapsed on top of him.

A long, silent time went by. Turner moved her to her side and held her for what seemed like hours. He got up and pulled the covers out from under her, then wrapped them around them both. They lay together, and she drifted off. As she drifted off, she was aware that Turner was not asleep. He was beside her, thinking. She could almost hear him thinking.

13
Loving You

Turner watched his wife sleep next to him. He was going to treasure every moment of this. It was the natural order of what their lives should be. They should be husband and wife, and their love should be a deep well to draw upon to help them through this life. They should be together like this, with the joy of their future awaiting them.

Sounded like one of his wedding ceremonies.

Turner pushed a stray red curl off Paris's nose, and she reached up in her sleep to brush the tickle away. He caught her hand in his and held it gently. He looked down at her empty ring finger. He should fill that finger with a wedding ring. But he'd like it to be real this time.

When she woke up, would Paris be different?

Would she surrender to this love, to this marriage? Or would she push him away again and lock her heart up in that prison that he couldn't find the key to?

What was the key? Where had things gone so terribly wrong for Paris? So wrong that she would be convinced her own babies would be better off without her? What made her so sure of her own horrible flaws that she would deny herself her own babies?

He must find out what had happened to her when she was a child. He knew the basic facts, but he needed more. He must find out every detail. He wanted the mother's medical records and the police files and the social services files. If he knew for himself what had happened, maybe he could help Paris.

Turner let go of her hand softly. He must find the answers he needed. Their children needed a mother, and he . . . well, he had never wanted anything as much as he wanted Paris. He wanted to have her be his partner in life and raise their children with him.

He had no idea when he'd fallen in love with her, but it had started long ago and begun rekindling when they'd been in New York. He'd seen something in her before he'd even known she was pregnant. Something special. Someone who needed him. He'd known at that moment that he'd married her as much for himself as for her—or any of the other reasons he could think of.

But what he wanted was looking pretty impossible right now, unless she had a big turnaround. This momentary evening of passion was wonderful, but in his heart he knew it was going to make her even worse. She'd be angry at herself, and at him.

He slid out of bed quietly, and after his eyes adjusted to the darkness, he gathered up his clothes, which were strewn all over the bedroom. Paris had really booked quite the suite, with a small living room separate from the bedroom. He left the bedroom and walked into the living area. He twisted the blinds open enough to enjoy the spectacular view of the Vegas strip. He probably would have chosen to face the mountains and desert, but he bet the lights made Paris feel more like she was back in New York.

Turner glanced in Paris's direction as he heard her move in the bed. She had just rolled over and gathered all the covers around herself like a cocoon. He laughed softly. She was nothing if not focused on self-preservation.

But then she'd been without parents since she was about eleven or twelve.

Again he felt compelled to find out the details of the story. He had an idea of where to start. St. Mary's had been her home since she was young. The priest there would be able to tell him something, surely. He might protest at first, but if he knew what Turner was trying to accomplish, he would undoubtedly give forth. Sort of professional courtesy—clergy to clergy. Turner would be sure and wear his collar.

Turner went over to the wet bar and poured himself a glass of water. The ice cubes clinked in the bar glass as he walked over to one of the living room chairs. He positioned it so he could watch Paris sleep and made himself comfortable.

She looked like a painting. Her long, wavy red hair flowed over the pillow and over her bare arm as if someone had arranged it that way. How he wished he were an artist so he could capture her beauty forever. She slept as if she were happy. The tangle of soft cotton sheets and silky coverlet hid most of her body except for her foot. It was a very nice foot.

He sipped the water and let the quiet mellow him. He hadn't realized how hard he'd been working and how nonstop he'd been worrying until just now.

Just for this moment he could stop and enjoy the pleasure of knowing she was peaceful, and well loved, and they weren't at each other's throats. Actually her throat had taken quite a bit of his attention tonight. Kissing her neck was amazing.

He sat back in the chair and relaxed, trying not to think about his to-do list, or future problems, or anything but just this moment. It was a good moment.

But it wouldn't last long. When she woke up the moment would be over. How can you love a woman so much and know that she was going to make you miserable at the same time?

Turner decided to leave her here in the peaceful, after-sex bliss of this moment and go back to his place. Then when she woke up in the morning she'd only have the memory of last night instead of a confrontation in the light of day. Good plan.

He finished his drink and got up out of the comfortable chair. His clothes were stacked on the sofa, and he quietly slipped them on. His wallet was still in his jacket pocket, and all was well. Maybe he'd grab a midnight burger on the way home from Digger's All Natural Drive-In. Best fries in the entire state of Nevada.

He better be sure about this because once that door closed behind him he wouldn't be able to get back in. He stood for one more minute in the opening to the bedroom, leaning against the wall, watching her. "I love you, Paris," he whispered.

Turner slipped his jacket on and went to the door. He slipped the chain off and wished he could lock her back in there after he was out. She'd be okay. Marla's room was right next door, and Anton's was on the other side. He made sure the door closed tightly behind him as he left.

"I see kitty has claws," Millie said.

"What?" Turner asked.

Millie put her finger on Turner's chin and indicated that he had a scratch across one side.

"Oh." Turner smiled.

"Tamed?"

"Not by a long shot. You're up late, Millie."

"The Hot Line was open late tonight. I had to wait till Sarah was asleep. She's such a wet blanket when it comes to stuff like this. Miss Goody Two-shoes."

Turner laughed. "Anything fun?"

"Na-a, just the usual."

Well, Turner thought, *it's safe sex at heart.* "Want some of my fries? Digger's Natural." He waved the brown paper bag made out of recycled paper in the air.

"Yum. Dish 'em," Millie said. She took up her usual place at the dining table, fuzzy slippers, curlers and all. She buttoned up her quilted robe high on her neck. The air conditioner was up high. He knew she liked it warmer. He went to the thermostat and turned it down.

Turner looked back at Millie and noticed that the dinette set was getting a little beat-up looking. He might have to get a new one soon. Its white plastic fifties top had seen a few too many nicks, and the chrome was fading on the legs.

Too bad they didn't have an actual dining room to put a new one in instead of the strange little bump-out at the end of the living room, next to the kitchen.

Another bathroom would be good, too. "Millie, my love, I think we're going to have to get ourselves a bigger dwelling. It seems I'll be having a pack of babies and you and Sarah, and heaven knows who else will show up." Turner went to the kitchen and got the ketchup bottle out of the fridge.

"True. We should get a place in the burbs with a fenced backyard and a sandbox, and maybe we'll get a yappy dog. And I'll get a cat. A Siamese cat."

"I figured as much. Want to go house hunting?" Turner asked.

"Sure. Now what happens if Miss Snottypants gets a grip and wants to play mommy?"

"That's *Mrs.* Snottypants, remember? I hope she likes the place is all I can say. I've got enough in savings for a down payment. Shall we ask her, or just surprise her?" Turner sat down in his usual place and tore the fry bag down the middle. He shook the ketchup, popped it, and squirted some squiggles on the fries.

"I say surprise her. She's been an awful brat."

"True. I'll think that over. A yappy dog, you say?"

"The babies would love it . . . eventually."

"It's not going to be a palace."

"We'll be fine. What about you, Rev, will you be fine?"

"I've got some work to do. We'll see. I have some ideas."

"Speaking of ideas, I think Sarah's got some ideas where you are concerned, in case you didn't notice."

"I sort of noticed, but I've been awfully busy with the chapel and Paris and all. I was hoping it would fade away in the face of reality."

Millie shook a fry at Turner. "It don't just go away. I'd say she's thinking she'll step in when you need her the worst."

"I'm in love with Paris, Millie."

"Isn't love just a stinker? You would fall for some ornery gal with a big chip on her shoulder. But what's to do? I've been there. I always seemed to fall for those good-looking slick talkers that played a good game . . . high rollers. They're fun for a while, but when their luck runs out they are just plain mean."

"I'm glad I've got you now, Millie. Are you up for a couple of rugrats?"

"You bet. We'll have to clean up our act a little, though." She popped a fry in her mouth. "I'll stick to selling fancy lightbulbs over the phone, and you better stop gambling."

"I don't gamble, Millie." Turner let Millie have the last fry.

"I know, I just couldn't think of anything else. You're just an all-around clean machine, Turner."

"How about next time a girl from high school I had a crush on shows up I won't marry her within four hours?"

"Sounds like a plan."

Turner got up and gathered the French fry mess. "I guess I get to sleep in the land of precious tonight, formerly my own room. I hope those bears let me have a corner of the bed."

"Holler if they give you any trouble. And Rev, make it clear to our little nurse-in-training, Sarah, that you're not interested. Up front is best."

He gave Millie a peck on the cheek. "I will. Good night, dear."

"Nag, nag." Millie smiled. "Good night."

The bed was occupied by six large lady bears with hats. He moved them onto the floor. He was beat. Tomorrow was the beginning of many things. He thought about Paris, in her lovely hotel bed. He wondered if she'd be angry because he left.

Hell, she'd be angry if he left or if he didn't. He was better off out of pitching-a-fit range.

Paris threw the covers off her and got out of bed. She walked from one end of the suite to the other, noting the empty bathroom with the door partly open.

Well, well, well. Turner Pruitt had taken a powder on her. She sat on the side of the bed and looked down at her toes while she still could. The red paint from Millie's pedicure day was chipped and faded.

That man. He'd done it to her again. Why was it she couldn't keep her panties on around him? Where were her panties? If he thought for a minute that this little momentary lapse on her part changed anything, he was delusional. She looked around the room in a daze and pushed her completely insane hair out of her face.

She was just going to have to be stronger where he was concerned. Paris got up and looked in the dresser mirror. That was a mistake. She rubbed at her face . . . dry skin. This desert sure hadn't done anything for her complexion. She was a mess.

Marla would be shocked to see her up this early, but she'd set up a massage, a facial, a manicure and pedicure, and a hair treatment, and that was going to take all day.

She smoothed her hands over her neck and suddenly remembered Turner's mouth, hot against her skin, making her crazy. That man was one amazing lover.

Paris decided not to think about last night. Fiddle-dee-dee, as Scarlet would say. She decided not to even think about it tomorrow. She was just going to indulge herself.

The phone was right next to the bed, and clearly marked buttons gave her room service in moments. She felt the urge to eat a New York kind of breakfast.

"Hi, can you bring up breakfast to 3901? Toasted plain bagel, smoked salmon, cream cheese, capers, no onions, fresh squeezed orange juice, two pots of tea, one peppermint, one English breakfast. I'll be here. How long for that? Fine."

She was going to have a great day. She wasn't going to think about Turner, or Millie, or that Sarah person, or anything else. After all, she deserved it.

"It was mighty nice of them to let you girls hang out with me."

"Um, Anton, I think it was the other way around." Marla's muffled voice came from the underside of the maternity massage table. "This is just heaven, Paris. You'll love it."

"I'm next." Paris's masseuse was an older

woman, but her hands were strong and she was making Paris's legs feel *so* much better while she waited for the special maternity table. They had just been aching something terrible lately. Probably the extra weight.

"I see naked women all day long in New York. Turn them upside down and they all look the same."

"So you told the staff. Now pipe down, Anton, we are trying to relax. If you don't have any good gossip, we don't want to hear from you."

"Well, let's see. Rita's been dating a prince."

"You mean like, a prince of a guy?" Marla asked. "What else is new?"

"No, I mean an actual prince of some obscure sort of Danish Copenhagenish province or something. He has an accent like a slab of budda on a brioche." Anton waved his hand downward, since he was on his back.

"Cut it out, you're gonna make me hungry, and I have many miles to go before I eat," Paris grumbled.

"Your turn, Mrs. Pruitt." The masseuse helped Marla up, and she and Paris switched tables.

"Mrs. Pruitt." Anton giggled.

"Paris Pruitt." Marla giggled too.

"You two are like . . . high school. And since you are so childish, you might as well know, my real name is Patricia. Patricia Pruitt. Now how in the hell did I end up being Patricia Pruitt?"

"I think it had something to do with a magnum of Rhoederer Brut champagne," Marla said.

"More like that magnum hunk of burnin' love, Turner. I have *never* seen a guy have so much sex appeal and not know it. It's positively alarming what happens to women when he walks into a room. Isn't it, *Patricia?*" Anton had another fit of giggles.

"I have to say, Anton is right. He reminds me of Elvis, Antonio Banderas, and Mel Gibson all rolled into a new package." Marla made a little growly sound.

"Geez, Meyers, did I lust after Rigley like that?" Paris grumbled from the underside of the table.

"Yes, you did. And it's Riley. I am Mrs. Riley."

"I am Mrs. Pruitt," Paris laughed. "In name only."

"Well I *am* Mrs. Nesbit, as Buzz Lightyear would say, and Mrs. P, I think it's a little more than name only from the looks of things last night. And this morning you have that *been done* smirk all over your face. Are we back in the saddle again?"

"It was a momentary diversion. Nothing has changed." Paris squirmed a little. She wanted to stop talking about Turner and get her pamper time. "So shut up, will you?"

"Oh, I think he's gonna think you're gonna do that again, and that you're gonna put on an apron and play nice. That's what I think." Anton's voice faded off funny.

Paris was hoping they slimed him with mud and that it would harden soon and make his mouth immobile. She would peek up and see, but this back massage was just heaven. Her back ached more than usual. Must be the high heels.

"I think he's right, Paris," Marla said. She sounded like she was mellowing into melted chocolate herself. "Would it be so bad? He's heaven."

"He's delusional. I'm . . . I'm . . . I have to leave this place and never come back. He better just get that through his head, no matter what happens. So I needed some sex. So what?"

"Well, when we're done here, you better go tell him," Marla said gently.

"I damn well will go tell him. But first, I want you two to shut up and only talk about toenail polish and jewelry. I'm having a pamper day, and I don't want to think about *all that shit!*" Paris's voice went up very high at the end. Then she slumped back into the indentation of her special pregnant lady table and took a deep breath.

"Ladies, ladies, we don't shout in ze spa. Zis is ze quiet place. Now all of you take a nice deep cleansing breath and relax. We bring you ze nice glass of fresh mango juice to sip through ze straw while our avocado mud packs percolate." The senior attendant started out sharply with her Swiss accent, then went into a very soothing voice. Somehow it just made you want to obey her, Paris thought. And that was something she didn't feel too often . . . the urge to obey anyone.

Marla was right, though, and she better get herself over to the chapel and have a chat with Reverend Pruitt later today. *Way* later, after her seaweed layers and her fresh mango juice and her avocado whatever. Now she was getting hungry again.

14

Crying in the Chapel

It was quite a walk from the Four Seasons to Graceland Chapel, but Paris was feeling so relaxed from her spa day that she practically floated along the sidewalks. She'd gotten a map from the concierge, and since the thing was a landmark, it wouldn't be hard to find—a little white church in the middle of a sea of tall hotels.

And hey, she was a New Yorker. She walked everywhere, and sometimes in high heels. But today, at least, she'd picked comfortable sandals. Her ankles were not at their cutest, that was for sure. She'd picked these shoes because at least she could get her feet into them.

She'd forgotten what the heat in Vegas could be like. Like an oven. A five-hundred-degree oven. Her wide black hat shielded her from the sun anyway, and her dress was billowy enough to keep a breeze going. She better switch to white though, black really sucked heat.

She'd gotten so mellowed out from the day of treatments that it was hard to work up to a pissy mood to confront preacher boy. Besides, he'd been really delish last night.

But he *had* left her there. That was sort of . . . low. She shrugged as she trudged. More like predictable, and she probably even knew why. He hadn't wanted to have a fight with her in the morning. He hadn't want to break the mood.

She looked down at her newly polished, bright orange toenails gleaming in the Vegas sun. Then she flicked her hand up to admire the matching manicure. She straightened up and walked tall. A few men on the street craned their heads around to take her in. That made her smile. The ol' redhead still had it. She sashayed a little.

Damn, it was hot. And this ten blocks was really feeling far. She should have brought a water bottle. Paris scanned the blocks for a mini-mart or something. Maybe she should stop into one of the casinos and have a cold drink.

No, she wanted to get this mission done with. It would ease her mind, and besides, she was going to go back to her fancy hotel room, take a shower and a nap, then have a lovely light dinner with Marla and Anton.

Maybe she'd look into getting her own apartment. She could use a different name, and Turner could just get his big "be there for you" and "watch the pregnancy" kicks by visiting and coming to all the doctor's appointments. Somehow she knew that wouldn't go over too well, but big damn deal. She was sick of that place.

Paris paused a minute and hung on to an iron railing bordering a line of shops. She felt sort of dizzy. She took a tissue out of her purse and wiped off her face. My, it was hot. Well, there wasn't much farther to go, and besides, she was curious about the chapel. She'd only been there once. On her wedding day. She'd have a drink of water when she got there.

She rounded a corner and saw the spire of the small white church in the distance. Only four more blocks. She could do it. She took the tourist map out of her slouch bag and fanned herself with it. This town had sure changed in all these years.

Her memories of being a young kid were all about her own neighborhood near Boulder City. If her parents had been more normal, it would have been a great place to grow up in. It had a small-town feeling. She remembered a playmate who'd lived on the same street. Carla something. Carla. She hadn't thought of her in years. They'd been inseparable. Carla with her great collection of Barbies. Until it had all happened, then Carla's parents had forbidden her to play with Paris.

A stab of emotion hit Paris in the gut. Man, why did she have to remember this stuff, anyway? Just being in this town was bringing it all up. It just made her sick! She needed to get out of here when this was all over. She'd go to Switzerland and check in to a spa and lose weight and buy herself a new wardrobe in Milan afterwards.

She adjusted her black sunglasses and kept marching up a small incline.

Why didn't my parents have more children sooner after me? she wondered. She searched through the conversations she'd had with her father, late at night, while he'd worked. He'd talked to her like an adult even though she'd only been a child. She seemed to remember her mother had lost one and then it had taken them a long time to conceive. So the gap between her birth and the birth of her sister was wide. That was it.

Her sister. Somewhere out there, she had a sister, raised by strangers. Maybe that was better than ending up in the Catholic orphanage like she had. Or maybe it wasn't better.

Another wave of pain hit Paris. She felt tears trail down the side of her cheek. What the hell was all this? She . . . she needed to think about other things. She needed to get mad at Turner.

She climbed the ramp up to the small chapel and pulled on the double doors. How *had* she ended up in this chapel that night? It was certainly off the beaten path. Well, closer to the Paris Hotel than the Four Seasons, but still, what an odd coincidence that she should have ended up in Turner Pruitt's chapel.

She swung the doors open and stood at the back of the sanctuary. Light streamed in on Turner through the stained glass windows. He wasn't in his Elvis duds, just a pale gray suit, a white shirt, and his reverend's collar. It was so amazing how handsome he was.

A couple stood in front of him, and a small group of people sat in the pews. They all turned to see who had opened the doors. Paris saw that the man at the altar had very white hair, and his bride was not some young thing but an older woman wearing a pale blue dress and a little hat with a short veil that perched on her short salt-and-pepper hair. She had a small bouquet of white roses in her hand, and white gloves. White gloves. Paris hadn't seen white gloves for ages. They almost glowed in a strange way. She rubbed her eyes to make that stop.

They all smiled at her. She saw a flash of light surround them all. How extremely odd. Then the light went out completely and a fuzzy darkness started like a frame around the picture of Turner and the couple. The frame faded and moved in on itself until the entire room was engulfed in darkness. "Turner?" Paris heard her voice echo through the dark room, then the room turned upside down, and the red velvet carpet was pressed against her cheek. That was the last sensation Paris remembered before everything went completely blank.

"She's going to be fine. She'll be fine," Marla repeated. Turner wasn't so sure. Paris looked very pale. The doctor had been doing that thing that made Turner nervous. Hovering and not saying a word.

"I'd like you all to leave the room now, please. I have to do some examinations. Mr. Pruitt, I'll be out to talk to you soon," Dr. Shapiro said.

A cart full of computer equipment came through the door, and Turner and Marla had to stand aside to let it pass.

"I like him, Turner, he's very intelligent." Marla held on to Turner's arm while they stepped out into the hallway.

Turner just shook his head and watched another nurse rush into Paris's room.

"Look, everyone is over here. Come on, we'll have Anton fetch you some coffee." Marla gestured for Turner to come.

He looked down the hall and saw a small waiting area straight ahead. There were palm trees in big pots and a painting of the desert on the wall in purples and oranges.

Millie, Sarah, and Anton were all sitting in orange armchairs, looking expectant. He wished he had something to tell them. He followed Marla to the group of friends. It was nice to see that Paris had friends.

Millie stood up and gave him a hug. "Sarah came and got me. Listen, buddy, she's just not used to this heat. She just fainted, that's all." Millie patted Turner's arm.

For some reason Turner just couldn't get himself to believe what everyone was saying. Part of that was the contradiction between the optimistic words and the rush of medical personnel. Also, when he'd run to her in the chapel and looked her over, he'd seen a spot on her dress that had turned out to be blood.

The truth was that Paris might lose their babies. He didn't have any words for anyone right now.

"Excuse me for a few minutes, will you? I'll be in the hospital chapel if they need me."

"Sure. I'll come and get you." Sarah stood beside Millie.

"Thanks," was all Turner could get out. He'd been in this hospital before, visiting some of his evening service-goers. He'd brought old Aldo Newsome here one night because he hadn't wanted him out on the street for his last day on earth. He knew where the chapel was. He'd prayed here before.

More orange chairs lined up in rows made two sections on either side of the small room. A large wooden cross was on the wall at the front of the chapel. The wood was carved so smoothly that it shone in the low light. He was grateful there was no one there but him.

"Where am I, what is this?" Paris watched the blur around her turn into people—in white coats. She felt very, very not okay, and scared.

Marla put her hand on Paris's forehead. "It's just us, honey. You fainted."

Dr. Shapiro leaned over Paris and smiled. "Hey. Don't try and get up. We've got you wired for sound."

"I'm fine. I . . . what's all this stuff?" There were machines to the left and right of her. One she recognized as an ultrasound. The other must be some sort of monitor. There was a do-hickey attached to her index finger with wires going somewhere. There was some big belt around her middle that went to another machine, which showed little wavy lines on a monitor.

"Can I talk in front of your friend, or would you rather have a private conversation?" Dr. Shapiro asked.

"Marla? We have no secrets."

"Yeah, now." Marla smiled at her in that way

when someone really worried about you tries to make the cheerful face. It made Paris worry.

"Well, you had a little heat stroke, but also you've had some bleeding and pre-labor. We've got that under control now. Your blood pressure was a little high and probably you've had some headaches?"

Paris nodded.

"Well, we're not sure what caused it, but we'll run some tests. It's actually lucky you fainted from the heat. It got you in here." Dr. Shapiro turned to Marla. "She's fine, and the babies are fine, now. But we'll have to keep her here for a while, and she'll have to be monitored after that. I'll need to talk to her husband."

"I'll get him." Marla gave Paris's hand a pat and left the room.

"What's a *while?*" Paris asked.

"Can't tell. At least three days or maybe more, depending on how things stabilize. You want to give those babies a fighting chance, now don't you, Mrs. Pruitt?"

Paris lay back on the hard hospital bed. "Yes," she said. Then she closed her eyes. She hated hospitals. Only terrible memories came from hospitals.

Except one memory—when Paris had come to see her mother after she'd had the baby. She'd been excited and curious, and her father had been great. He'd bought her a big sister present—a teddy bear with a ballerina outfit. And they'd had dinner in a restaurant that evening while her mother had stayed another night.

Her little sister had been so tiny. Paris had taken her hand in her own, and the tiny fingers had curled around her bigger finger. The baby's hair had hardly been there, but it'd been red, just like hers, and her mother's. Daddy had said, "Here we go again, all my redheaded girls."

Her mother hadn't meant for everything to go so wrong for that baby. She'd had every intention of giving the baby a happy life. Bonnie. Her sister's name was Bonnie. That was the first time Paris had thought of that for years.

Something in her heart felt sad and heavy. She didn't want anything to happen to Turner's babies. He was going to be a wonderful father. She had to fight for them to have a good start in life.

"Turner." Sarah lay her hand on Turner's shoulder. "She's awake."

He looked up at her. "Is she—"

"She's going to be okay. And the babies are fine."

"Thank you." Turner got up and walked out of the chapel, leaving Sarah behind.

Sarah looked up at the large mahogany cross. She couldn't help how she felt. She'd loved

Turner since they were kids. He might love Paris now, but there was still a chance. When Paris handed him two infants and walked out the door, she would still be here. She would be the one there for him. Even if it took years, she would wait. Sarah sat down in the orange chair still warm from Turner's body and said her own prayers.

Turner headed down the maze of corridors and quickly strode through the door of Paris's room.

"Dr. Shapiro."

"Mr. Pruitt, we're out of the woods. Just in the last half hour we've seen no further labor, and her blood pressure is down to a normal level."

"Labor?"

"Talk to your wife. I have to see to something for a moment, but I'll be back shortly. I'll fill you in on all the details together." Dr. Shapiro stepped out, and they were alone.

The early night sky was still bright with stars and sunlight as Turner came up beside Paris. He noticed light patterns from the curtains dancing on her bedcovers. He found her free hand between the wires and held it up to his lips for a moment.

"I was coming to yell at you." Paris smiled weakly.

"Any particular reason?"

"General stuff. Making love to me, expectations, you know the drill."

"I do."

"I'm sorry, Turner, I didn't know taking a walk would make me go into labor."

"It's not your fault." He thought that was probably the first time he'd ever heard her say she was sorry for anything.

"I promise I'll do everything I can to take good care of your babies. I'll listen to the doctor and eat right from now on, and behave."

Your babies. He wanted to correct her, but she was showing the first maternal instincts he'd seen in months, so he didn't want to break that moment. "You're going to be fine. We'll make sure of it."

"I'm a brat, Turner."

"But so cute." He bent over and kissed her forehead. She looked up at him with her emerald green eyes, and he thought for a moment he saw tears well up on the edges.

"Don't start thinking things are different now. My plans are still the same. But I like you, and you deserve good things. I know you really want these babies."

"I want you too, Paris. And if something had happened today, I would have still wanted you."

"I can't do anything about that, Turner, but I

can make sure and do the best I can with this pregnancy." She turned her face away from him.

He was sure she was crying, in that silent way in which women sometimes cry.

Dr. Shapiro came in. "Okay, folks, let's pull up a chair and go over the facts. I like to have all the facts, don't you?"

15

Playing for Keeps

All her spa time down the drain.

"I cannot stay flat on my ass in bed for four months. That's impossible." Paris crossed her arms and fumed. What were they thinking, she would like . . . pee in a bedpan twice a day? She shuddered. "Get me that throw, Meyers."

"Say please and behave yourself," Marla retorted. She picked up the throw anyway and came to tuck it around Paris's shoulders.

"Please."

"Good girl. They let you get up to go to the bathroom," Marla said.

Paris perked up. "Well, thank God for small favors."

Sarah stood in one corner, glowering at Paris. *Now what's up her bonnet?* thought Paris. Sarah was such a priss, Paris wondered how she could become a nurse being so prissy.

"Anton and I are going back to the hotel, Paris." Marla kissed Paris on the cheek.

Paris swatted at her and missed on purpose. "Stop that."

"Marla's going to send you a laptop computer so you can learn to e-mail us. The Internet is full of fascinating places, Paris. It will keep you occupied for months. And out of everyone's hair. Speaking of hair, if you don't behave I won't fly back here and do your roots for the whole four months, and you'll look like an old woman with all the gray that's going to grow in." Anton cackled. "I've got special natural dyes just for pregnant women, too."

"You would fly back here and do my roots?" Paris asked.

"Sure, honey. No one knows your formula but me. Well, and that one guy at the hotel," Anton answered. He'd been sitting on the side of the bed while Marla had been fussing with Paris. He got up to leave.

"I can't believe you two are abandoning me." Paris stuck out her lower lip.

"Only because we know you are in such good hands." Marla winked at Turner.

"Yeah, look at these hands!" Millie held her hands up in the air and made fists.

Paris saw her flex her old lady muscles and was pretty impressed.

"I'll keep her in line," Millie continued.

"She will, that's true." Turner laughed.

Paris made a face at him. How could life get so weird as to leave her locked up with crazy Millie and sour-faced Sarah for four months? And just when she'd planned her escape so well. She'd been hoping to take an apartment near Turner's place. She'd plotted it all out on her walk up to the chapel. She'd been going to tell Turner he could visit her there and watch her be pregnant from afar, because she was sick of his one-bathroom loony bin.

"Well, darling, we'll come back in the morning. We've got a late flight out tomorrow."

"I'll have your things sent to the flat." Marla gave her one last over-the-bed hug.

"Call me." Paris's voice broke.

"I will. You can bet on it."

"Don't be a brat, and don't let anyone touch your hair." Anton gave her another bed-hug.

Paris thought she might cry, but she bit her lip instead. "Scram. Give Ripple a big sloppy kiss from me when you get back."

"I will," Anton smirked.

Marla smacked his arm. "No, *I* will!"

"No, *I* will," Anton countered. Turner put his

arms around each of their shoulders and walked them to the door. They kept repeating that same game until Paris couldn't help but laugh out loud.

Turner returned. "I'm going to run Millie and Sarah home, Paris. I'll be back."

"Save it, Turner, I'm bone tired. I'll just get some sleep. You can come back in the morning." Paris pulled the skimpy covers up further toward her chin, trying not to knock into the wires. "Tell them to send in about five extra blankets. They really have the air cranked up in here."

"I will. But I'm coming back. We are going to talk."

"Whatever."

"Come on, Sarah, get out of here before she puts you to work," Millie said.

Sarah took one step forward. "Actually I have a shift tonight. I get to rock babies all night. I volunteered while we were here. I'll take a bus home or get one of the other gals to drop me off."

Turner and Millie stood still. To Paris they both looked surprised. The mouse had come out of her corner.

"I'll be fine." Sarah smiled at Turner.

Turner came over to Paris's side. He kissed her cheek before she could move it. "Hang in there, tiger."

"Go away."

"We're going, but I'm coming back," Turner

said. Then he and Millie left the room—finally. That just left candy striper Sarah.

Paris actually felt a little frightened by her. She had a really mean look on her face. Well hell, what could the woman do to her anyway?

Sarah came over to her bed.

"You don't have to stay here, Sarah. Turner has seen you pretend to care about me. That's all you needed," Paris said. She was in no mood for this woman.

"Do you think everyone just pretends to care about people, Paris?"

"I'm not having this little talk with you. Leave me alone. I wish I'd had a miscarriage. Then I could leave this town and not have to deal with any of you." She knew it was horrible the minute she said it, but it came out anyhow, and Sarah looked so shocked that Paris wondered if she might slap her.

Paris watched Sarah turn away from her for a moment. She looked overcome with emotion. Then Sarah's whole posture seemed to change. Paris got very, very scared for some reason.

"I'll be right back," Sarah said. She said it all kind of hard and spooky. Not her usual, mealy-mouthed self.

"Don't bother." Paris did her usual snappy snap-back without thinking.

Sarah just stared at her. She turned and stamped out of the room, her little flat heels punctuating the quiet except for the beeping of a few machines.

What the hell? Was nurse junior going for Jell-O? Was she determined to sit by Paris's side and keep an eye on her because of her secret crush on Turner? Keep an eye on the goods so Paris didn't do anything stupid? Paris got very uncomfortable and shifted around a bit. Damn all these wires.

Time ticked by, empty as the room. Paris heard voices in the hall, then nothing. She watched the sky darken. If this was what the next four months were going to be like, she would undoubtedly go nuts even before the birth. That made her feel even more spooked out. She shivered.

Sarah came back in the room like a gust of wind. She had an orderly with her, and another nurse. Dr. Shapiro's nurse. The nurse came over and took some readings off Paris—blood pressure, some blippy stuff—then took her temperature.

"What's up?" Paris mumbled through the thermometer.

"Quiet," the nurse ordered. She had that same look in her eye that Sarah had had earlier.

Paris had read bad books like this. She tried to scrunch under the covers.

"She's good to go. Keep her flat." The nurse unhooked a few wires.

"No, I'm not! I'm not going anywhere! Where's Dr. Shapiro?"

"I just spoke to him. He approved a brief trip down the hall," the nurse said sharply. She moved machines against the side of the room.

The orderly stepped out and returned, pushing a rolling gurney.

"I don't want to go down the hall." Paris scrunched down further. She was going to be mistaken for someone having a gallbladder operation. She was going to end up with a tonsillectomy!

Sarah came over to her and helped the nurse strip the sheets right off her.

Paris screamed, "Get away!" She tried to pull her skimpy hospital gown down to cover her bare ass. The orderly smirked as he butted the gurney up next to her bed. He came over to one side and pulled the bottom sheet out from the corners.

"We're moving you, so hold on. On my count. One, two, three." The nurse and Sarah picked up one side of the sheet, and the orderly caught the other. They lifted her over to the rolling gurney.

"I'll scream."

"Go ahead. No one on this floor is going to pay any attention to you," Sarah said in a steel-cold voice.

"You can have Turner! You don't have to kill me to get him." Paris couldn't believe it as she watched the orderly wrap her tightly in the sheet and fasten two straps over her.

"Kill you? Maybe later. Right now we want to show you something. So pipe down," Sarah commanded.

Paris was scared out of her wits. She felt her heart pounding. They pushed the gurney out the hospital room door and headed down a bright corridor. Sarah walked beside her with quick steps. The lights were so bright that they made Paris squint, but her hands were sealed up in the straps so she couldn't cover her eyes.

They stopped, and the nurse dug through the sheet for Paris's arm.

"I'm telling Dr. Shapiro on you."

"Go right ahead. I'm sure he'll take me out to lunch." The nurse kept a stone face while she took Paris's pulse and blood pressure once more.

"Okay." She spoke to Sarah. "I'll be right at the nurses' station. Holler when you need me."

"Thanks, Rosie. Lennie, I'll page you when I'm done." Sarah took the wheel, and Paris watched Lennie the orderly wink at Sarah.

Well, great. She was now the prisoner of psycho student nurse Sarah. Who she was then going to be *at the mercy of* for another four months.

"Just remember in four months I can get up and pound you, Sarah, so whatever your evil plan is, I'd just remember that. I'm bigger than you."

"Before we go in, I want to say what I have to say." Sarah glowered over her.

Paris thought about grabbing Sarah or smacking her with her now free hand, but it occured to her that might not be the best strategy.

"Get it over with. You want Turner, I take it. Well, I'm sorry he fell for me, but if you wait around a bit, I'll toss him to you for free."

"You are without a doubt the most selfish, self-centered woman I have ever encountered in my entire life. You think everything is about you. You don't deserve to spend a minute with Turner, and I'll be glad to see you go, because I actually believe you when you say you would be the worst mother on earth."

That actually hurt. Paris fell silent. She would not be the worst mother on earth. She was doing these babies a favor. They'd be with a loving father. She'd be away from them where she couldn't crack up . . . maybe even hurt them. Sarah was crazy. "You don't know what you're talking about."

Sarah pushed the gurney into a room with less light. They stopped rolling, and Sarah pushed a brake with her foot. Paris could hear the thud. Another nurse nodded to her and moved to the far end of the room, busying herself with charts.

"I want you to look at these babies. Turn your head and look."

Paris thought about not doing that, but she figured Sarah would twist her head if she didn't. She turned and saw a row of incubators. In each one was a tiny, tiny infant. She couldn't believe how small some of them were. They had bindings over their eyes, and they were hooked to all sorts of tubes and monitors. She gasped at the painfulness and strangeness of it all.

Sarah's voice was low, but so, so nasty. "Some of these babies only weigh a pound. They might make it, they might not. If they do, they might be blind, or damaged in all sorts of ways. Do you understand what I'm saying to you?

"All I've heard is how inconvenient everything is for *you*. How staying in bed would be so difficult for *you*. You eat what you want, you do what you want, and you order everyone around. You are a spoiled, horrible woman. Well, this is what is going to happen to your babies if you don't get a clue. If you don't start focusing on the needs of the infants you are carrying, you'll deliver early. If you do, they might actually live. Then you'll be free to abandon them and Turner will spend the rest of his life caring for them."

Paris wiped at a tear with her one free hand. "I . . . I don't want anything to happen to them. You don't understand. I might be a danger to them."

"Whatever this thing is that you've got going in your head, I have no doubt that the truth is you can't be bothered with being a mother because your enormous ego doesn't have room for that. I have never seen anyone so heartless and cold as you, Paris.

"I don't know why God gave you Turner's babies, but I'll be damned if I'll let you hurt them before they're born. You can do whatever you like after that. We'll buy breast milk from the milk bank, because did you know that preemie twins need breast milk? Do you know *anything* about your own pregnancy? Have you read a single book? And all twins are basically preemies, because it's very rare to make it past thirty-five weeks."

Paris stared at the infants in their glass enclosures and felt shame—for once in her life. No, it wasn't the first time. She'd felt shame when she'd gone to school and when people had known about her mother. Her teacher's look of pity had made her feel shame. The nuns had made her feel shame for what had happened to her parents. Should her babies feel that same shame?

"I don't know what planet you are on, Paris, but I'm going to see to it you stay in bed, and eat right, and do what any decent mother would do, even if I have to tie you down. Turner doesn't *deserve* a wife like you. He is a saint."

"Take me back," Paris sobbed.

But before anything else could happen, she saw Turner's face framed in the doorway. She had never been so glad to see Turner Pruitt in her entire life.

"Turner, *Turner.*" She couldn't even get more words out.

Turner took Sarah by the arm and escorted her out into the hallway. The doors closed behind them, so all Paris could see was their silhouettes on the glass. Sarah had her face turned directly up to his, and whatever she was saying was pretty harsh. Her body language, as far as Paris could see, showed no remorse. It seemed like it took forever.

Then Turner stepped back into the room without Sarah.

"Thank God you came back. Can we leave this place now? I can't stand it," Paris wailed.

"Be quiet, Paris, there are infants sleeping."

"Then take me out."

"No. We're going to stay here for a few minutes." Turner was oddly silent. He looked around the room. "Is it true you said you wished you'd had a miscarriage?"

Paris felt herself getting panicky. That horrid bitch Sarah would have to tell Turner that she'd said that. "I didn't mean it, Turner. I had no idea they'd be like this."

"Our babies are fighting for their lives, Paris."

"I won't do anything to hurt them," Paris sniffed. She wiped the tears off her face with her hand.

Paris saw movement—the nurse with a mask at the other end of the room, checking each baby. Turner watched her. She saw a deep crease form in Turner's forehead.

A woman came in—probably a mother—and went over to one of the glass boxes. The nurse came over and talked to the woman, then helped her tie a medical mask on her face. Paris watched as she pushed her hand through an opening in one of the incubators and into a glove sort of thing. She heard her talking to her baby in soft tones. Then the nurse rested her hand on the mother's shoulder for a moment.

Paris snuffled. The mother looked up at her. After a few more minutes the mother removed her hand from the opening and walked over to Paris.

She put her hand on Paris's hand. Paris looked up at the woman's eyes and saw the pain there. But she saw something else, too.

The woman dropped her mask down and spoke to Paris. "Is your baby in here?" the woman asked her.

"No. I . . . a friend of mine wanted me to see."

The woman looked confused but passed over that thought and held Paris's hand. "I'll pray for you," she said.

Paris felt a terrible sting of emotion hit her. It hurt so bad she thought she might cry out loud. "I'll be fine," she murmured, her voice breaking a little. "I'll pray for you, too. I will. My husband is a minister." Did she really say that?

The woman looked up at Turner, who nodded quietly to her.

"Thank you." She took Paris's hand in both of hers and held it for a minute. "He gained two ounces," she said.

Paris saw tears in the woman's eyes. "I'm sure he'll be okay," she replied.

The woman dropped back and wiped her eyes with her gown sleeve. "I better get back. It helps them to have their mother's voice and touch. Even if it is a glove."

The nurse stepped over to Turner. "You better take her back."

Turner grabbed the end of the gurney and pulled Paris out of the room.

"I swear to you, I won't let anything happen. I want them to have a good start," Paris choked through her tears.

Sarah was standing in the hallway. So was Lennie the orderly.

Sarah leaned over her. "I have nothing more to say to you, Paris, but if I hear you whine about how laying on your back is ruining your hair, or complain about how put-upon you are, I swear I will slap you myself."

"I can be a very strong person when I want to," Paris said quietly.

Turner just stood there and let that woman

talk to her like that. Then he let the orderly take the gurney from him and roll her back down the hall. He stayed with Sarah. Paris felt sick to her stomach.

"My, my, we've really pissed someone off, haven't we?" Lennie leered at her.

"Apparently."

"I'd behave if I were you. Dr. Shapiro's nurse, Rosie, is one scary lady."

"I hear ya."

Lennie got her back to her room, and Rosie the scary nurse came in. They undid her straps and did the sheet transfer again. Once she was back on the bed, Rosie reattached all her wires and belts and took another round of readings. They remade the bed around Paris and gave her several warmed blankets off a tray. They felt so comforting that Paris started to cry.

"Get some sleep, Mrs. Pruitt. Dr. Shapiro will see you in the morning bright and early. I suggest you follow doctor's orders to the letter. He's a very good doctor. Keep flat. Ring the bell if you want to go to the bathroom. We'll use a pan for the next twenty-four hours. After that, if Dr. Shapiro says it's okay, you can get up for that only," nurse Rosie said.

Paris had nothing to say, or any ability to say it.

The nurse tested each machine, watched the reading, then seemed satisfied. She turned and padded out of the room with her soundless white shoes. Lennie rolled the gurney out after her. "G'night Mrs. P," he called back.

Turner came in the room. He stood next to her bed and felt her cheek. "Warm enough?"

"Y-yes."

"Your chills are from your blood pressure dropping down after being too high. Dr. Shapiro gave you some medication to make it drop."

"That won't hurt the babies, will it?"

"No, it won't." Turner was deadly silent between his short answers. "It's good of you to ask."

"I'm not as much of a monster as she thinks I am," Paris said.

"It's not about you anymore, Paris. Unless you can make some kind of shift in thinking, I don't see much hope for a good outcome with this pregnancy, or with us. I am seriously concerned."

Paris looked up into Turner's face. His usual warmth was gone. In its place was something else—anger? Disappointment? Whatever it was, it hurt her more than anything Sarah had said. She was shocked at how much it hurt. It made her ache with pain.

"I thought you said it wasn't my fault?" Her voice was betraying her feelings, and she didn't like that. She bit her lip.

"It's not about fault, Paris. You didn't mean to get sick. But what happens next *is* up to you. I've watched you push people around for months now. I'm hardly surprised one of them pushed back. But you are carrying two little lives that are depending on you to think of them first from now on. I don't know if you are capable of that, and it makes me terribly sad to think that my faith in you has been a mistake."

"What are you talking about?"

"I've held the belief that you had the capacity to love. That once we faced some of your early pain, and you began to heal, you might find yourself capable of giving and receiving love. Sarah doesn't seem to think you have that ability."

"She hates me."

"She doesn't know you like I do, but I've been waiting to see some effort on your part. A sign of recognition that you have been entrusted with the care of two lives. Maybe I've been a fool, like Sarah says."

For the first time, Paris thought that Turner might leave her. For the first time, she understood why.

"If you want to leave after the birth, I'm not going to stop you, Paris. I had high hopes we'd make a real family for our children. But I'm only one man. I have a great deal of love to give, but I can't fix this, Paris." His voice was so hard and broken at the same time. She could hardly stand it.

"I—I'm sorry, Turner. Sorry for everything. I can change, I promise."

"Prove it," Turner replied. Then he walked out of the room.

Paris lay flat on her back in the hard hospital bed with her eyes wide open, tears streaming down her temples. Outside the window she saw the neon competing with the stars, making them dim. Out in the desert, not far away, the stars filled the night sky like nowhere she'd ever seen before. The desert was beautiful. A good place for her children to grow up.

She wanted them to grow up. She wanted them to have a wonderful father like Turner. She had been a horrible woman for so long that she didn't know how to change. She cried for being horrible and hard and unloving, and for the tiny little babies she'd seen in the preemie ward. Why did Turner even bother with her?

At least she could give him the gift of his babies, well and healthy. Paris thought for a moment about Turner, and how much she cared whether he hated her or not. She didn't want him to hate her. She . . . she loved him. She lay awake until the light of morning streaked a rainbow of pink and yellow light into her room, thinking about love, thinking about her children. Thinking about Turner.

16

Don't Be Cruel

Turner hadn't slept much. He stood at the window staring at the morning sky. He ran his hand over his face and rubbed his aching forehead. The smell of perking coffee hung in the air. The pot made gurgling noises.

Sarah opened the front door quietly. She looked startled to see him there.

"Turner?"

"I couldn't sleep."

"The babies are doing fine. I checked before I left."

"And Paris?"

"She's fine."

Turner heard the edge still in Sarah's voice. How could she not think badly of Paris if she didn't know the inner turmoil Paris was having? He'd been so respectful of Paris's privacy, but it was costing her the love and support of other people in her life.

He knew Paris probably didn't care about that. But he did.

This probably wasn't the time to talk to Sarah about it, though, after a night shift.

Sarah hung up her sweater on the coatrack and came over to where Turner was standing. "It's a beautiful sky today, isn't it? Millie says you're thinking about house hunting. Is that right?" she asked.

"It's going to get pretty crowded around here with two babies," Turner said softly.

"There's no hurry, though. When Paris leaves you'll have your room back and we can rig up a nursery in there with you pretty easily. Or we'll just turn the living room into baby world while they're still infants." She laughed a little, in a forced way.

Turner looked over at Sarah and tried to read where she was coming from. He didn't understand her sometimes.

"I'm hoping that Paris will change her mind."

Sarah took a step over to the table and pulled a chair out. She sat down hard and crossed her arms across the sparkly white linoleum tabletop. "Turner, why would you want her to stay? I get that the babies would do better with her for a short time, but she obviously doesn't care. She is the least maternal woman I've ever seen. She shows you no affection, and frankly, sometimes I think you've lost your mind. I know you are an optimistic, godly man, but sometimes we need to cut our losses and get on with life. We'll all pitch in and make sure your children are surrounded with love. That's more than their so-called mother would ever do."

Turner let her get all that out. After all, this was the first time Sarah had actually said it out loud to him. The bitterness in her voice told him that she'd been holding it and twisting on it for a very long time.

He was bone tired. "Let's have some coffee." He walked to the kitchen and took down two cups. He saw Paris's Garfield cup on the shelf. How could a woman who brought her cartoon cup from New York not have a soft side? It must be in there somewhere.

"Another round of coffee around the table is not going to make this all better, Turner." Sarah sounded like she was going to cry. "And besides, I'd rather have tea. Just micro me a cup." She wiped at her eyes and slumped in the chair.

Turner filled a cup with water and pulled out a peppermint tea bag. He stuck it in the microwave and punched the buttons. The machine whirred. He poured himself a cup of coffee from the Mr. Coffee. That was Millie's phrase for the electric coffeemaker. She liked to call things by their brand names. The Amana. The Frigidaire. It made him smile.

"We need a new house, Sarah. We don't have a washer and dryer. That's seventeen-thousand diapers a day," he joked. He didn't know why he picked that moment to joke—just trying to cut the tension.

"I see your point."

The microwave dinged, and he pulled her tea out. He balanced a small dish on top for the bag and brought both his coffee and her tea to the table. This kitchen table was getting a lot of talk time lately. It used to be Millie's favorite spot until the hordes had come. This table had seen some mighty hot talk on her Hot Line. He smiled as he sat down.

He held his hot coffee cup in his hands, warming them. It seemed like there was a chill in the room, but he knew it was just the discomfort of the conversation.

"Sarah," he said quietly as he sat down next to her. "There's something I feel I need to tell you. I'd like you to keep it as a confidence, the way I have. I know you are an honorable person, and will do that if I ask you to."

"Yes."

"Paris has very personal reasons for believing she might be a danger to her own children. She is convinced she will repeat her mother's medical history of postpartum psychosis. I've tried to convince her this is a new era, with new treatments, and that she most likely won't even have this problem, but she is basically scared out of her wits."

Sarah was very quiet. She stared at Turner like she was taking it all in slowly.

"Does this make sense to you? She had a very bad time of it as a child. You know her parents are both dead. She was put into an orphanage."

"I didn't know," Sarah answered. "That's unfortunate."

"Yes. The best I can do at this point is track down the records. If I can show her what could be done today under similar circumstances, I think she might listen. I've been reading up, and this one book in particular has very solid evidence that natural progesterone therapy can make a significant difference. Plus we've made major medical advancements in the treatment of depression."

"I saw that book on the table. Katharina Dalton, right? I read some of it. It's actually a shame more OBs don't read this research. It seems to me women should be aware of the various options."

"I know. At least Dr. Shapiro read it. We've talked some, but I've decided the best hope lies in recovering the true information about the past and getting her to face it. She was quite young, and she has her own version locked in her head."

"Locked is right," Sarah said. She picked up her tea and sipped. Turner could see her hand was shaking.

"I'm telling you this so you can understand she's not quite the coldhearted creature she appears to be. She's in a great deal of pain, really. And fate has given her to me. For my own reasons, I am very much in love with her. I don't know what will become of that, but I'm determined to find out. She's a unique person, full of spirit. She just needs healing."

"And you think you are the person to do that?"

"I do."

Sarah put down her tea as if it were heavy in her hand. Turner saw that her face was pale. He took another gulp of his coffee.

"I was a little rough on her tonight," Sarah said. She looked down into her cup, as if she might be slightly ashamed of herself.

Turner wondered just what "rough" meant. "Do you want to talk about it?"

"I wanted her to understand that the health of her babies was more important than the discomfort she might have to endure. I was angry at her for complaining and . . . for being so coldblooded about leaving you—and them."

Turner had caught part of what she had said

to Paris, but not all. He was upset with Sarah, but he understood. Besides, Paris needed a wake-up call. Maybe Sarah was meant to be the messenger. He couldn't control everyone's reactions to Paris. Paris was going to have to start taking responsibility for her own actions. He listened to Sarah and watched her emotions play out on her face.

"I said some terrible things to her right before you got there. And you already know I arranged that visit to the preemie ward. I'm sorry, Turner. If I'd known some of this, I wouldn't have been so harsh." Her cheeks were red with embarrassment. "What can I do to help?"

"Actually, you can do some medical research for me at the college library, and if you find anything about new advancements in treatment, bring them to me. Other than that, you said what you felt was the truth. Maybe Paris needed to see those babies, and hear your words. I'd just like to suggest you have some compassion for Paris now that I've told you the whole story, and try and understand where she's coming from."

"Please let me know what you find out about her parents. It might help me focus the research." Sarah took another sip of her tea, pushed the cup aside, and got up from the table abruptly.

Turner saw that her eyes were starting to brim with tears.

"I'm going to get some rest. I'm sorry, Turner.

I hope you can help her." She left the room quickly.

His coffee was moving toward lukewarm. He got up and poured a refill from the pot, then leaned against the counter and sipped from his favorite black cup.

What would it be like to have been ripped from his family and put in an orphanage? He knew St. Mary's was a decent place, but the nuns could hardly substitute for the love of a mother and father. The internal pain she must have endured was hard for him to imagine.

He'd been in the most loving of families his whole life. He missed them right now, badly. He looked at the kitchen clock. It was 6 A.M., 4 A.M. on Aitutaki Island. He'd have to wait till ten or eleven to catch them at a decent morning hour.

If he could take Paris there, let her see what his family was like, that would be such a gift. That, and the white sand beaches, the lapping waves, the palm trees in the warm wind. He would just have to make that happen sometime soon.

Right now, he had a very pressing engagement to get ready for. Turner finished his coffee, rinsed out the cup, and put it in the "Whirlpool" dishwasher. He was headed for a hot shower, a suit, and a meeting with St. Mary's parish priest. But first he'd stop at the hospital. He had left things badly with Paris.

Turner wondered if Paris was capable of rising

above her old demons. He had to be prepared for the worst. But while he had her, he was going to do battle with everything he had in him. He looked out the window at the bright sun. The desert was famous for cleansing the spirit. He must have faith that Paris was in his keeping for a reason.

"Wow, you've got your regular reverend duds on." Paris sat up slightly, surprised to see Turner so early, and with his collar and a suit. He looked very . . . preacherlike, but very sexy too, which she was sure must be a sin on her part to even think. Maybe. She forgot what the rules were. She tried to sound light with him. As if she weren't devastated by what had occurred between them last night. She wondered if her levity was working.

"You look very tired."

"I can't sleep in hospitals. Nurses slapping those white shoes on the floor all night, intercoms, it just gives me the creepies," Paris lied. She could have slept if her mind would have shut up for a minute. It hadn't left her alone at all last night. It had gone from one worry to the next in quick order, and she had felt completely powerless to stop it. Particularly when she hadn't been able to numb herself with a sleeping pill or a glass of wine or a martini, the way she'd been doing for the last ten years.

Turner brought a chair up close to the side of the bed. "Has the doctor been in yet?"

"Yes. He poked around and mumbled and said something about keeping an eye on me for another day. You didn't miss much. He said he'd be back after lunch."

"I have an appointment at ten, but I'll come back after that. I want to talk to him."

"Hey, we're doing fine. You don't need to watch me watch soap operas and eat Jell-O." Paris gave him a weak smile and pulled up the blankets.

Turner looked surprised. She could hardly blame him. Her voice didn't have its usual acid bite. Her words probably sounded *reasonable,* for pity's sake. That was a shock, she was sure. But she'd spent the whole night thinking about Turner, and what a raw deal he'd gotten, marrying her, and how horrible she'd been over the last five months. At least she could make the next part of this time less difficult for him.

"I brought you some things. Here's a nightgown and some other stuff." Turner pulled out Paris's small bag and unzipped the top. "And here." He handed her one of her bears. Actually it turned out to be one of her favorites.

"Wow. Alice Vanderbear. Thanks."

Turner planted the bear next to Paris and smiled at her. "I figured you might want a few things from home."

Home, Paris thought. Did she have one? Even her place in New York was sort of the condo of the year. She'd sublet it without much thought or emotion. Paris stared at the bear. She didn't have much emotion about things or places, or even people. She was either mad as a hatter or numb. She hugged the bear and felt like she was going to cry. But she didn't.

She looked up to see Turner looking at her. His deep brown eyes held a well of feelings, she could see that. But things had shifted between them, and it made her ache with emotion.

"I've got something for you. I picked this up this morning and got it activated." He handed her a tiny purple box.

She opened it up. It was a pager.

"So if you need me, just push this button, and it will page me."

"Thank you, Turner." She meant that. She knew it was all about the babies, but maybe it should be. She didn't exactly deserve any consideration from him, considering her terrible treatment of him.

"Sorry it wasn't a diamond bracelet, I'm a bit short of jewelry money these days. But it is purple, and kind of shiny."

"This is much better than jewelry. Which reminds me, I have insurance."

"I just gave them mine so they'd let you in the place. We've sort of skipped over some of the business parts of being married. I'll get some paperwork together and we'll talk about it."

Turner Pruitt was being business-like with her. She tried not to cry. A sharp pain crossed her temple. She reached up and touched her head until it passed.

"Also we'll need to talk about money. But that can wait till you are feeling better."

"What about money?"

"Well, I'm going to shift some funds out of a trust account I have, and I've been thinking I'll need to buy a house. There's just not enough room for everyone. . . ." Turner dropped his thought. "And we'll have to be a bit more careful with our grocery bills and that sort of thing for a while so I can pull in some extra to pad the down payment. The trust only goes so far."

Paris couldn't believe what an idiot she'd been, eating Twinkies and watching soaps for months, not even offering up funds for her own keep. Well, she had paid for all the expensive linens and any shopping channel moments she'd had, and what, a few take-out dinners? She'd been the worst guest imaginable. She was the worst *wife* imaginable.

"I'll buy you a house."

"What?"

"You heard me."

"I can't let you do that. I'm not a kept man, Paris. I can manage." Turner looked very stern.

Here he was, doing weddings, gathering collection plates at late-night services, paying the food and shelter for three women. What a sweetheart, trying so hard. He'd done a pretty good job so far, and she'd been a completely selfish pig. Paris was seeing herself in a new light today, thanks to Sarah, and it was not pretty.

"This isn't 1959, Turner. I can damn well buy a house for the two children I'm accidentally bringing into the world. It's the least I can do. Were you going to ask me for child support? I doubt it. You could use a few lessons from me about being less giving, Turner."

"Don't be so hard on yourself."

"So maybe I have a lot to make up for, and maybe I'm going to have a bunch of guilt, and this will make it feel better."

"I have to tell you, my male ego is just not handling this well."

"So what? Are you man enough to take a gift from a woman?"

"I'm not sure I am."

"Let's change the subject. Where were you thinking about living?"

"Some sort of neighborhood situation that would be nice for the kids. Playground, that sort of thing. I'll have to research the best schools," Turner said.

"Don't send them to St. Mary's, Turner," she said softly.

"I wasn't planning on it." He looked at his watch. "I've got to go now, Paris, but we'll talk more about all of this later." Turner got up and pushed the chair back quickly. It scraped against the linoleum floor.

"I'll be here," Paris said. She tried to sound brave.

"I'll be back about one. Page me if you need me."

She held up the purple beeper and smiled. "Beep beep."

Turner all but bolted out the door. Paris smiled to herself. A house. It felt so good that she decided buying that house was a must-do.

She reached the phone without any trouble and called information. She didn't even know the number for Turner's apartment, and she wanted to talk to Millie. Millie would just love this. Millie had been so straight up with her. She owed her a big apology.

17

If We Never Meet Again

Turner surveyed the wall of fine leather-bound books in Father Gibbs's office. A large antique-looking globe stood on a wood-and-brass stand in one corner of the room. A beautiful illumination of Mary hung on the Spanish stucco wall. It looked to be from the Byzantine era. The frame was ornately carved and overlayed in gold.

As he'd entered the school, escorted by Father Gibbs's secretary, his senses had been filled with the familiar scents and colors of St. Mary's. As he'd walked in he'd been surrounded with the aroma of candles burning in the sanctuary, the sounds of students not so quietly going from class to class, the bells, and the bustle of nuns moving down the tiled hallways. Some places just stayed exactly as they always were, and visiting was like stepping back in time.

Actually, much *had* changed. The nuns had modern habits now that looked more like street clothes. The students were still in uniform, but he'd seen some wild hair go by.

Turner shifted in his chair as he heard footsteps.

"Turner Pruitt. I am so happy to see you again." The priest entered the room.

"Father Gibbs, you look wonderful." Turner stood and shook the priest's hand. He meant that, too. Father Gibbs looked only slightly older than he had fifteen years ago. He had on the same clothes Turner always remembered him in—black slacks, black shirt with a clergy collar, his sleeves rolled up, ready to pitch in and work at whatever needed doing.

"I gave up coffee, booze, cigarettes, sugar, and anything else fun, plus I started taking a daily walk about ten years ago. I take handfuls of vitamins, and we put a universal machine in the school gym, so I go up there and work out three times a week. It was a big sacrifice for me, a basically indulgent old man. But I figured, hey, I'm asking everyone else to give up this or that, I should try it myself just in case it actually works. That's a little Catholic humor there."

Turner didn't remember Father Gibbs being this relaxed back in the old days. He laughed and sat down across from him in the heavy Spanish-style wooden chair. Father Gibbs took up the chair next to him instead of sitting behind the large desk.

"Boy, these things are hard as a rock. I'll have to have these reupholstered. A little stuffing helps our old bones ache less."

"I'm with you there. I remember sitting in them, waiting for you to deliver a lecture. They're even harder when you're young, Father. So, Father Gibbs, how did you manage to keep this assignment? I know the church usually relocates people every ten years or so," Turner asked.

"When it was my time to go I guess the nuns and the students made such a big uproar you could hear it all the way to Rome. I was given special dispensation to stay. I am a very lucky man."

"St. Mary's is lucky to have you, Father."

"I hear great things about your work with the chapel, Turner. I've kept track of you. I hear your night services are very well attended. God needs people like you out there, my friend. It's just a shame we didn't snag you for the priesthood."

"Sorry about that, Father, my parents were Free Methodists, you know. They just chose St. Mary's for its educational reputation and the fact I could board here for my senior year and be close to my aunt."

"You're forgiven." Father Gibbs slapped his

knees and laughed. "Are your parents still in the Cook Islands?"

"They are. It's their home. I miss them terribly. I called there today, as a matter of fact. They sounded wonderful."

"And what's this you mentioned in your call about you marrying Patricia Jamison? Or I guess the terror of St. Mary's is now the famous Paris James. Poor little thing. I'm sure your parents were very surprised."

"I'd written them about it before, but I had news to tell today. We are expecting twins. That's one of the reasons I'm here."

"My my, twins, is it? Congratulations, Turner. I was most interested to recieve your call, and I spent a great deal of time looking for the records for you. Of course you realize these are private records. But for the life of me I can't think of why I shouldn't give them to you after what you've told me."

Father Gibbs looked at Turner with true compassion. "She was a live-in student here, no adoption took place, so there's no legal issues. It's purely a matter of whether we feel it is in the best interest of the person involved," he said.

Father Gibbs got up and went to his desk. He poured a glass of water out of a large pitcher. "Can I get you a glass of water?"

"I'd like that." Turner felt very anxious to delve into the file he saw sitting on Father

Gibbs's desk, marked with Paris's former name. "I think in this case, it is in Paris's best interest, Father. As I said, she is convinced that she will repeat the same patterns. I've tried to get her to see reason, and so has her doctor, but she is shut in a tower of fear and pain. I think the only way out is for her to face the real facts of what occurred when she was a child."

"I see your logic there. Many times a child's view has shadows lurking in it, and because they had no one to discuss it with, or weren't able to put it into words, the shadows just stay in place and grow into monsters until they drag them out into the light as an adult. It's a painful process, you know." Father Gibbs handed Turner a cut-crystal glass full of water.

"I know. I'll be there with her."

Father Gibbs seemed to be considering his position on the matter. Turner hoped he wouldn't change his mind. The priest took a long drink of water, then set the glass down next to the pitcher. "And Patricia has not expressed an interest in these records herself?" He sat back down behind his desk this time.

"No, unfortunately. Everything that reminds her of her past she seems to run from. But now my children's future is at stake. I will do whatever it takes to try and heal this situation. They need their mother, Father."

"I see your point," Father Gibbs replied. He

picked up the file and opened it. "This is only going to take you so far, though. You'll have to get some medical records, and that will be much harder. The mother was originally in South Vista hospital, which was a division of the main hospital in Henderson. She was only there for a short time—two months. Then they transferred her to Harmond. Harmond is a state facility. Are you familiar with it?"

"Yes."

"Mrs. Jamison was still in Harmond when the husband died. Patricia was made a ward of the state at that point. St. Mary's became her legal guardian, and she came to board full time. She had already been attending school here for the previous two years, so it was a natural transition and, we felt, in her best interest, since there were no living relatives."

Father Gibbs looked up. "We tried very hard to give her love and guidance. Many of the notes in the file were made by Sister Claudia. She took a special interest in Patricia."

Turner was confused by what Father Gibbs had just said, about the order of things, but he heard the hint of concern in Father Gibbs's voice and focused on that for the moment. "I have no doubt that St. Mary's did their very best, Father. Patricia's problems center around her mother and father as far as I can see."

"Such a tragic story. We heard from the

mother a year after her release from Harmond. Here is a copy of the letter she wrote, and the legal form in which she relinquished all parental rights. She vanished after that. By that time we'd decided not to try and find adoptive parents for Patricia, since she was already fifteen. Those things sometimes go so badly, and Patricia was a difficult child."

"What did you say? The mother was released from Harmond? I'm confused. Did she die *after* that?"

"No, she didn't die. As far as we know she was still living when Patricia graduated. We checked the state records for her current address to update our files. Of course that was fifteen years ago. She could have died since then." Father Gibbs fingered through the thick file and pulled out one piece of paper. "This lists her in Mill City."

"In Nevada?" Turner felt a rush of shock hit him. Could Paris's mother still be alive? "Why didn't she come for Paris?"

"Here is a copy of her letter. I remember it. She said Patricia would be better off not knowing. That Patricia had suffered enough pain from her parents, and that St. Mary's had been a good home for her child. Seems like the mother and the daughter do have something in common."

"Why does Paris think her mother is dead?"

"I can't say for sure, but I'm guessing Sister

Claudia might have decided it was kinder to tell her that rather than tell Patricia her mother chose never to see her again."

Father Gibbs took off his glasses and rubbed his eyes.

"The money from her father's life insurance came to Patricia when she turned eighteen, and, if you remember, she left for New York the day after graduation."

"Is Sister Claudia still here?" Turner asked.

"No, I'm afraid not. You know Patricia has been very generous with St. Mary's over the years. We have been very grateful for her donations."

"Paris donated money to St. Mary's?"

"Yes, quite a sizable amount."

Turner still could not believe what he had heard. He took a drink from the glass he was holding and set it down on the coaster protecting the small table beside him.

"And you never told Patricia yourself that her mother was still living?"

"Believe it or not, the subject never came up between us. I'm sorry to say I left the more emotional matters to Sister Claudia. When I was with Patricia we talked about her future plans, her grades, that sort of thing. She seemed so determined to put the past behind her."

"I understand." Turner ran his hand over his chin. "Thank you, Father. I'm assuming I can borrow this file?"

"You may keep this. These are all photocopies, except for the letter. I'm giving you the original. I'm entrusting this to you for Patricia. To help her bring the shadows into the light." Father Gibbs handed the manila folder to Turner.

"I'll do my very best," Turner said. He got up from the chair. "My wife has a strong spirit despite all that has happened to her, Father. She just has to believe in herself again."

"I'll pray for you. We all will." Father Gibbs rose and extended his hand to Turner.

"Thank you."

The priest walked Turner to the carved wooden door of the office. "I'll let you find your way out," he said, opening the door.

"I'd like that. It's good to be here again."

"Let me know."

"I will." Turner headed down the corridor and left Father Gibbs standing by the door. The father looked a bit paler than he had when their conversation had started. The larger consequences of what Turner had uncovered were no doubt running through his mind as well. Turner could hardly comprehend them.

In all his work, in all his study of the psychology of how people deal with life, he'd seen how people repeat patterns, sons following the destructive patterns of their fathers, daughters duplicating their mothers' patterns in relationships, women who had been raised in abusive homes marrying abusive mates, unless they learned and grew and broke the hold the past had on them.

But he'd never seen a case like this. Paris was unconsciously repeating the pattern her mother had set. Even without knowing it. Somewhere inside her, Paris was repeating what her mother had set into motion. The mother who was afraid to cause her daughter more pain by being in her life.

His footsteps echoed in the halls. The students must be in the north section having lunch. He could smell something vaguely southwest in flavor.

His heart ached for Paris. How would he tell her? And would the shock somehow endanger the pregnancy? He thought of having a talk with the doctor—could his wife stand up to an emotional shock this big?

But his next stop in this search was going to be the county office. He wanted to check the last city directory and some other records. Her mother might have been alive fifteen years ago, but she might not be now. He better get his facts straight before he made any huge blundering announcement to Paris.

Right now he was going to get back to the hospital and catch Dr. Shapiro. Turner felt like his mission was much clearer now, but also much more difficult than he'd ever imagined. He was going to need his deepest inner strength to face this development.

18

Farther Along

"I think it's Kevin's baby. Remember last month when the twins caught him and Kaylee making out in the barn and the horse spooked and kicked Chrystal in the rear end?" Millie insisted.

"There is just no way Kevin had time to boink her. It's Stone's baby, obviously."

"He's too old to be the father. I think he had a vasectomy when Shanna got pregnant last year."

"He had it reversed when he married Zoreena," Paris countered. "Pass me those carrots," she added.

"Three months of lying in this bed, me teaching you, and you still haven't learned to say please. Tsk-tsk." Millie held the bowl out beyond Paris's reach.

"Oh, I'm sorry, Millie, I forgot. I'm not easy to retrain. Pu-l-eeese, you old witch!"

"Cackle cackle, just call me Sabrina the old-age witch. Here, eat hearty."

"I hardly call this hearty, I'm dying for a double cheeseburger."

"I believe we decided you were gaining a whole lotta weight and didn't want to end up being a giant pig besides the giant load of babies in there."

"We. I love that when you say *we.*" Paris munched on her baby carrots and glowered at Millie. Of course she was right. For the first three months of her pregnancy she'd eaten the most bizarre things, like ten oranges or six cream cheese Danishes, in between yakking all the time. For the next two she'd eaten everything that moved, with a Twinkie on top.

Then they confined her to this bed and weeks upon weeks of soap operas and the Food Channel. Finally she'd come to understand that if she didn't do the healthy thing, she'd blimp up so bad she'd never be able to work it off. As it was, she was an elephant. But a small elephant. Dumbo, not Jumbo.

"Ouch!"

"Kicking again?" Millie reached over to feel the movement.

"Why does that foot always go into my bladder?"

"Lively bunch in there, aren't they?"

"It's the three-o-clock jump. Every day when *General Hospital* comes on, they play trampoline."

"Isn't it time for your stretches? Maybe if Mommy moved, they'd quiet down."

"Have I told you what a nag you are lately?" Paris rested her hand on Millie's.

"Not for at least an hour."

"Have I told you how much I appreciate you?"

"Not for at least an hour. Now get those gams out and let's do our Richard Simmons thing horizontal."

"Yes, ma'am." Paris obediently started her stretching routines. She'd found a true friend in Millie, who had a real knack for keeping her in line. Cranky women understand each other.

That was without a doubt the best rendition of "How Great Thou Art" Turner had ever heard. Danny Vernon was a natural. Turner was so glad Danny was there to be Elvis, because the last thing he felt like doing was climbing into a sequined jumpsuit tonight.

The pews were packed. The ceiling fans whirred above him, creating a nice breeze. On a night like this, Turner always thanked God for air-conditioning.

He'd finished his short sermon about trust, and Assistant Pastor Danny had belted out quite the inspiring number. He saw that it had affected everyone. The gift of a good singing voice was a wondrous thing.

Two of the older men picked up the collection plates and walked the aisles, gathering a few dollars here and there. Turner would make sure a good portion of it went to the Las Vegas women's shelter. That was his favorite place to drop off an unexpected bit of cash. He liked to talk with the women there and encourage them to stick with their new life-plans. He always brought things for the children, who, despite being uprooted and traumatized, seemed to find their peace being out of harm's way. They loved to play in the children's center there. It seemed to him they were building up some trust in life again.

Trust. He was having a hard time with that one. And when he was wrestling with something, he usually wrote a sermon about it.

He was sitting on a very big secret, and he had to trust that the right time to tell it would reveal itself. He sure knew it hadn't been right for the last few months. Without revealing the nature of the information he was holding, he'd asked Dr. Shapiro whether Paris could take a shock.

The doctor had advised him not to upset her until he felt her condition was stabilized. That was good advice, and as the months rolled on, Turner could see that very clearly.

Millie had been Paris's conspiratorial buddy, and ever since the laptop computer had arrived from Marla in Indiana, Turner had heard less television coming from his old room. Millie confessed they'd been house hunting on the Internet.

She'd confessed because she'd seen a place with a fenced-in garden, a little fountain, and a patio. She'd always wanted a garden spot.

But the ladies had refused to show him the picture. They'd given him a choice. How far would he be willing to commute, and something about golf. He'd said thirty minutes max, and that meant a car, and he didn't play golf, but he could learn if pressed to the green.

He was also trying hard to trust that letting Paris buy a house was . . . acceptable. That was just *so* hard for him. The protector in him screamed out that it was his job to provide for all these women. He still hadn't surrendered to that one. He was looking for a way to contribute to that purchase himself.

It truly hadn't occurred to him that Paris might be a rich woman. He had no idea what she'd done with all her modeling money and thought maybe she'd blown it all on expensive shoes and bears. Her condo back in New York hadn't reeked wealth, for sure. But what did he know about Manhattan rent other than the fact that it was extremely expensive?

Anyhow, that was the least of his problems right now, and as his father had said to him on the phone back in August, the way through rough times was to set your priorities—and pray. Whether or not his wife was amusing herself shopping for a house she apparently had no intention of living in was not first on the priority list.

Turner's biggest concern was the fact that the possible due date for his children was coming close and he still hadn't located Paris's long-lost mother.

It was as if she'd vanished into thin air. He'd hired a locator and had them run a check on the entire country, and he'd still come up empty.

Paris's mother could have changed her name, or remarried, though he'd gone over the Nevada marriage records for the relevant years and still found nothing. Maybe she'd changed her name *and* remarried.

One thing was becoming obvious—Lucy Jamison didn't *want* to be found. He worried about that a great deal. Maybe he'd hung his hopes on this idea of a reuniting and healing too much. The last thing he wanted to do was find the woman and have things get even worse. She might not be receptive to the idea of meeting the angry thirty-year-old daughter she'd abandoned.

Turner jumped up to the sound of the doxology Darlene Goddard was pounding out on the electronic keyboard that pinch-hit for an organ. Darlene was the daughter of one of his regular Sunday night ladies, another former showgirl. Darlene played in a rock band on Fridays and Saturdays. Having her play here was her mom's way of keeping an eye on the girl. Darlene seemed to enjoy herself anyway, and once in a while she added quite a rockin' riff to the hymns. She was very talented on that keyboard.

Turner took the collection plates from his two ushers and placed them at the front table. There was something very soothing to him about the repetitiveness of chapel services. And he knew that his regular attendees felt the same way.

When he got home he was going to talk to Paris about what kind of life she'd like her children to live. That would get her thinking. Maybe if she could visualize them in a happy life she might be able to overcome some of her fears and trust that together they could overcome anything. Maybe he was crazy.

What could he do to get her to see that? What could he do to get her to trust him? If he couldn't find her mother, would he be able to help her heal the past enough to overcome her great fears?

Turner walked to the back of the church and thanked everyone for coming. He said a prayer over them and himself—a prayer of healing and trusting.

* * *

Sarah pushed the file drawer back in and sat down at the hospital records archive desk with what she hoped was the key to Turner's quest. She knew it wasn't her business, but she hadn't been able to help herself one day when he'd been away and Paris had been power shopping on the Internet. She'd found the file he kept in his old desk, which was now crowding the tiny living room back at the apartment.

Actually she'd had to find the key first. That had been easy; it had been hanging on the Siamese cat wall rack with all the other keys. Turner had a lot to learn about security.

She'd seen him put the huge expandable file away several times. She'd known it had something to do with Paris's past, and she'd been compelled to know the whole story, not just the amended version Turner liked to give her. He'd only asked her to research postpartum psychosis in the college library, but that left a whole lot of the story out.

What she'd found there was pretty powerful stuff. Paris's mother in a mental hospital, an infant child given up for adoption, the father dying, and Paris put in a boarding school. Such a young age for a child to have that much tragedy in her life. That file had furnished the pieces of the puzzle Sarah had been looking for.

Now she had names, dates, and even some

photographs that Father Gibbs must have given Turner.

She flicked on the desk lamp and opened the manila folder. This was the list of nurses active in the visiting nurse program. Hopefully she'd find the information she needed.

She scanned the list with her finger for the name of Emma Foley. Emma had worked at Harmond hospital during the years Lucy Jamison had been there. Four-year patients are hard to forget. Sarah had gotten Emma's name from another nurse who'd worked at Harmond, later. It had taken a bus ride over to the facility to get this far. That, and a sob story to the records nurse on duty about how Sarah was trying to find her lost aunt. A lie, but for a worthy cause. The woman would never have given Sarah the names without thinking it was her own relative Sarah was seeking.

The records nurse at Harmond, Peggy Hubbard, had looked up former nurse employees still actively practicing. Emma Foley was one of the few on that list. She was a visiting nurse now. But the home listing for Emma was old and marked inactive and incorrect.

The others on the list of five were either deceased or retired.

She'd spoken to one lady but had gotten nowhere with her. When Sarah had asked her if she remembered a woman named Lucy Jamison, the woman had decided it wasn't proper to talk about. Sarah hadn't wanted to push her and have her report the odd interview, so she'd backed down politely and asked her what it had been like working in a mental facility. Sarah had covered and said she'd been contemplating that path herself.

She flipped through the hospital records, scanning the names. There it was. Emma Foley, visiting nurse, specializing in post-delivery infant care. Now that was an interesting twist.

Sarah took a pad from the desk organizer and carefully copied Emma Foley's address and phone number from the visiting nurse list. She lived in Henderson, very close by.

Sarah pushed the rolling office chair back and refiled the folder. She probably could have found this information on a database, but the hospital was less interested in a nursing student that volunteered to refile records in the archives than one who wanted to poke around the active computer data directory.

She sighed and turned to look at the stack of records she'd have to file now to make her visit here legitimate. Might as well get to it.

Turner would be angry that she'd read his file at home, but she'd thought up a way to help that he hadn't considered yet. An inside path—the path between women. She wanted to help Turner. If he found what he was looking for, things might work out with Paris. He had a good theory in that. Heal her, she'll stay.

It made Sarah's heart twist in pain to know he would most likely end up with Paris instead of her. But somewhere in the last months, watching Paris make an effort to guard the health of her unborn infants, and watching Turner be an honorable husband to her day after day, bringing her videos of all her favorite movies, cooking her healthy food, and sitting in that room with Paris, Sarah had grown to understand that Turner, for some reason, loved Paris, not her.

A cruel twist of fate, to be sure.

She suspected that Turner's obsession with Paris was partially due to his drive to fix all things in the universe and set them right. Perhaps when he'd succeeded in fixing Paris—if he did succeed—then the spell would be broken.

But Paris did have her charms. Sarah had heard laughter—deep, heart-filled laughter—coming out of that room. Turner and Paris, laughing together. She knew they weren't having sex, or even being physically affectionate. She'd heard Millie talking to Turner about how hard that must be for him.

He had answered that his time would come. He had complete faith that Paris had been sent to him for a special purpose. And that his love for her was strong enough to weather the storm.

Turner had said he'd believed the vows they'd said—those words *in sickness and in health, for better or worse.*

And that had been the hardest thing of all for Sarah to hear.

However, as things stood, Paris still had no intention of staying in Las Vegas with her two infant children or Turner. So who knew, really, how things would turn out. Whatever happened, she, the quiet, steady one, would be here. And it served many purposes for her to help Turner on his quest.

It was late—past ten—and Turner would probably be finishing up his Sunday night chapel service soon. She'd gone to several and watched him deliver sermons that had made her cry. She couldn't imagine anyone in the chapel not having their heart softened by his words. He'd spoken of simple things; kindness, helping each other, forgiveness, joy. But his voice and his words had been touched with something special. She'd seen the looks on the faces of people who came to hear him.

One time he'd spoken longer than usual about how the sadness of the world is so hard to take, and that we should not despair—that we have each other. His last words had been "do not despair." And she'd seen people wiping their eyes. She'd seen them through her own tears.

And she'd thought of Paris and the despair that must have surrounded her at the time her mother fell ill. How Paris, just a child herself, had tried to care for her baby sister and then her depressed father by herself, and how that had all fallen into the depths of misery and all had been lost.

She had read the sad account of this in the records that Father Gibbs had given Turner. They'd been written by one of the nuns at the time, and she had spared no detail for some reason. Perhaps so someday someone would understand Paris.

Paris did deserve happiness. It was a shame Paris didn't believe that herself. At least she was making an effort for her children.

Sarah finally reached the end of the stack of filing and picked up the note she'd written with Emma Foley's name on it. She tucked it in the pocket of her uniform.

She still had time to catch the 11:15 bus or call Turner to pick her up.

Maybe she'd let Turner get home to his wife early. The bus was fine. There were always other nurses to buddy up with for the trip.

Tomorrow she'd borrow Millie's car and drive over to Henderson. Millie and Turner had taught her to drive when she'd gotten here, since on the Islands there had really been no use for a car. She'd picked it up fast and had passed her test last month.

It was still a little scary to drive the highways by herself, but she had somewhere to go. She had to go see Emma Foley. She had a feeling about Emma Foley. She could be the turning point in Turner's search.

19

She's Not You

Paris's fax machine made some beeping noises and dumped out a pile of papers. Paris caught them and read for a few minutes.

"Yippee! We did it."

Millie looked up as Paris waved a bundle of papers in the air.

"We got it, Millie. The offer was accepted, our agent drew up the papers, they got their big fat check, and we can move in as soon as we can get our asses over there. It's the Desert Rose, remember? I loved it, you loved it. Look—look, here's the floor plan. It's got a bonus room on the first floor, just steps away from the kitchen. That will be great for Turner. And look here, there's an office over here. He can set up shop for counseling clients and work right from home." Paris was obviously excited.

Millie set down a puzzle piece on the small table beside her and got up from her chair to grab the paper from Paris. "Yup, I remember this one. Wow, you bought it. You bought it without showing Turner. Hmm, aren't we sort of reordering his life? I know we are brilliant and all females know best, but maybe we should have asked him about that?"

"I did show him. This was one of three I showed him, and he turned green and said it was terrific, *but* blah blah blah and something about money. I stopped paying attention after 'this is terrific.'" Paris groaned as she shifted herself around in the bed. "Augh. Could these two get any bigger? What did they do, invite a few friends in?"

"They're having a baby convention. They told me all about it."

"They talked to you through the walls of my body?"

"Sure they did. I talk to them all the time. Hey, wow, I *did* like this one too. Oh, look, this is the one with the granny suite with its own bathroom and closet and wet bar. Now that's a great plan. A wet bar in my bedroom."

"I think they intend that to be a breakfast station, not a get-drunk-on-your-ass-before-noon station," Paris smirked at her.

"Speak for yourself. Spring Valley. Sounds very pretty."

"This is the neighborhood with the nice school district and a park built right into the development."

"It's swell."

"I can't believe how much house you can get around here for a measly mil. It's a freakin' palace. There's a golf course across the road too. Maybe Turner can golf. We should get in there as soon as possible. Jenifer Shipley is dropping the keys by tomorrow. It's amazing what a little money can do. We'll hire a couple of cute moving guys to cart all our stuff over there and set up house. Would you be willing to oversee things until these two decide to come out and play?"

"It's a very nice neighborhood. I'm going to love lunching at the clubhouse with all my gal pals and showing off the twins. I'd have thought a New Yorker like yourself would do the downtown condo thing, not the old suburban two-cats in the yard deal."

"It's not for me. It's for them," Paris said quietly.

Millie watched Paris's face carefully for signs of getting a grip. Millie had been doing hunky stars jigsaw puzzles and watching soaps with Paris for months now, and she knew that Paris had made a whole lot of progress in the decent human being department. Why, the woman just *asked* if she was willing to take charge instead of ordering her to.

But not much progress had been made in the stick around and be a mom department. Millie just couldn't understand how Paris could get this far, with babies kicking around in her, and not have an about-face. From everything Millie had seen—and that was a whole lot—Paris would never be able to make the break once she gave birth to those precious babies. So why couldn't she just say so?

Just take the buckets she'd cried over some soap opera scene where the woman gave up her baby to the father. Paris could say all she wanted; and she still said she was giving them to Turner, but that was her head talking, not her heart.

Sometimes Millie just wanted to slap her. Like about twice a day.

But the house thing. That was hopeful. They'd scoured all the new developments in a wide radius from the Graceland Chapel and found some pretty good houses. They'd almost made an offer on one, but Paris had decided that wasn't good enough.

This must be the hundredth floor plan Millie had looked at, and she had to give it to Paris, this one was perfect. She'd thought of everything. This house had room for Sarah, for Turner, for old Millie and her Siamese cat collection, room for twin babies to grow and play, room for everyone but Paris. Millie stared at the plan for a long time.

She looked up and watched Paris staring at her own copy of the floor plan and exterior picture. Millie could see that Paris was imagining her life in that house. She had a faraway look as she studied the paper.

She'd seen her do this before. First the look, then Paris would get mad. She'd find something—lunch or the television or the computer—to yell at. And sometimes Millie had seen a few hot tears roll down Paris's cheeks.

Millie knew Turner had a plan, and he'd been working on it for a long time now. She'd listened at the door to him talking to Paris about what their babies' lives were going to be like. He'd decided to only do private counseling and a few weddings at the chapel before the children were old enough for school. He'd told Paris that he was preparing for that with his associate, Reverend Danny Vernon, so everything was ready to go. Of course since he owned the chapel, he'd bring in an income from all events there.

But Millie knew Turner had something up his sleeve, and she knew Sarah did too. She just wasn't sure whether Sarah's sleeve was a good one or a bad one.

Well, they better get into the house fast. Millie

had been shifting Paris's baby purchases around for months now, all still in their boxes and wraps. She was getting a little tired of winding her way around boxes of fancy baby baskets and imported strollers—from *Sweden* yet. Paris had told her these Emmaljunga ones were the best. Then her friends Marla and Anton had been sending scads of boxes of tiny baby clothes. Girl clothes. They knew now it was two girls.

She and Paris had really had a blast opening things. Marla had a bent toward frilly, impractical bonnets and dresses. Anton was pretty darned creative—he kept sending bright-colored light knit outfits that those babies could really use here in Las Vegas. And they had all sent the cutest baby shoes she'd ever laid eyes on. Italian shoes for babies. Paris had ordered two of each style in each size that would last till the little darlings were at least age three.

Obviously Paris was overcompensating for the impending desertion of her two children.

Millie had never had children, but her sister had, and she'd held her sister's babies and watched them, and there was no way Paris was going to be able to leave. Sometimes it was right for a woman to let her child go to a better life. But this time wasn't one of them.

Okay, here it comes, Millie thought. Time to duck and run.

Paris threw the paper on the floor beside the

bed with an angry movement. "Millie, this tea is like *rancid*, and it's freezing cold in here. Can't you crank up the heat? It's winter, you know."

"Yes, Your Majesty." Millie curtseyed.

"I'm not royal."

"You are acting like a tyrant queen."

"Am not," Paris said. She crossed her arms and sat against the pillow like a crazy redheaded queen.

Millie half expected her to shout *Off with her head!*

Come to think of it, Millie was feeling a whole lot like that white rabbit in *Alice in Wonderland. We're late, we're late, for Paris's due date!* Well they weren't late, but Paris was huge. Millie couldn't believe she'd made it past week thirty-five. Neither could the doctor, who visited once a week now. He'd wanted to put Paris in the hospital for the last week, but she'd stubbornly refused. She'd said an aide car could make it there in thirty seconds, and there was no reason to waste the money in that stinking, horrid hospital. She'd said her babies were better off at home.

The doctor had to agree. Paris had done such a great job of staying off her feet and taking care of herself that all of the danger had passed. But the doctor had said he didn't want to take any chances. After all, we were on the home stretch now.

Millie yawned loudly to express her opinion

and picked up Paris's iced tea glass. "I'll bring you water. It's late. You should go to sleep now."

She left the room quietly while Paris undoubtedly had the remainder of her fit about not living in the beautiful house she'd finally chosen to raise her children in.

Millie had left her own copy of the house plans on the bed where Paris could reach it, just in case she wanted to have her stupid circular thoughts all over again. Millie figured that after the thousandth time of convincing herself she would only make her children's life miserable, Paris might get tired of it.

Of course the whole show they'd watched on *Oprah* about postpartum psychosis hadn't helped at all. It was tragic and horrible, and as far as Millie was concerned the doctors should be horse-whipped for not paying attention to their patients and checking up on every single mother they delivered. Doctors were all idiots as far as she was concerned.

Even the books that Turner had gotten from the baby doc had said there were ways to fix this if people paid attention—if *doctors* paid attention.

And Paris seemed to be oblivious to the fact that Millie was planning on being there for every single moment of those babies' birth and life after birth. If anything was going to stir up in Paris, Millie would be there to make sure she got help. Paris was so stuck in her own head that she just couldn't see the light at the end of the tunnel. Turner better get her fixed fast. This big ol' white rabbit was getting very scared.

Turner closed the door quietly and headed toward his former room to check on his very pregnant house guest. He twisted himself sideways through a pile of boxes containing baby equipment—two of everything. He better start putting some of this stuff together. Monday was his day off, so tomorrow he would round up some tools and put all these swings, high chairs, bassinet, playpens, car seats, and bath things together. It was damn scary to think two babies needed all this stuff.

It was hard to believe the amount of trouble one woman could get into from her bed. Well, his bed. Well, it used to be his bed. Now it was transformed into Paris central. She had a swing-over desk with the laptop Marla had sent her. She had files on a standing rack, and some sort of mini-office contraption. She had a remote pocket, which Millie had designed to hold all the VCR, music, and television remotes beside the bed.

He turned the knob of the bedroom and cracked the door open enough to see if Paris was sleeping. A sliver of light illuminated the room.

She was. She looked like Sleeping Beauty. Her

red hair was tangled in curls all over the pillow. She had on some sort of pale green silk nightgown that looked beautiful on her. She must have fallen asleep with some stapled-together papers in her hand, and they were about to fall off the bed.

Turner slipped inside the shadowy room and gently removed the papers from her hand. As he looked down at her face, he was amazed at the peacefulness he saw there. He hoped her dreams were good. He leaned over and kissed her forehead softly.

He was in love with his wife. He loved her spirit, wounded as it was. He imagined that if she could heal enough to let in the joy and love he had to offer her, she would turn that intensity to devotion. He could see that she would be a fierce and amazing mother. She had so much to share—her energy sparkled like a sky full of fireworks when she was happy. He'd seen it before. When they were young, she had filled his life with magic. Now it was a deeper, more amazing magic.

Over the last few months they'd had conversations about how she saw her children's lives evolving. Her imagination and her positive nature had bubbled to the top, overshadowing the fear and anger that sometimes posessed her. He loved to see her like that.

She stirred, and Turner stepped back from her

bedside, into the shadows. He didn't want to disturb her, with the small amounts of sleep she was getting lately.

He wished he had something to tell her. He was almost ready. But he had to be sure it was the right thing to do.

Goodnight, Paris. He slipped out the door. Everyone must be sleeping. But he wasn't sure whether Sarah was in or out.

He wove between the boxes to the kitchen table. Millie had made a sheet cake that was sitting in the pan, one square removed. It looked like carrot cake with cream cheese frosting. Millie baked when she was riled about something. Probably Paris.

The papers he'd taken from Paris were still in his hand. He sat down at the table and looked them over. It was the floor plan and exterior elevation of a house. A very grand house, grander than anything he could afford. Six thousand square feet. Wow. He pressed his hand to his forehead.

He was going to have to have a long talk with her about this. He knew it was for her children, but they were married, so she should discuss it with him.

Except they weren't really married. She had no idea about his finances, he had no idea about hers. They operated independently. He paid the chapel bills, and some groceries, but lately Paris had taken to having loads of groceries delivered on her own credit card. He paid the rent, he found out she'd already paid it. Then she buys a million-dollar house on a golf course . . . with a park . . . near schools. He read all the amenities on page two while he ranted in his head about his manhood.

After the floor plan and elevation was a letter from that real estate lady who'd visited Paris about twenty times in the last months. From what he read in the letter, it looked to him as if Paris had put escrow money down on the house and that it had been accepted.

He remembered that this house had been on her final three list, which he'd actually been shown and had commented on but tried to avoid talking about since he was unable to face the fact that his wife might buy him a house. Correction. She was buying it for her children, in reality.

The sound of a key in the front door made Turner shift his gaze. Sarah came in and closed and locked the door behind her. She set down her bag and took off her coat.

"Hey, Turner. I thought you might be up," she said.

"Millie has been baking again. Want a piece of cake?" Turner put the papers he'd been reading down on the table.

"Actually, I'd love one. With a glass of milk." She walked into the kitchen and poured two glasses of milk, then came over to the table and sat down next to him. There were paper plates, napkins, and forks already on the table, as if Millie had been expecting them. Sarah cut a piece of cake for each of them and handed one over to Turner. "This baking of hers is going to catch up with us one of these days."

"I know this is so, yet I keep hoping that day doesn't come." Turner took a bite of the carrot cake. "Mmmm."

"I'm glad you're up. I wanted to talk to you."

"How was your shift? Did you get to do anything fun, or are you still on bedpan duty?"

"I was filing in the basement archives. I guess when I finish my second year I can move up to taking temperatures and sticking poor unsuspecting children with immunizations." Sarah took a bite of her cake and drank her milk.

"You'll have your LPN pretty soon, won't you?"

"One more semester. It's good I started in the summer, and that I had my college requirements out of the way. All that cyber college learning came in handy."

"Then what?"

"Slightly less than three years to complete my RN degree."

"That's not bad." Turner pushed his empty plate away. He must have been hungry. The burger he'd wolfed down before chapel services hadn't done much for him except remind him that it would be nice to get one of Millie's home-cooked meals again.

Sarah pushed her empty cake plate aside as well. "Turner, I have something to tell you. I know you're going to be mad, but I think I found a way to help you with Paris."

"Why am I going to be mad?" Turner looked at Sarah's slightly pink face.

"Because I read the file you have on Paris's family." Sarah lowered her voice to a whisper. "I know you are trying to find her mother. That she might not be dead."

It took quite a bit to shock Turner, but he felt a rush of surprise to think that Sarah had unlocked his desk and gone into his papers. He was surprised to find out she even possessed a devious side. He didn't know what to say.

"I know, I know. Bad me for going through your papers. I'd explain it all to you, but right now I think it's more important that we work together. I know you want Paris to heal some of those old wounds. I know that would make you happy."

"Sarah, I'm so surprised at you I can't even think. That was private."

"Well, I guess I cracked."

"I guess." Turner leaned over to speak quietly. "I hope you haven't discussed this with anyone else. I can't even tell you how private a person Paris is."

"No, I haven't. Now listen. I found something.

I took the search on a different angle than you did." Sarah rose from her chair and walked to the front door. Turner saw her take something out of her tote bag and come back to the table.

"Look at this. I've heard so many stories from all the old nurses, I thought maybe if we could find one that worked in Harmond while Lucille Jamison was there, we could get some information. I tracked down five nurses. Some have died, or moved, one just wasn't too keen on talking. That leaves this lady—Emma Foley. I thought we could call her tomorrow and maybe go see her."

Turner read through the information Sarah had compiled. "Where did you get this?"

"I went to Harmond and got the records clerk to give me a list of names of nurses that worked there during that time. I've been tracking them down since then. The address was old, but I found her in the hospital visiting nurse records. I have a good feeling about her. Can you go tomorrow?"

Turner set down the paper. He felt very strange about letting Sarah in on his plan. It felt so private. So much between him and Paris. But she'd found a pathway that might actually help. He stared intently at her, trying to read her sincerity. "First, thank you for your efforts. I see you've found a way I didn't even think of. I should have been more expansive. I've been focused on records and documents, and I really hit the wall on that one. Of course the adoption records for her sister are closed, and no one but Paris or the sister herself could even petition for that information. Even then, I doubt they'd give it to her."

Turner toyed with the fork he'd propped on his cake plate. "I'm very uncomfortable with this. It's a very private matter for Paris. You'll have to agree to be discreet. I'll be very blunt here. I know you've had your doubts about Paris, and I hope you would never use this information to hurt her."

Sarah looked down and shifted in her chair. Turner saw her cheeks blush pink.

"I'm sorry about that, Turner. I'm sorry about a whole lot of things. I know you care for her deeply. I'd like to help you if I can. I think I understand what you are doing. If she sees her mother, if she understands that life can go on, she can stop being so dead-set on leaving you alone with two babies. They are going to need her. I want what is best for your two children, Turner."

"This could all go very bad on us, Sarah. Paris could be extremely angry and just refuse to believe this. Plus, her mother might not be alive, or even worse, she could be a wreck, and we might end up opening a terrible can of worms."

"We'll just have to take things one step at a

time." Sarah folded her hands together on the table.

"Starting with tomorrow. I promised myself I'd put together some of these baby things, but we can call Mrs. Foley and see if she exists."

"Why put them together if you are moving?" Sarah pointed to the house plan printout sitting next to them at the table.

"Paris is in her last weeks. There is no way we're going to make it into a house before she gives birth."

"I wouldn't be so sure. That woman can work miracles when she wants to. Even confined to bed."

"That would be a miracle. I'll at least be sure there are two baskets ready for them in case they decide to arrive any day."

"She's done really well with all this. And Millie has been a saint."

"Millie knows she and Paris are kindred spirits. Millie used to be a beautiful woman, you know."

"I know. I saw her scrapbooks. She looked fabulous in feathers."

"No one ever thinks about what happens to women whose lives were based on their looks. It can't last forever."

"Tell that to Paris."

"I won't have to. I'll just be there when she needs me."

"You're a wonderful guy, Turner."

"Thanks, Sarah. And you've really surprised me by helping Paris this way."

"I guess I owed her one. And you. I'm so excited about tomorrow. I can hardly wait to see what we come up with."

We. Turner thought about that and felt a rock in the pit of his stomach. He used to be such a trusting person, until he'd married a woman whose face had been on every major magazine in the country. Now he felt overprotective. But maybe there wasn't such a thing as overprotective where Paris was concerned.

"Yes, tomorrow. Don't get your hopes up. So many patients go through those doors. Emma Foley might not remember anything. And now, you are in my bedroom, and we should all get some sleep." Turner gestured toward the lumpy sofa.

"So I am." Sarah got up and gathered the dishes off the table.

"Here, I'll take the glasses." Turner helped her, and they cleared off their mess. Sarah opened the dishwasher in the kitchen and loaded things in.

"We're a good team," Sarah said.

Turner looked at her and saw her sadness. He wished things could be different for her. "There will be someone for you, Sarah. Someone special."

"I know," she said and turned her face toward the dishes.

Turner had the sense to walk away.

20

Love Letters

It wasn't cold in Las Vegas very often, but this December day was downright nippy. Turner pulled up his jacket collar and wished he'd worn gloves. He stood on the steps of a modest stucco bungalow in an old section of Henderson and rang the bell.

"I didn't think it got this cold in Nevada." Sarah stamped her feet and rubbed her arms to warm them.

"About once every hundred years or so it snows. Or is it twenty? I forget. It hasn't ever snowed since I've lived here. We've had a few cold days. But this year the weather has been very strange."

A woman opened the wooden door and stood behind the screen. "Reverend Pruitt?" she asked.

"Yes, and this is Sarah Eastman. She's a student nurse at Mercy."

"Come in, please. My, it's chilly out there. My geraniums are going to freeze. Just pick up that pot there, will you? Bring it right in."

Turner smiled and picked up the white plastic pot of geraniums while Emma Foley unlocked and opened the screen door and let them both inside.

"Just set it right there. Thank you so much. Come in, please."

Emma was a tiny woman with sharp features. *She must be all of five foot three,* Turner thought. But she had a strength in her face that said so much, as if she had seen a lifetime of happiness and sorrow and it was all written in her eyes. As they moved through the small house, he noticed pictures on the wall—grandchildren? Maybe her daughter, in a wedding dress?

"What a lovely family," Sarah said.

"That's my daughter, Ellen, and those are her children, all girls," Emma said. "We've been a very lucky family. My husband passed on three years ago March, but he left me well fixed. He was a very smart man about such things, bless his soul." She led them into the living room, and they sat on the yellow striped sofa. The room was cheery and clean. Turner propped a floral pillow behind himself so he could sit up straight.

"I was most interested in your phone call," Emma said. "Coffee?"

"Yes, please," Sarah said.

Turner helped Mrs. Foley pour and watched Sarah drop two cubes of sugar in the small cup for herself. He was nervous. He poured a splash of cream in his coffee. More caffeine probably wasn't his friend.

Emma sat down in a pale blue club chair across from Turner and Sarah. Sarah kept her distance from him on the sofa; which made him grateful, for many reasons. Emma rocked her chair a bit.

"We are so glad to find you. I realize this is going to sound somewhat odd, but we have a very good reason for coming to see you," Turner said.

Sarah started talking. "His wife's mother was in Harmond during the same time you worked there. It was such a tragic case we were hoping you remembered her. The name, as I mentioned, was Lucille Jamison. She had a baby, and a little girl. Her husband died while she was hospitalized. That little girl is Reverend Pruitt's wife, and we feel it is of vital importance we find Lucille Jamison if she is alive. It's a matter of hereditary medical conditions and her . . . peace of mind."

Turner tipped his head at Sarah and gave her an exasperated stare. He'd planned on a gentle lead-up, heading toward a reassurance of their utmost discretion and sincerity. So much for that.

Sarah stared back at him blankly. She obviously had her own ideas. There was a short but weird silence in the room. Sarah picked up one of the homemade shortbread cookies Emma had put out on the coffee table. Turner sighed and picked up one himself but didn't eat it.

"Oh, my, yes. How could I forget? Such a sad case."

Was Emma Foley really going to tell them all about a mental patient that might still be alive? She'd be violating a whole lot of privacy issues. Turner felt extremely weird even asking the woman to compromise all that.

"Poor thing. I took a special interest in her case. I saw the father bring those two children in to visit her. For the longest time she didn't even recognize them." Emma leaned back in her chair and seemed to be reaching into the past for bits of memories.

Turner—and Sarah, he noticed—stayed so still a breath would have been noticeable.

"They'd given her shock treatments. They'd actually had some success with shock therapy in cases of severe depression, and she was so depressed, so locked away inside herself. She heard voices. It was sad . . . I can see why you are concerned. How is your wife doing, Reverend?"

Turner took that breath he'd been holding in. "She's actually about to deliver twins sometime in the next few weeks, and she is confined to bed. She is extremely concerned that the birth will trigger a similar chemical depression in herself. Her memories are very traumatic."

"She looked so frightened when she came to visit. Harmond was a frightening place for children."

"It was believed that Lucille died during that time, but the priest at St. Mary's school tells me this is not the case."

"No, she didn't die while she was there. But the death of her husband set her back severely. She'd been almost ready to be released. She blamed herself most terribly," Emma said.

"But she was finally released?" Turner asked.

"Yes, and I feel quite proud of that. I spent many hours with her, talking and getting her to eat properly. I had a theory myself, and I had her take long walks with me. I think the fresh air and exercise added to her recovery. These doctors think they know everything, but sometimes the nurses know better, isn't that right, Miss Eastman?"

"Sometimes they miss the simple things. Like having someone that cares take the time to walk with a patient. You are a wise woman, Mrs. Foley," Sarah said.

This seemed to please Emma Foley greatly.

She sat up on the edge of the rocking club chair and poured a little more coffee in her cup. "I don't get to use the good china much. My friend Sally from next door and I eat dinner together every night, but we keep casual. We take turns cooking. She's a Mexican lady, and she can cook like nobody's business. But she loves my tuna casserole."

Turner smiled at her and did his best to look reverend-like. "I'm so glad you are blessed with a good friend."

Emma sipped her coffee. "I'm not sure how God sent you here to me today, Reverend, but I do have much to tell you. Are you certain that your wife has never heard from her mother?"

"Patricia is under the belief that her mother died. The nuns at St. Mary's thought it better. There was a letter." Turner talked carefully.

"His wife is convinced this thing will happen to her. Turner feels that a resolution with the mother is the only hope of getting Patricia to understand. Even if he can't accomplish that, if he could just talk with her, it would help." Sarah did her blurt-out thing again.

He looked at her sharply again. She ignored him—again. He guessed women had a different way of going about things.

"It's a shame Lucille felt so much guilt about the father, and about Patricia, and the baby. That was the one thing I couldn't get her to let go of. I can see it has prevented her from reaching out to her daughter. What a pity. At least she found Bonnie."

"Bonnie?" Turner looked at Sarah, but Sarah just shrugged.

"The baby. Bonnie Jamison. Well, I might as well tell you that Lucille wrote to me for many years after her release. Like I said, I don't know how, but you've found me for a reason. I'm sure the Lord has his mysterious ways."

Turner felt a rush of excitement, and sadness, and impatience, and awe all at once.

"It's best if I just give you her last address. I don't feel I should say so much more. But she and her daughter Bonnie, the baby that was adopted out, were reunited. Bonnie traced her mother through the adoption agency after she turned eighteen. They let you open the records after that, you know."

"Yes, I see." Turner set down everything he had in his hands so he wouldn't drop it all. He saw Sarah do the same thing.

"She and Bonnie had a good talk, and now they know each other, and that's good for both of them."

"Lucille sounds like she pulled her life together."

"Well, she met a nice man at the hospital. A patient. I liked him. He was recovering from exhaustion and a terrible trauma. He's just a fine fellow. I got to taking him on our walks, so I feel sort of like I got them together, which helped both of them."

"Love can really heal people," Turner said.

"Best medicine. Well, they didn't have any other children, but they did get married, and she wrote me a few times after that. I have a Christmas card from her for every year."

"This year?" Sarah's exitement was hard to miss.

"Yes. It's right here." Emma casually reached for a stack of letters sitting on a table next to her chair.

Turner could not believe they'd found someone who actually knew Paris's mother. "Is she in Nevada?"

"She lives over by Lake Meade." Emma handed the card and its torn-open envelope to Turner.

"I had a feeling she was close by."

"That's less than an hour's drive," Sarah said. She sat back on the sofa, apparently stunned by this information.

"There's something else. After she got well, she became a nurse. She's an LPN that specializes in postpartum care, of course. That only makes sense."

A chill ran through Turner as he thought of how strange it was that they had found Emma Foley. How Sarah had followed an instinct and led them here. Even how Sarah had come into their lives, perhaps just for this reason, and how odd it was that she was becoming a nurse herself. The universe truly was amazing, and the more Turner opened himself to recognizing that thread of coincidence, the more he was convinced of that.

And underneath it all, there was his love for Paris, and perhaps her own mother's love, reaching out to her, no matter what.

"Thank you so much. I know Lucille will want to help Patricia."

"It will help Lucille, too. She needs to know that Patricia doesn't hate her, or fear her, and that she turned out okay. I don't know why she couldn't ever get over the thought that Patricia was better off without her," Sarah said.

"Sometimes the wounds are so deep they just can't be overcome without someone else's help," Turner said quietly. He stared at the card he held in his hand. A bright angel with glittering wings hovered above Mary and her infant child.

Inside, the handwriting was carefully done, as if Lucille had a tendency to write badly so she'd taken time to make the words readable. *"With great love, Lucille and Bill Worth."* Her new name. No wonder he hadn't been able to find her. They even married in another state, so no records were on file for Nevada. He hadn't gotten to the

Utah or Arizona records yet, with so many years to cover.

He started to put the card inside the envelope and noticed a photograph. He pulled it out and saw a woman who looked like she was in her fifties, a nice-looking gentleman, and a younger woman—that must be Bonnie, because she looked exactly like Paris. Turner felt a twist of emotion hit his heart so hard that he could hardly speak.

"I'm sorry I don't have a phone number," Emma said.

Turner found himself and answered her. "You've given us everything we need. Thank you so much, Mrs. Foley."

"You let me know how things turn out, won't you?"

Sarah stood up and came over to the elderly woman. "I'll call you myself." Emma got up out of her chair, and Sarah gave her a hug.

Turner reached over and shook her hand. "Thank you. We'll hope for the best."

On the car ride home Sarah was quiet. Turner had a million thoughts going through his head. Lucille sounded like a reasonable person. He just couldn't understand why she didn't track Paris down. Would Paris ever be able to forgive her for that? So many years had gone by.

One thing was for sure: Sarah needed a wake-up call.

"Thank you for helping me find Mrs. Foley," Turner said. He gripped the steering wheel and kept his eyes on the road. This was going to be hard. "I have something to say to you that is rather overdue. I've let you help me with quite a few things. I might have given you reason to think we were more than friends. When you came here I was happy to help. I still am, but we need to set a few boundaries between us."

"I know. I knew this was coming."

"Let me just be clear here. I don't want you to have anything more to do with this hunt for Paris's mother. It's between my wife and myself from now on. Do you understand? I feel very uncomfortable that you went this far into the whole thing. I'm grateful that your lead paid off, but now I have to insist that you redirect your energies into your own studies and your own life."

Sarah was silent again. But he wasn't done.

"It's been wonderful of your parents to send money for your school tuition and expenses. I really appreciate that. And I want to see you finish up school and become a nurse. It's a great calling. Your parents should be very proud."

"They are. Yours are too. They are all very supportive," Sarah said quietly.

"When we make this move to this house Paris has managed to find, I'd like you to stay in the apartment. It's closer to school, and it would be your first apartment on your own. The rent is extremely low, and with the two bedrooms you could get a roommate and reduce that cost even more."

"Millie is going with you?"

"Yes." Turner glanced at Sarah and saw that she was fighting back tears.

"That is a good idea. I could take the apartment." Her words were choked with emotion.

"I think that's best. My wife and I have some things to work out. I love her very much, Sarah."

"I know."

"I'm going to drop you off at the college. I know you have a class this afternoon. Do you have everything you need?"

"I brought my bag with me in case it got late. I have some work to do in the library. I'll be fine. Drop me off."

The rest of the ride was dead silent. Turner had said all he wanted to. Sarah was a good friend, but he had never thought of her any other way. It was a kindess to her to make her understand that.

And things were going to change with Paris, right now. He had no more time left. He wanted to set their lives in order before his children were born.

Paris felt so very pleased with herself. On her trip to the bathroom, the only walkabout she could make, she found that all the boxes of baby things had already been taken away. God Bless Jenifer Shipley for being the best agent ever. It had been a good sale for Jenifer, and she had personally taken charge of the moving, bringing in a decorator for some color consulations and placement decisions for the nursery.

Paris figured this must be that nesting instinct she'd read about, because she felt hell-bent on getting that nursery set up today. She'd shown the decorator a picture of the perfect nursery from *Baby Style* magazine and told her to basically duplicate it. As of now, she was pretty sure some mural painter was sizing up the wall for a picket fence and flower motif. Hopefully they'd move full speed ahead. She'd added a sizable bonus to Jenifer's already very nice commission on the house and given Millie the checkbook to a bottomless line of credit.

She'd like to see that beautiful room. She would. But she was stuck here in bed being a good girl. Plus, she'd already decided the best way to do this was to make a clean break and let Turner take them to their new house after they were released from the hospital. She'd go directly to the Sonoma Spa and spend three weeks being miserable and fat and that would be that. Back to work. If she got crazy, the spa people would have orders to check her in to some private hospital where no one would find her.

It would be better this way. Then the girls

would never see their mother hit her head against the wall, trying to make the voices stop, until her forehead bled. Or see the pain of a father trying to deal with all of that and a new baby, too.

And what if she didn't go crazy? Would she come and see them? Would she come back and stay? Would Turner ever consider taking her back?

Paris started to cry. She ran—or sort of waddled—for the bed and crawled in. Millie was out at the new house, Turner had gone off with Sarah somewhere, and she was alone. Where the hell had everyone gone for so long? It was almost dinner, and Turner usually came and spent the evening with her if he didn't have a wedding. Did he have a wedding? It was almost Thanksgiving, and he'd said something about a few this week, plus he and Danny Vernon were trading off weeknights.

But no, he was off with Sarah. She felt a rush of heat in her cheeks. That Sarah—at least she could wait till it was all over and she left town before she put the moves on Turner.

She pulled a pillow up close to her face and cried hard. She'd really screwed everything up this time. She wanted to find another way, but her head just couldn't seem to see clearly. It was like she'd set herself on this twisted, dark path and a fog had descended on her and she couldn't make it lift, or find her way off the path, or find anyone to help her.

She couldn't help herself anymore, and she cried until she hiccupped.

After a while she couldn't cry anymore. She reached her hand out toward where the tissue box should be. Instead, someone handed her one.

She pulled back the covers to see Turner sitting beside the bed.

21

That's When Your Heartaches Begin

Paris reached out her hand to him. He held it with both of his. Then he put hers to his lips and softly kissed it.

"Things have to change now, Paris."

She let go of his hand. She mopped her face with the one Kleenex until it was shreds. "I don't know how."

"I know. I'm going to help you. You have to let me, though."

"What can you possibly do?"

"I stopped by to talk to Dr. Shapiro today. He told me you'd done such a good job that he might let you get up and at least lounge around the house. He said your butt must miss a chair."

"Very funny. It's flattened out from all the

weight, I'm sure." Paris sniffled and blew her nose.

"All of this is about your mother's illness, Paris."

"You know I hate to talk about it."

"I know. How about I talk instead." Turner pulled his chair up close to the side of the bed. He rummaged under the covers and found her hand again.

"I have been working on something. I started out just researching what happened to your mother. But I found more than I bargained for."

Paris looked up at him with such pain in her face that he almost couldn't continue. But he knew this was going to be hard, no matter when, or where, or how. At least they could face it together. "Remember Sister Claudia? She was at St. Mary's."

"She was a good person."

"She cared about you. She didn't want you to have any more pain."

"Did she die too?"

"I don't know. She isn't at St. Mary's anymore."

"You went there? Why?" Paris asked.

Her breath was quieting down some. He wanted her to stay as calm as possible.

"To ask about what happened to your mother."

"Well that was a dead end. She died alone in some horrible hospital."

"Paris, she didn't die. Sister Claudia just told you that because she thought it would be better that way."

Paris pulled herself completely up and sat against the hard wooden headboard of the bed. Turner reached over to help her and put a pillow behind her. She shoved him away.

"What are you talking about? Who told you this?"

"Father Gibbs."

"He's senile."

"There's a letter."

"Let me see it."

Turner got up and pulled his leather briefcase onto the end of the bed. He opened it and found the expandable file folder he'd been using for his reasearch.

"Give me that," Paris demanded.

"It's not all relevant. I'll find the letter for you."

"Let me see that whole thing *right now.*" Paris went beet red.

Turner came over and held the file out to her. "I'll go through each thing with you. We are going to do this together, Paris."

Paris grabbed the file and dumped the entire contents on the bed. She shifted through the papers like leaves, some dropping to the ground, until her hand fell on the picture. It must have come out of the envelope. He watched as she picked it up. He saw her fingers shake. She shook so badly that he reached toward her and touched her shoulder.

"Paris."

A horrible cry came from her. To him it sounded like it came from the depths of Paris's soul. She rocked back and forth, and tears streamed down her face.

He pushed off his shoes and climbed in the bed next to her, his arm encircling her. She leaned her head against his shoulder and rocked and cried.

Surely, she would see how she couldn't do this to her own children. For a moment, resentment for Paris's mother boiled up in him. Not for being ill, but for believing for all these years that Paris would be better off without her. Everyone always assumed Paris was so strong and capable. She was all those things, but she was also someone who needed love more than anyone else he'd ever known.

If only her mother had understood that. But that was the past. The Lucille Jamison he'd gone to see today was not the same one that had left Paris. She'd been more than willing to help. He was absolutely sure that talking to her would help Paris be able to move on.

At the moment he wondered if Paris could

take it. It wasn't going to be easy. He felt the pain wash over her and wished he could take it on himself.

But they were out of time. His children would be coming into this world very soon, and they needed their mother.

"Paris, I went to see her."

"You went to see her? When were you planning on telling me about this?" Paris's words were clear despite the fact that she was fighting back deep, rasping sobs.

"When I found out whether it would be worse or better for you to meet her."

"I don't think that's your call."

"I have to agree with you. I made a mistake. I've been protective of you and the pregnancy."

"How did you find her?"

Turner was so hoping she wouldn't ask this question. He could lie, but he didn't lie. He could omit, but that would be the same.

"Sarah found a woman who had known your mother long ago."

"Sarah? You told Sarah about this?" She shifted her body out of his arms as best she could. "You're telling me that you and Sarah have been conducting this search together? That the two of you have known about my mother being alive for what, months? And yet you never told me?"

And would he tell the truth about Sarah to

get himself off the hook? Should he say how Sarah had broken into his desk and found out for herself?

Paris took a pile of tissues and dumped water from her bedside glass on them. She blotted her face and looked like she was trying to calm herself—she breathed deeply to slow down her hysterical hiccupping.

"She only came into this at the end. She wasn't aware of things until lately. It wasn't intentional. But she did help. She gave me the last piece of the puzzle that led to me finding your mother."

"Where does she live?"

"By Lake Meade. On the Arizona side."

"So close. Is this the address?" She held up the envelope that the Christmas card from her mother had come in.

"Yes."

Paris got very quiet. She got so quiet that it made Turner move and look at her. What was she thinking?

"Are you all right, Paris?"

"No, but life goes on. What are your plans tonight?" Paris made her voice level and quiet.

"It's my day off. I was going to stay here with you and cook some supper. Maybe set up the bassinets just in case." Turner put his hand on her hand. She moved hers away.

"I bought you and the girls a house. Millie is

out there. My realtor Jenifer took her out. You should go see it. Then you can bring Millie back later." She wanted him out of here *now.*

"I should stay here with you, Paris. This can't be an easy thing to learn. I want to be here with you. The house can wait."

"Nonsense. I'll get over it," Paris said coldly. She would, too. But she had something to do first. How the hell was she going to get Turner out of here? He'd never let her do what she wanted to do.

"We should talk. We'll arrange a meeting with your mother. She can come here."

"I don't want to talk, Turner. I want to be alone. Go to the new house. You'll like it. Besides, I had the movers take all the baby stuff out there. You could set things up. We want to be ready, don't we?" she said, trying to appeal to his sense of responsibility.

Turner slid out of her bed and stood up. He leaned against the mattress and looked closely into her face. "I'm not going to leave you, Paris."

"Get out, Turner. I need to cry and carry on for a few hours. I don't want anyone around to see that." She tried for his therapist side. She sniffed and held up a tissue to her eyes, even though they'd gone bone dry with anger.

"Nope. I'll go make you some dinner. I'll shut the door and you can cry."

Damn him! He was so damn stubborn. She thought quickly. She always thought quickly when she felt overwhelmed with emotion and chaos.

"Turner, you know what would make me feel better? To know that you were over at the new house setting up the nursery. I had a painter do a mural on the walls, and it's probably done. Then I could know it was finished and that would make me happy. Maybe I could take a drive out there tomorrow. I'm really tired. I can't take any more today. I'd like to just take a long nap. We'll have a late supper later," she lied. She wasn't the least bit tired, for once.

Turner wavered. She saw it on his face. Score. Turner had this need to fix things, she'd figured that out. And if you told him what would make you happy, he'd have a hard time not doing it. If it weren't for the fact that she'd ruined his life, she would have loved to have had him for a real husband. But she had ruined it. Somewhere down the line he was going to resent the hell out of all of this. She knew that. Then things would get ugly and sad, and that would be terrible. He probably already did.

"If you really think that would make you happy. I'll ask Dr. Shapiro if I can take you over there tomorrow."

"Go. Take your toolbox. I'm so tired. I need to rest." She gave him a weak smile, then pushed herself down into the bed and pulled the covers up. "Can you shut off that light?"

"I'll be back, Paris. And you have your pagers? One for me, one for the hospital?"

"Yes, yes." She made her voice sound tired.

Turner dimmed the light and shut the door to the bedroom. He found himself standing in the living room, which was uncharacteristically bare. Never mind the fact that the woman had purchased a house for him. He couldn't go into that right now.

He felt dazed. Maybe sleeping was her way of dealing with emotional overload. Turner ran his hand over his chin. It was rough with an afternoon shadow. Sarah would be back after her class, so someone would be here soon. Maybe getting the nursury set up was Paris's way of taking a step toward acceptance.

His head was spinning. He'd had a hell of a day. His visit to Lucille Jamison had been shocking. She'd looked so much like Paris, but with a depth of sorrow that lined her face and gave a darkness to her eyes.

He went to the kitchen. There was old coffee in the pot from this morning. He poured it in a small brown cup from his mother's old china set. It always looked like cream was dripping down the sides of the brown glazed finish. She'd given him the set when he'd found an apartment and settled in, but Millie had packed up most of it and bought something with butterflies and flowers on it.

Tonight he needed something with some family warmth built in. He poured in the coffee, added a splash of water, and warmed it in the microwave—the Amana, as Millie would say. It beeped, he pulled it out, and sipped. Really, really horrible. He took it anyway and sat down at the table to gather his wits.

He had never missed his family as much as he did now. He'd written them several times about everything that was going on. He'd talked to them on the phone. They'd made plans to come in December, for the holidays, after the babies were born. He had to laugh, because if he had one childhood trauma, it was that his parents had always focused on their flock for the holidays. He'd even resented it a few times, but their generous hearts and spirits made their home an open door for everyone, and even more so during the holidays.

So Paris had bought a house and set up her idea of a life for her children, and for him, and even Millie. Everyone but herself.

He didn't feel good about it, but if she could see the place, maybe she could step into her own picture. Tomorrow he'd talk to her about seeing her mother. He wanted to be there for her—take her there. He'd be damned if he'd let her face this alone. It would defeat the whole forward growth idea if he let her push him aside. That just wasn't going to happen anymore. He wouldn't let it.

Turner drank his bitter coffee. He'd grab a sub sandwich on the way to the house. He had to develop some normalcy around his life, and fast. He was about to be a father. He wanted order for those babies. Warm dinners, story reading time, rolling a ball and playing in the grass time. Those were more important to him than a fancy house. But it looked like he was stuck with it for now.

The sounds of people in the hallway distracted him. The walls were pretty thin in this place. The door opened and Millie and the real estate gal—Jenifer—walked in. Millie had on her jeans and a sweatshirt with a Siamese cat on it, under a quilted jacket. He thought that was weird. She was usually lounging around in velour, or pajamas, or a jogging outfit. Both women stood there in their coats and hats. They were both wet from the rain.

"Turner, we came to get you. You and some tools, and the bassinettes in my room. I've been hoarding them in there. I didn't want those babies to have to sleep in a dresser drawer if they popped out early. But we need a man. Come on, man. You'll love the place." Millie yammered nonstop. "Come on, come on! We've got Jenifer's minivan and we're rarin' to go. Plus we have to stop for some takeout. We're starved. Come on, the crew went home at four. We need you to help us play."

Her name was Jenifer Shipley, Turner remembered. She was about fifty, with shoulder-length gray hair. She smiled, then came over and shook his hand. "Turner, we've crossed paths a few times, but I don't think we've been properly introduced."

"I've seen your name on a few papers. Jenifer Shipley, right?"

"I've seen your name on a few papers, too. The deed to the new house, for one."

He stopped shaking her hand, surprised. "I hope she put her own name on there as well."

"We'll gab about that later. Come on, get these things out of my closet and give us a hand." Millie actually came over and aimed Turner at her bedroom, then gave him a directional push.

"Millie, you are one pushy broad, did you know?" Turner let her plow him forward.

"I know."

He went in her room and saw two beautiful wicker baskets with pink satin-and-lace ribbons woven through them. There was a pile of comforters and other linens in pink gingham still in their wrappers beside the baskets. He stacked the top portion of the baskets together, loaded up a few linens, and left the bases for the next trip up the stairs. His life was going to be one long, pink, gingham story from now on, so he better get used to it.

"Good, good, we'll take the comforters. You get the bases on your next trip, then the tools." Millie directed traffic.

"I can carry the bases. They're just awkward, not heavy." Jenifer grabbed them up and followed Turner out the door.

A few trips later they were loaded up and ready. Before he left for the last time he looked in on Paris again. She was sleeping soundly. He felt very uncomfortable leaving her. But she'd said this would make her happy. In his heart he'd thought that his being here with her tonight would have been the thing that would have made her happy. Maybe he needed to listen more carefully to people and quit making assumptions about what they needed.

He slipped on his heavy jacket. He couldn't remember a colder November. He wasn't ready to give up on helping Paris yet. Something in him just wouldn't let go. Maybe it was the moments when, at her most vulnerable, she reached for him or put her head on his shoulder. Or when he made her laugh. He loved to make her laugh. He closed the door quietly behind him and walked out of the building.

Paris threw back the covers the minute she heard the front door close shut. She eased her body out of bed. My God, all these months lying around had really made her weak. She'd noticed when she'd gone down the hall a few times a day, but right now she needed strength, so she'd better find it. The kick of a baby inside her made her grab for the wall to steady herself. *"Shhh. We're going on a little trip,"* she whispered to them.

She made it to the window in the bedroom, where she could push back the curtain and make sure they'd all left. She'd heard their plans. It'd been a stroke of luck for her, Millie showing up with a ride for Turner. Otherwise she'd have had to hire a limo to make her little trip.

While she'd been pretending to sleep, she'd figured that if Turner didn't leave, she'd wait till he was asleep and sneak out. That would be hard—a very large woman not waking him up. She'd noticed that he slept pretty soundly though, as she'd passed by the sofa on her way to the toilet each night.

The laptop computer was logged in and ready, and she stood in front of the swing-away table by her bed to enter data. Paris pushed aside the covers and picked up the envelope with the Lake Meade address on it. She accessed Yahoo maps and entered Turner's apartment address in one side, the Lake Meade address in the other, then she hit driving directions, then print. The printer booted into action.

She dressed herself in clothes, which was a big

change from the huge flannel nightgowns she'd been living in. The only thing that fit was a big black jumper and a white maternity turtleneck Marla had sent her. Even that she had to pull down across her enormous belly with a big yank.

She'd had some amazing moments being pregnant—feeling the life within her grow and jump and move had been an experience she'd never forget. But other than that, what the *hell* was God thinking making women do this? Or maybe hell was more like it, because only the Devil could have thought up something this weird—swelling up like a hippo, craving sardines and mustard on rye, two aliens rolling around inside you, kicking your internal organs, and let's not even get into the birthing process. Stephen King couldn't have thought it up any weirder.

Now how was she going to get socks and shoes on? She rummaged in the tiny closet and found a pair of big boots from her earlier days. Well, socks were overrated anyhow. And underwear, for that matter. She held on to the closet doorjamb and pushed her bare feet into the boots. Thank God they weren't zip-up.

She caught her reflection in the full-length mirror on the back of the closet door and had to hold on to the doorjamb again. Wow, she looked horrible. Her face was pale and blotched with red from crying, her hair was a rat's nest. She stared at her image in the mirror. She looked like one of the nuns from school in her black-and-white jumper and top. Well, a very fat, pregnant nun.

Something inside her kind of snapped, and it wasn't a foot in her ribs this time. For once in her life, she didn't give a damn about what she looked like. This woman could either take her the way she came or forget it.

She'd prettied up for people her whole life. She was sick of it.

She grabbed a scrunchy black hat off the rack and stuffed it on her head, tucking in her wild red hair. Her purse was hanging on the bed, credit cards nearby for shopping emergencies.

Paris grabbed the envelope with her mother's address on it, the directions, and the photograph. She lumbered out of the room and went toward the front door. She found the Vista Cruiser keys on the rack.

Every movement she made was awkward and difficult, and as she slowly moved herself out of the building and toward the car she realized that no undies and no socks had left her with a mighty big breeze under her black jumper. She was freezing her butt off. How could it be so freakin' cold in Vegas?

She squeezed herself behind the wheel of the Cruiser and pulled her coat over her legs the best she could. It had been a very, very long time since she had actually driven the freeway, but she used to get around here just fine as a teenager. She'd always had a boyfriend with a car, and she'd done plenty of driving with plenty of those cars. She knew the way she needed to go. She lay the directions beside her in the seat and adjusted the bench back so her large-size self could fit behind it. If she wasn't so unbelievably upset, angry, and freaked, it would be funny.

She doubted that she could ever forgive Turner for telling Sarah about her mother before he'd even discussed it with her. Not only that, he'd gone to *see* her mother. He'd seen her before Paris had even known she was alive. What the hell was he thinking? He'd taken overprotectiveness to a new extreme.

She started the car and let it warm up. She felt a rush of excitement at the thought of seeing her mother. Paris didn't know so many mixed emotions could be inside one person. She was hot with anger, cold with fear, and terribly sad at the same time. She pulled the car out of the parking space with some jerky movements and put her foot down on the gas.

Turner was right about one thing: Everything had to change now. Right now.

22

All I Needed Was the Rain

Turner stood in the new nursery and wondered at all his wife had accomplished in a few days, or weeks, or months, without him knowing about it. The room was beautiful, with its walls painted like a picket fence with flowers and birds and a country scene in the distance. Of course her bears were here, as well. It looked as if Paris had given all her bears to the babies.

He had set up the bassinets, although he figured they might end up in the master bedroom at first. Even though this room was right next door, he felt like he wanted to watch them every minute for their first few weeks. He had absolutely no experience with children. Millie had some at least, although she'd been reading up like crazy. Every time Turner was done with a book, Millie snatched it from him.

But he was pretty sure books only gave you the merest hint of what to expect.

Paris had really outdone herself with this house. The neighborhood looked great. She hadn't gone for the exclusive gated community but had opted instead for a mid-exclusiveness. That made him more comfortable. After all, Daddy was a minister with a wedding chapel in Vegas, not a stockbroker.

Turner checked his watch. He wanted to get back to Paris very quickly. The nursery was good enough for now. He'd had a bad feeling ever since they'd walked out the door of the apartment.

"Millie, what's our time frame? I want to get back to Paris."

"What's the rush? You said she was sleeping, and she has your pager, right?" Millie had been folding up baby things and putting them in the drawers of a hand-painted armoire.

"Turner, honey, you can take my car over and check on her if you want. We're having too much fun to stop. I've sold lots of houses, but helping set one up is just a blast," Jenifer Shipley said. "But I sure understand why you want to keep an eye on Paris. Those babies are really getting big."

"I'd appreciate that. I'll go back and fix her

some supper, then bring the car back by eight. Is that too late?"

"Heavens no. We've got two feet of sub sandwich here to keep us happy, and Suzy Wingate is going to drop by with window treatments in an hour. Here, you take my cell phone just in case." Jenifer went to her purse in the corner and dug around.

"Believe it or not, I've got one." Turner pulled the tiny cell phone out of his pocket. "I figured I might need it with the babies arriving any day now. I'll write down the number for you."

"Great. Here's the keys to the Quest and my card with my cell number. You go on now. We'll be fine," Jenifer said.

"Worrywart," Millie said.

"That's me." Turner made his exit, went to the kitchen, and found a scrap of paper. He wrote the cell phone number down, then headed out the door to Jenifer's minivan. He might as well test one out; his life was headed for minivan territory, although he wished they made one that was hybrid electric gas, because they really ate fuel.

It was a short trip back to the apartment, only twenty minutes, but the traffic was still heavy, and the strangest part of all was that the light rain had turned into snow. Snow. It only snowed once every fifty or a hundred years around here. The weather had been so odd all year.

Of course the odd snow made everyone go even slower. It was making him nuts. Every mile he went he felt less at ease about having left Paris. He pushed on the gas and moved around some crawling cars. He needed to get back home.

Paris couldn't believe it was snowing in Nevada, and Arizona too. As she crossed the border she watched the flakes build into a dancing blizzard. But she was used to snow. She'd been on the East Coast for the last ten years.

And yet she'd come back to the warm desert for her thirtieth birthday bash. That was the last decent work she'd had as well. What had made her take that job anyway?

She'd been to Vegas for a few shoots since she started modeling, but in general she avoided contracts that took her here, because of the memories. She'd thought she was old enough to breeze into town and not think about growing up around here. She'd thought she could skim over her pain and stay on that oblivious roller coaster ride she'd carefully developed, forever.

But Turner had changed all that. Turner had changed everything in her life. In the last months he'd been beside her every day. No matter how cranky and whiney she'd gotten, he'd just rubbed her back, painted her toenails, or read her stupid newspaper articles about fish that could walk on land or some woman in Texas who had six babies. And now he'd found her mother for her.

She'd locked herself in a corner for sure. The fear rose up in her and almost made her sick. She just couldn't let her babies live through what she'd lived through. She had no faith in herself, no trust that she'd be able to rise above. But she couldn't just leave anymore. If there was just some way she could know for sure—without a doubt—that she wouldn't turn all crazy like her mother had.

Maybe her mother could tell her what had happened. Paris couldn't believe her mother was alive—that she'd hidden away from her all these years. Oddly enough, Paris understood why. Her head spun with the whole thing. It spun so much that she had to pull the car over and let it pass.

The snow was powder dry and swirled in the wind. She'd pulled over to the left so she could get out her own door and take a breath of fresh air—cold, fresh air.

She felt sick. This was probably a bad idea. But she couldn't wait another minute to look into her mother's face. And she didn't want Turner with her. She wanted to do this alone. No one could understand what had happened but her . . . and her mother.

In less than an hour Paris was standing at the address given to her by Turner. She wished she could have called first. She felt as frightened as a child. Actually, she felt exactly the same as she had when she was little. She pulled her long wool coat around herself as a chill overtook her.

Paris took a deep breath and leaned on the doorbell. The door opened so quickly she almost fell inside. She caught her balance and looked straight into her mother's gray-blue eyes.

The emotion hit her so hard she balled up her fist and covered her mouth as a cry escaped her lips.

"Mother?"

"Patty, oh, Patty." The woman put her arms around Paris as best she could. Their cheeks touched. Paris's cheeks had tears streaming down them. The snow drifted onto their hair.

Paris had no words. She couldn't find herself. She was completely lost in the moment of seeing this woman again. The woman she'd thought was long dead. Paris touched her mother's once-red hair as if to feel that she was alive. She felt the dusting of snowflakes, and the soft waves of her mother's hair. Everything about her mother was the same. Years had hardly changed her.

Lucy took Paris's hand and led her inside.

Turner knew immediately what had happened. He went to the computer and pulled up the last page viewed. There were the driving directions to Lucy Jamison's house. He hit print, then dug in his pocket to find the cell phone and Jenifer Shipley's card.

"Jenifer, I'm going to need your car. It's an emergency. No, Paris has taken off. Can I speak to Millie? Thank you."

"What the hell has that broad done now?" Millie asked.

"Went to see her mother."

"Oh. That makes sense. The mother she thought was dead. Was that what you've had up your sleeve all this time? Well, heck, that can't be all bad, can it?"

"I'm going after her. She shouldn't be driving anyway. Jenifer said her husband can come and pick you all up. Tell her thanks again. I'll speak to you later."

"Don't worry Turner, she's a big girl."

"Yeah, way big right now."

Turner said good-bye and flipped the phone off. He replaced it in his pocket and grabbed the printout. His wife should not be driving on a freeway pregnant with twins, in the snow, upset as hell, and after being in bed for many months. He didn't care what she thought was right or wrong; he was going to get her.

He ran out of the apartment and got in the van Jenifer had loaned him. Paris was even driving the Vista Cruiser, which didn't have the best tires in the world. What had possessed her to do this crazy thing?

Well, that was easy to answer. To learn that her mother was living an hour away must have been more than she could stand. When Paris got a mind to do something, nothing stood in her way.

Turner spun out of the slick cross street they lived on and headed for the freeway. When was she going to let him in? He would have taken her there. He would have stood beside her. Turner hit the steering wheel with his fist. Damn her!

He'd had enough of being patient. He'd be damned if he was going to let Paris go. She was about to be the mother of his children. He loved her, and anything that happened, they could deal with together. Why couldn't she see that?

She had to rise above her fears and allow herself to have a life—and love. He'd found her again, and this was the end of that road. She was either going to face the music and be a wife and mother and learn to trust, or she was going to get out of their lives, just like she'd sworn she would.

He'd truly believed he could find the way to her heart, but maybe he had failed. Either way, this would be the end of wondering. The snow was coming down hard, and the freeway was almost empty. Nature could dump a blizzard or a hurricane or a twister out on him—go ahead. Nothing was going to stop him from making this trip.

When he finally arrived on the street of the

Lake Meade neighborhood, he found the simple home of Lucy Jamison Worth, with the Vista Cruiser parked in the driveway.

Turner pulled in behind her and shut off the car. Paris, Paris, how could she drive herself this far in her condition? He thought about that for a moment. Many women kept working up until they delivered. She was a tough girl, but her pregnancy hadn't been easy. He prayed she was all right.

When Turner knocked on the door, Bill Worth opened it. "They are in the bedroom. Lucy made her lay down." He didn't even ask who Turner was. Turner figured Lucy had told him about his visit and he knew everything.

"Is she okay?"

"I think so. They've been talking for about two hours."

Turner wondered if that was enough time to make up for over twelve years. "I need to see that she is all right."

"Come in and have a cup of coffee. It's mighty cold out there." Bill Worth gestured to Turner. He looked like a very friendly man. Turner had hoped he would be understanding about all this. "I think it would be good to give them a little more time," Bill said.

They went to the kitchen, as everyone does during a crisis. Turner smiled as he sat down at their kitchen table. Bill went to pour coffee. It seemed like their whole life over the last year, since last April, had been a long, drawn-out crisis around the kitchen table.

Bill brought them both mugs and sat down across from Turner. He pulled the sugar bowl over and added a teaspoon to his own coffee. "Cream?"

"No, thanks." Turner warmed his hands on the thick white mug.

"I know you talked to Lucy earlier. She was expecting to come and see Patty. But she said to me that she wasn't surprised that she showed up here. Patty was always a very brave girl."

"She had to be."

"Don't think I don't know what you're thinking. I've been through it with my wife a hundred times. After five years I stopped. Then when Bonnie found her, I thought it might make Lucy find Patty. She has all her magazine covers, you know. Bonnie has tried, too. But Lucy forbid her to contact Patty. Lucy felt that Patty made a new life for herself, and the ghosts of the past should be buried."

"Did she know Paris thought she was dead?"

"No, she didn't. I didn't either. I figured Patty . . . Paris . . . would track Lucy down sooner or later. Lucy was convinced Paris didn't want to find her. How people get into these circles of thinking is so hard to figure. I'm for straight-out talking."

"Me, too." Turner was starting to understand things better now. Lucy hadn't thought Paris wanted to see her. She'd figured Paris knew she was alive but didn't care to look into Lucy's life again. But that left a whole lot of years when Paris had been too young to make that decision. Lucy had made it for her, with just the same kind of emotional pain that Paris had. The two of them were frighteningly similar.

And Paris must have known that in her heart. That's why nothing had been able to convince her that she would be different from her mother. She knew they were made of the same stuff.

But that was many years ago. Medicine, and alternative medicine, had come a whole long way since then. Turner had convinced Dr. Shapiro to get Paris started on natural progesterone therapy this month. He remembered reading that beginning before delivery was a very good thing. And she'd cooperated for once. Actually, she'd been making a big effort to cooperate with Dr. Shapiro ever since she'd left the hospital. She really had made a change, but she'd be the last one to admit it.

Paris started to get up from the bed, when Bill knocked on the door and opened it.

"Lay back down, now. It's just my Bill," Lucy said.

"I feel fine." Paris smiled at her.

"Turner is here," Bill whispered.

Paris heard him plainly. "I'll talk to him. God, I owe him a huge apology." Paris shifted herself up and felt a very uncomfortable twinge. It wasn't a new kind, though, it was just the same as all the uncomfortable twinges she'd had over the last week.

She didn't get far, because Turner stood in the doorway of the bedroom. It wasn't a big bedroom, so Lucy and Bill excused themselves, and he moved to let them pass.

"What part of 'I want to see you through this' didn't you understand?" Turner said.

"I'm sorry, Turner. I didn't think. I had to see her."

"I'm going to take you home now. Tomorrow we're going to see Dr. Shapiro. I don't care anymore about the off chance that you might repeat your mother's postpartum depression. I've had enough of this. I've had enough of your lack of faith in yourself, and me, and in our ability to deal with whatever comes up."

Paris bent over and held on to the bedpost. "I've been such a complete idiot." Her voice was pained.

"You've had your reasons. But that's got to end now. We've got to come to a clear understanding. Whatever happens between the two of us, you cannot leave your children and run off. They need you. I know you are a strong woman, but we have to go through this *together*, not separately." Turner was practically yelling at her. He'd never done that, ever.

"You are a stronger woman than your mother was, Paris, and I am a stronger man than your father was."

"Turner, we're going to have to finish this conversation later," Paris said.

"I'm not going to be put off any more, Paris."

"I see that, but I think I'm in labor." She held on to the post for support.

"Really?" Turner came over to her and took her in his arms. He stood next to her and pushed a strand of her hair out of her eyes, then kissed her forehead. He put his hand on her belly. Not that he could tell anything from that. "It could be. I'm going to get your mother. Did she tell you she was a nurse?"

"Yes. She told me."

Turner ran out of the room. "Lucy, Paris is in labor."

Lucy came to him in the hallway. "I thought that might happen. She might have had a mild contraction about an hour ago." Lucy looked at her watch. "We're about forty-five minutes from your hospital, so we better get started. But don't panic, this is her first, even if it is twins. First deliveries are notoriously slow. Did her doctor say anything about position or whether he'd planned on a C-section?"

"He said they were in the best possible position. I took the Lamaze class without Paris, since she was stuck in bed. I tried to translate as much of that as possible to her," Turner said.

"Well, that will help, but in Patty's case I'd say not for long."

Turner wasn't used to anyone calling Paris Patty. He'd tried to gain understanding for Lucy after talking to her, and he'd felt clear that years of misunderstanding had been straightened up. But he was still wary of her. He wanted this delivery to be as calm as possible for Paris, if such a thing was possible.

She seemed to read his mind. "I'll help you get her to the car. We'll come tomorrow," she said quietly.

"Thanks," Turner said. He went back to Paris and helped her get her coat on.

"We've got plenty of time, Paris. I'll drive you to the hospital."

"So this is the 'slight discomfort' the books talked about? They must have been written by a guy."

"You'll do fine. You're an Amazon woman. Think of Zena, warrior princess."

"You think of her," Paris groused. But she let Turner help her down the hall and toward the front door of the bungalow. Her mother and Bill Worth were standing by the door.

"Mother, I want you to come along," Paris said. She didn't know why she said that, but it felt important. There was an unfinished circle that she needed to close up.

Paris could tell she had surprised Lucy. "We'll follow you." Lucy looked at Bill, and he hurried off to get whatever they needed.

Turner leaned over to her. "Are you sure?"

"I want her there. I don't know why, but it will help finish it, Turner."

"I'm fine with that," he said.

She wondered if that was true. His face looked disturbed. Outside, the snow was amazing. In her eighteen years in Nevada, she'd only seen a cold spell, never snow. "Oh, man, I would pick today."

"It will be memorable." Turner helped her into the minivan.

"What the heck is this?"

"Jenifer Shipley's van. She loaned it to me." Turner closed Paris's door and came around to the driver's side.

Paris settled into the seat and felt for the adjustment buttons. She moved it to a slight recline. That's when the first really big contraction hit her. She grabbed the door handle and groaned.

"Wow. That was big," Turner said.

"I like how you get to comment from the side."

"The population curve would cease if men had to give birth. They'd ban it. We only need forty-five minutes or so, Paris. We'll make it fine. You aren't going to have them in forty-five minutes, right?"

"No, but I can have a whole lot of labor. They should show a movie of labor and birth in high school. It would be the perfect birth control."

"And we're only getting warmed up."

"We?" Paris laughed a pained laugh.

Turner took out his cell phone and called Dr. Shapiro. That gave Paris a good feeling to know that Dr. No-nonsense would be there at the hospital when she arrived.

Paris saw Lucy and Bill's car pull out of the garage, then Turner moved the car out of the drive so they could follow him. The minivan moved slowly through the snow. Very slowly.

"Turner, are we going to be okay?"

"We are. We'll make it. Once we get to the freeway, we'll do better."

Paris tried not to think panicky thoughts. She tried to rest. She'd never had such a day as this. She was already exhausted from *feeling* so much.

She couldn't believe her mother had actually thought she hadn't wanted to see her all these years. It was so hard to understand. But once they'd talked about the horrors of that time, she could see that her mother was still filled with guilt—years of heavy guilt—for getting sick, for derailing their lives, and for the death of her father. And for her and Bonnie.

That had been a real miracle in her mother's life, Bonnie finding her. Paris could hardly wait to meet Bonnie. Lucy said she came twice a year to visit. Bonnie had paved the way to her mother's healing.

Paris had to admit that all Turner's talk of fate and coincidence and cosmic order was the best explanation for some of what had happened in the last year. To think that her mother had been here, so close, so alive.

Paris felt true shame for what she had put Turner through. After several hours with her mother, she'd had to face what she'd done. To think she'd actually spent the last months convinced she would give birth to these beautiful children and leave town. Why, they'd end up feeling the same pain she'd felt about her own mother. Even finding her after all these years couldn't erase that pain.

And she would have ended up just like her mother—full of guilt, unable to break free of the past. All the things Turner had said to her night after night, and how she'd tried to make him shut up because she hadn't wanted to hear them: They all made sense now—how she was letting her fear destroy her chance at happiness. They'd just been words until she'd seen her mother. Now all his words were giving her the strength to face what a horrid thing she'd almost done.

How could she have been so blind? The past had gripped her like a sickness.

And the *present* . . . was currently gripping her in pain. She tried to remember that breathing thing Turner had taught her, but for some reason, all she could do was scream. "Ahhhhhhhhhhhhhhhhhhhhhhgh."

"Hey, you're supposed to be breathing through those."

"I'll try and remember that," she panted. "Turner, the roads. I'm scared."

"We're almost to the freeway. Hang tight."

Paris felt a wave of panic that made her heart beat quickly. She tried to breathe slowly. She had so many fears in her. All her old fears about being a mother—they felt like an old story she'd told herself a hundred times, and believed, but now, she could see a different ending.

But her new fears were even bigger. Maybe Turner had given up on her. It had been a long, painful period of time, with her insisting she was going to dump two children on him and run.

She shifted herself so she could watch him. She wrapped her coat tighter around her legs. How ironic would that be? Here's this wonderful guy, standing by her through all sorts of hell, and she waits too long to come to her senses and loses him in the end.

Her chest hurt with that fear. She sucked in her breath and tried not to cry. She was afraid to say anything to him because she was already so upset she'd probably get hysterical for the second time today and not be able to concentrate on the task at hand. Another wave of pain hit her hard.

She had to admit it was pretty damn hard to concentrate on anything else but that contraction when it took over your entire body.

"I've decided we should do this another day," Paris said when she caught her breath.

"How about next week, is that good for you?"

"Sure." She reached over and put her hand on his cheek. He put his hand on hers, then moved it back to the steering wheel. He must be so angry with her. She just couldn't lose him now. What could she do to make Turner love her like he had before?

Through the crazy, wind-whipped snow, in his rearview mirror, Turner watched in shock as Lucy and Bill's car slid off the highway and down an embankment. He'd slid past that slippery patch just a few seconds before them, but their car hadn't made it.

"Damn, *damn*. Your mom's car just went off the road."

"Oh my God, we have to see if they are okay." Paris twisted around in her seat.

Turner eased the van over to the side of the road. "You stay here. I'll go." He set the brake and fought his way out the door against the wind and snow. What else could happen? He looked up to the sky and let snowflakes pelt him in the face. He had to get his wife to the hospital. He could feel a serious urgency here. He prayed that Lucy and Bill weren't hurt. He'd have to call for help if that was the case.

The embankment was steep. Turner made his way down and opened up the driver side door.

"You folks all right?"

"Sort of. Let's get Lucy to your car. I'm sorry, Turner, I guess this isn't the best car for snow."

"No apologies. How often does this happen? Let's get you both in the car."

In five minutes they were back on the road, and Turner was trying to drive as carefully as possible, while picking up speed. Lucille Worth had a bump on her head, but nothing serious.

He was very proud of Paris for hanging in there. He'd been timing her contractions on the car clock, and they'd gone from thirty minutes apart to fifteen.

She was such an odd mixture of strength and weakness. He had a feeling that the little girl part of Paris was going to get a big awakening in a few hours. She'd been focused on herself for a very long time. Thirty years. But how else would she have survived her early years except by protecting herself like that?

He felt sure that she was going to let the strong part of herself rise up and take charge of these two babies. But whatever happened, he was ready for it.

Paris sat quietly in the car and tried to rest between contractions. How come Marla Meyers had never told her this part? She'd had her second baby in October and had somehow glossed over the part where the giant forces come and twist your uterus into a wringer, then squeeze it again just for fun. Paris was going to have to have a little talk with that Meyers woman. And to think she did it *twice*. Like once didn't teach you anything.

At least she had the sense to have two at a time. She clutched her huge belly and wailed as another round hit her.

"Fifteen minutes apart," Lucy said. "We may be delivering them in this van in a snowstorm. She's moving awfully quickly, Turner. It must be their position."

"We're less than thirty minutes from the hospital exit. Paris can do it. She's going to make it."

Paris was grateful to hear her husband sticking up for her. Her husband. He *was* that. She'd almost forgotten.

Lucy reached over the seat and put her hand on Paris's shoulder. "Tell us if you feel the urge to push."

Paris thought about that and groaned. She suddenly figured that the only way through this was not to think about anything but the moment. Maybe that's what she should do with the rest of her life as well. "I'm glad you're here, Mom. Turner is going to get me there. I trust him."

Paris glanced at Turner and saw him look at her with surprise. But she did trust him. She trusted him with her life, her children's lives, and everyone else's. He had never failed her. Not even when they were kids. She'd led him into all sorts of wild situations, and he'd always been there to protect her.

So basically, nothing about Turner had changed. Maybe after this she could make things up to him. She didn't know what she had to offer him as a partner, except for one thing. If she let herself, she could love. She could show him what she felt in her heart. It would take a while, but as far as she could see, Turner was the most patient man in the entire universe.

She proved that point by screaming at the top of her lungs and digging her fingernails into his leg. He flinched but kept the car on the road. What a guy.

* * *

"Are you ready, Mrs. Pruitt?" Dr. Shapiro was gowned up and peering at her from between her legs.

"Thanks for not saying *we.* Just give me drugs and I'll be the best little laborer you've ever seen. I've had enough of these nasty contractions."

"I'm sorry to say it, but there's no time for that. I want you to do exactly what I tell you. Can you do that?"

Paris was going to think about that, but another contraction hit her. "Okay, whatever you say."

Turner was sitting behind her head, rubbing her temples. Her mother was gowned up and stood to the side. Paris was glad her mother was there. She could show her that not everything in their lives had to be terrible. She could share something good with her.

But most of all she was glad Turner was there.

23

Anyone (Could Fall in Love with You)

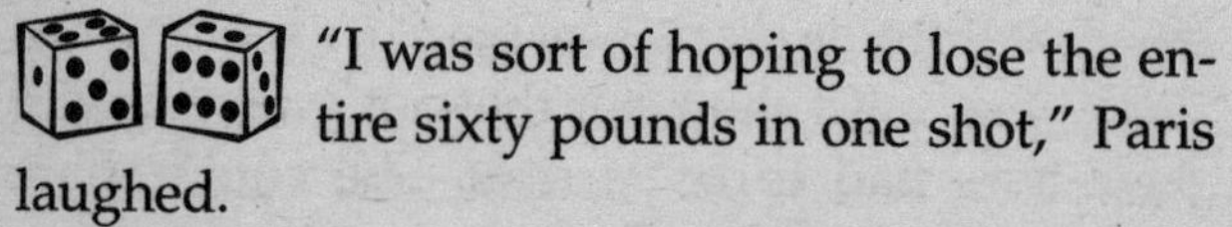

"I was sort of hoping to lose the entire sixty pounds in one shot," Paris laughed.

"Well, here's six and seven ounces, and another six and five ounces." Turner held two babies, one in each arm. Turner couldn't believe what they looked like. A tuft of red hair on each head, Paris's nose, and his mouth. At least that's what Paris had said.

Lucille Worth held her daughter's hand. Turner could tell she'd been crying. He'd also seen Paris comfort her. What a twist.

"Give them to me, Turner."

He brought them over to Paris and tucked one on each side. He looked into his girls' sweet faces and watched them make little mewing noises as they slept. They'd been through a big night. Hopefully Paris could get a little rest, too. She'd hardly had a chance last night. The morning light was streaming in the windows now.

"I want you to promise me something," she said.

"Today I'll promise you anything. You are queen for the day."

"This has to be a forever promise. I want you to never ever tell these babies how completely ridiculous their mother was before they were born."

"Family secrets aren't good, but I'll make an exception in this case." Turner hoped this meant she'd seen the light. "I promise."

"I know what you're thinking, Turner, and I didn't have time to tell you yesterday. I was busy."

"You were."

"Mom, could you leave us alone for a few minutes?"

"Sure. Thank you so much, Paris, for letting me be here for the girls' birth. I can't even tell you what it's meant to me."

"I understand, Mom. I'm glad you were here."

Lucille exited the room and left Paris and Turner alone. Well, as Turner saw it, this was the most alone they were going to get for many years. "What else did you want to tell me?" He moved over by her side and watched baby one sleep. They sure needed to think up some names.

"Actually, it's more of an ask than tell. Turner, I fell in love with you. I don't know when, maybe it was the time you painted my toenails Kiss Me Pink, but I figured that out yesterday as I was driving to see my mother. I know I'm not the same girl I was back in April. I'm fatter but wiser. You've seen some really bad days with me. I've pushed you away over and over again. A man can only take so much of that. I've been a heartless, confused woman."

Turner sat quietly. He knew in his heart that he was deeply in love with his wife, and not one moment of this time had changed that. He'd had his doubts, and he'd been ready for her to walk out, but somehow he'd known his love would finally make a dent in her. He'd seen it in her laugh, and in her tears too. But it wouldn't be bad to hear it from her own lips. He smiled and listened.

"So what I'd like to know is, will you marry us for real this time?" Paris gave him a tearful look and pulled the two girls up close to her.

His wife was a wreck. She had no makeup, and no brush had been near those scarlet locks of hers in a good two days. Her face was tear-stained, her eyes were rimmed with red, and he saw freckles for the first time ever, spattering across her nose, which was chapped from blowing. The babies didn't look too much better—their heads were a little lopsided, one had a blotch on her forehead—from her sister's foot, most likely.

But really, he had never seen a more beautiful bunch of women, and they were all his.

"Paris, for me, it was for real the first time, and I'd marry you again in a minute." He came over to her and tipped her chin with his finger, then kissed her with all his heart. This time, for the first time really, she kissed him back with all her heart. He could feel it. Even with her arms full of babies.

"Mmmm." He brushed her cheek and let his hand rest there. "I know a nice chapel not far from here," she whispered.

"Very funny." Turner saw his wife blush for the first time in his life.

"I wanted to ask you yesterday, but things got out of control. Besides, I waited till I had some leverage." Paris nodded to the sleeping babies.

"You already had leverage, Paris. You just didn't give yourself enough credit."

"I know that now."

Turner kissed her again. He was flooded with happiness knowing that Paris had found her way to him, and to their children.

"I think I'm going to need some therapy, though, and I'm still fairly terrified about what might come up in the next few weeks, but my mother is willing to work things out with me. She said we should go to counseling together."

"I'm going to be with you through whatever

comes up, Paris. I'm in this for the long haul," Turner said.

"I owe it to them . . . and you, to get my head on straight. Which is not to say I won't still be a raving bitch sometimes."

"Yes, but you are *my* raving bitch."

"I love you, Turner. I guess we are going to have the best holidays ever."

"I love you too, Paris." He bent to kiss her again. The door to the room opened with a quiet knock. Paris's mother was there, and behind her was a lovely redheaded girl who looked to be in her twenties.

Paris gasped. Turner figured it out pretty quickly. It must be her sister Bonnie. He gathered the babies up. "I'm going to take the girls for a walk, Paris. We're going to the nursery for a while, but I'll bring them back." He nodded at Bonnie as he passed by.

Bonnie pushed past her mother and flew right into Paris's arms. He heard a whole lot of crying, and he smiled at Lucille. "Thanks."

"She caught a hopper flight from Fresno," Lucille said. "It's been quite a morning."

"Is your head okay?"

"Just a bump. But the inside of it is a little overwhelmed."

"I'm going down the hall. Come and join me after a while," Turner said.

"I will."

Turner walked his daughters down to the nursery and had the nurse tuck them into their bassinet. She put them together. She said she had a theory that twins slept better together at first. He sat in the resident rocking chair and watched them sleep.

His whole world had been turned upside down in the blink of an eye. He thought back to April first of this year, when Paris had whooped her way into his life. He thought about the young Paris, howling at the moon with him on a desert night. She was still that girl, and he was glad his daughters would grow up with her free spirit. He thanked God that his prayers had been answered.

"Now you've got a handful," Millie's voice came from the doorway to the nursery. The nurse checked with Turner, but she asked Millie to wait outside in the hall anyhow. Turner stepped out to join her.

"Redheads up to my eyebrows." Turner gave Millie a hug. "She asked me to marry her."

"Did you say yes?" Millie joked.

"I did."

"I knew she'd crack."

"I'm sure you helped with that." He hugged her again. "And Millie, we're going to need you, so pack up your scrapbooks and come to that big house."

"I'm already in there. Preacher Pruitt's house is quite the joint. Are you sure you want an old showgirl like me around?"

"Who else can teach them to high-kick? But no more phone sex, okay?"

"Darn, and I so enjoyed it. Turner, I can't even begin to thank you. I never thought I'd be a grandmother, since I didn't have any kids of my own and all, so you've given me quite a gift."

"Don't worry, you'll regret it later."

Millie reached down by the wall to a shopping bag she'd brought with her and pulled out two Raggedy Ann dolls. Turner could see they were handmade, complete with loopy red hair.

"You did these? They are beautiful."

"Lookit those girls." She turned and pressed her nose to the glass nursery window. "What are you going to name them?" Millie asked.

"I don't have a clue. I'm trying to figure out how to tell them apart."

"You're going to be a hell of a daddy, Turner. We'll just call them Thing One and Thing Two for a while."

"Your children are beautiful, Turner."

Turner turned to the sound of Sarah's voice. She was right behind them, wearing her student nurse uniform. "Thank you. They're doing very well. It was an extraordinarily easy delivery."

"Easy for you to say," Millie added.

"I saw her name on the chalkboard. I came over to say congratulations."

"Thanks, Sarah. It's been a long haul, and you helped out a great deal."

"She's going to stay, isn't she?"

"Yes."

"I knew she would."

Turner saw the sadness in Sarah's eyes. He reached over and took her hand. "You are always welcome with our family, Sarah, and we're here if you need anything."

"Thanks, Turner. As soon as I'm finished with school, I've decided to go back to the Islands. They need nurses there, and I actually miss my folks," Sarah said.

"That sounds wonderful. Until then, you've got the apartment, and I guess we've moved. I think the only things left in the house are my leftovers."

"We're leaving most of the furniture. The princess went shopping," Millie said.

"Hey, it's her specialty. She's good at it," Sarah smiled.

Turner refocused on his babies and enjoyed watching them sleep. From everything he'd heard, this was a rare moment. Millie danced a Raggedy Ann in the window and made faces.

"Oh, you're going to be great. You'll get them all excited, then hand them back to the weary parents," Turner said.

"Heh-heh. Now you're getting the picture."

Turner was glad Sarah had come to make peace. He felt, at this moment, completely blessed.

Epilogue
A Big Hunk o' Love

Three years later

"And waltz, and turn, and very nice ladies! Emma, pull your tights up. Little ladies can't have saggy tights." Paris tried not to laugh as her two three-year-old terrors danced together behind the much older preteen girls who had signed up for Paris Pruitt's School of Girl Power. Millicent and Emmaline Pruitt weren't ready for manners yet, that was for sure. Paris was lucky to get them dressed in the morning, and without Granny Millie's help, she doubted anything would ever get done.

The girls turned and headed down to the other end of the long mirrored studio space, her daughters doing the toddler two-step behind the older girls. The bright music put more wiggle in them than grace.

And they never listened to her, only their daddy. Of course those two were wise women already, because if she'd just learned to listen to Turner sooner, she wouldn't have wasted a minute resisting his charms.

After meeting his parents, it was easy to see where Turner got his patient and loving spirit. Not to mention his good looks. His dad was an equally handsome older version of Turner, and the nurses in the hospital had flirted with him shamelessly.

Mr. and Mrs. Pruitt were so gratful to Paris for making them grandparents that they instantly accepted her into their fold. She didn't even want to think about what Turner had told them, but once, as they'd been washing a giant load of baby things together, his mother had said she and her husband had prayed together every day and night that all would be well for Turner and Paris.

Even in the weeks following the birth, when she'd felt the edge of darkness fold over her and a very mild depression start, they'd all been there beside her. Her doctor, Millie, her mother, and her in-laws all helping out. She'd survived it. She'd done no harm to anyone, and she'd learned an amazing lesson about love.

But Turner had been the best. Her husband had made sure she took all the treatments on time, and had made her round-the-clock snacks to keep her blood sugar even. He'd made sure she'd gotten enough rest, and he'd shouldered more than his share of baby care, along with his parents and Millie. She was one lucky woman to have Turner in her life.

She'd come to see that although her mother's problems had had many facets, not all were passed down to her.

She'd never been so grateful to a man in her life for standing by her through good times and bad. No man but Turner ever had.

She had quite a family now, including Millie. Something she'd never even dreamed of. And it was a good thing, because it was going to take a village to raise these two rascals. Her own mother and sister had pitched in when they'd been able to, and it was so wonderful to think that the girls had an Aunt Bonnie now. Paris and Bonnie never let a day pass without talking to each other on the phone. Hopefully Bonnie could swing a move to Vegas as soon as her husband found a new job.

Her mom's suggestion to open this school had been brillant. Paris had loved the idea. She could teach these girls a thing or two, like it was great to be pretty, and makeup was extremely cool, but a girl has to tap into her inner warrior princess once in a while, because life can kick you in the butt unexpectedly.

She'd drifted off into her own thoughts, and she hardly noticed when the music changed from Strauss to Elvis. The familiar opening guitar riff to "Jailhouse Rock" came blasting out of her stereo system.

And there was her husband, the hottest Elvis that ever lived, in his white studded Elvis duds, playing air guitar and singing, "Let's rock, everybody let's rock . . ." The girls went wild, including his own two. They ran smack into him and he lifted them like airplanes, one under each arm, while he twisted like Elvis. Paris thought they'd yak from squealing so much.

The older girls were doing their own squealing, and it was just all too funny for words. That's what she got for buying the building behind the chapel and opening her studio where Turner could come and bust up her classes anytime he wanted. Although it had been a long time since she'd seen him *in the Elvis.*

Paris walked over to Turner, who put down his redheaded daughters and grabbed her. She'd figured out long ago that she better know how to jitterbug with this Elvis, and at least now he could lift her in the air after three years of low carbs, aerobics, and Pilates torture.

He spun her out and all her girls started rocking around the room, the waltz abandoned, the beat of fifties rock and roll fully embraced.

As he dipped Paris backward and she saw the smiles on the faces of her daughters—upside down—Paris knew she was completely blessed. Fools like her that rushed into crazy love must truly be looked after by the angels in charge of Las Vegas wedding chapels.